INTRIGUE IN
ISTANBUL

Books by Erica Ruth Neubauer

MURDER AT THE MENA HOUSE

MURDER AT WEDGEFIELD MANOR

DANGER ON THE ATLANTIC

INTRIGUE IN ISTANBUL

Published by Kensington Publishing Corp.

INTRIGUE IN ISTANBUL

ERICA RUTH NEUBAUER

KENSINGTON
PUBLISHING CORP.

www.kensingtonbooks.com

KENSINGTON BOOKS are published by

Kensington Publishing Corp.
119 West 40th Street
New York, NY 10018

Copyright © 2023 by Erica Ruth Neubauer

All Kensington titles, imprints and distributed lines are available at special quantity discounts for bulk purchases for sales promotion, premiums, fund-raising, educational or institutional use. Special book excerpts or customized printings can also be created to fit specific needs. For details, write or phone the office of the Kensington Special Sales Manager: Kensington Publishing Corp., 119 West 40th Street, New York, NY, 10018. Attn. Special Sales Department. Phone: 1-800-221-2647.

Kensington and the K logo Reg. U.S. Pat. & TM Off.

Library of Congress Control Number: 2022948694

ISBN: 978-1-4967-4115-8

First Kensington Hardcover Edition: April 2023

ISBN: 978-1-4967-4117-2 (e-book)

10 9 8 7 6 5 4 3 2

Printed in the United States of America

For Zoe Quinton
and
Katie and Trevor.
To the moon and back.

CHAPTER ONE

After so many months abroad it was a little surreal to be back in my hometown of Boston. The streets were still bustling and nothing about the city had changed, but I certainly had. I was a much different person than the one who set off to Egypt. Not only that, but I was now bringing home a man to introduce to my father, something I never thought would happen again.

Yet here we were.

We'd taken a train from New York after spending several days there, and then a taxi from the train station. I was very much looking forward to a few days without the hustle and bustle of travel, and to showing Redvers around Boston. He'd been here plenty of times before, but he said he was interested in seeing the city through my eyes. I wanted to take him to my favorite park, and the little bakery where I often had coffee and watched the world pass by, and a thousand other places where I passed my time at home.

First, he had to meet my father, however. I was both excited and nervous at the prospect of them meeting, curious about what they would think of one another. Would my father take Redvers and his mysterious profession in stride? Would Redvers find my absentminded but amiable father charming?

The taxi driver had unloaded our trunks and bags onto the sidewalk and I sighed at the notion of dragging them into the house. Father kept a housekeeper, but we didn't have any other staff so getting all our luggage inside would fall on our own shoulders. Apparently, I'd gotten a bit spoiled after staying at so many places where such things were taken care of for me.

Our home was part of a long red brick building, a series of row houses stretching up both sides of the narrow street and lit by gas lanterns. Black shutters lined white windows, front doors slightly offset from one another due to the buildings being built along the upward slope of the hill. This area was historic by American standards, but certainly not by European ones. The street was paved with cobblestones, which I still found charming despite having grown up here and despite the fact that they were somewhat difficult to walk on—it was easy to catch a shoe on them. We were at the edge of the fashionable neighborhood of Beacon Hill, where many of the city's rich and powerful lived. But since we were neither, we were able to enjoy our peaceful little street.

I had my keys at the ready, and pushed open the front door, calling into the quiet beyond. "Father? I'm home!" There was no answer.

"Does he know you're coming? Perhaps he's out," Redvers said from behind me.

I stepped fully inside and cocked my head. It was dead silent, but the kind of silence that lingered. The air also felt stale, as though fresh air hadn't come through in a while. That was strange in itself since the housekeeper normally stopped by several times a week, but it felt as though no one had been here in some time.

It was odd, but nothing seemed amiss, so we dragged our trunks and various other pieces of luggage into the row house and left them in the small foyer for the time being. I took the opportunity to show Redvers around the house, starting with the cozy sitting room, where I'd spent countless hours reading by the fire. Redvers took it all in quietly, including the framed portrait of my mother sitting on the mantel.

"This is your mother?"

I nodded, coming to stand beside him.

"I see the resemblance."

I laughed. "That's kind of you to say, but I look much more like my father."

"I'll need to meet him first before I can be the judge of that." Redvers' tone was lighthearted, but he was an observant man, and I knew he was taking everything in. I also knew we were both wondering where my father had gone. Everything was in its proper place, but I noticed there was a fine layer of dust covering everything. Which meant that not only had Father been gone for a bit, but our housekeeper, Mrs. George, hadn't been by in some time either.

But I was curious about something else as well, and I cocked my head at him. "Who do *you* most resemble?" I'd never even see a photograph of the man's family, which suddenly struck me as strange since I was going to marry into it.

My fiancé gave a casual shrug, now studying me with a fond smile instead of the portrait. "I'm told I look more like my father, but who's to say?"

"Me, I suppose. Once I meet him." Although I didn't know when that would be—we hadn't discussed traveling to Redvers' hometown to meet his father. I did know that his immediate family was now just his father since both his mother and brother had passed away years before, so it would be a small reunion when it did happen.

"Plenty of time for that," Redvers said, pulling me into a warm embrace.

We broke apart a few moments later and I continued my tour, showing Redvers through the dining room, popping our heads into the kitchen before ending in my favorite room of the house, the library, which also served as Father's office. It was lined with books of all shapes and genres, where literature and history sat beside current novels and ancient texts. It was a hodgepodge, and I loved it.

I took a seat in the wooden chair behind his well-worn wooden desk. It was strewn with papers, which was nothing new. But the stacks of unopened mail were. I flicked mindlessly through the envelopes, puzzling over where my father could have disappeared to and why Mrs. George hadn't been here in what was at least a week, judging by the dust.

As I flicked through the envelopes, it suddenly struck me that several of them were from our bank. I frowned, glancing up at Redvers who was wordlessly perusing the bookshelves. I dug around and found Father's letter opener and slit an envelope open, pulling the paper out and briefly glancing at it. The words "repayment" and "repossess" jumped out at me and I slowed down to read the notice in full. Alarm bells sounded and I opened another envelope and then another.

"Is everything all right?" Redvers asked.

I looked up, worry evident on my face. "These are all notices from the bank." I gestured to the array of now-opened envelopes before me. "It seems as though Father took out a large sum of money against the house and the bank is calling for their note to be repaid."

A frown furrowed Redvers' brow. "What would he have wanted the money for?"

"I haven't the faintest idea. But it looks as though we only have a few short weeks to return it before they will repossess this row house." I felt panic rise, but tamped it down. Surely there was an explanation. And surely we would find my father later today and have him return the money and all would be well. Once that was settled, Redvers and I could carry on with our relaxing time here in Boston.

"Why would he ignore the notices?"

I shook my head. "He hasn't opened a single one of them. And some of these have been here for some time. He's a bit . . . absentminded. I've taken care of the accounts for years." I usually took care of the mail also, and well, every-thing. Father taught his classes at the university and usually lost himself in his research. I'd been a little nervous about leaving him behind while I traveled with his sister, but Mrs. George had assured me that everything would be fine.

But Redvers was asking an important question—what *did* he need all that money for? It was enough money that we were now apparently in danger of losing our home. How long ago had he taken it out, and where was it now?

CHAPTER TWO

A quick sweep of the rest of the house didn't reveal much except that my father's battered old trunk was gone. Where to was anyone's guess, although I thought it was worth a trip to see Mrs. George to find out what she might know about my father's whereabouts. If his trunk was missing it meant that he was farther away than a day trip—this business with the bank wasn't going to be resolved as quickly as I'd first hoped.

And the bank was our first stop, so we set off for a walk. It was only a few blocks, and after the train ride I was happy for a chance to stretch my legs even if the weather was quite brisk. Late November wasn't the most pleasant time in New England, but it wasn't as though the weather was much fairer back in regular old England either. And with my leather gloves and wool cloche hat and jacket, I was fairly well protected against the biting wind.

The trees were nearly bare, and the few dried-out leaves on the narrow sidewalks blew past our feet as we made our way to the square where our bank was located. I released Redvers' arm as we pushed through the door to the lobby, but he stayed close behind me.

"Good morning, Mrs. Wunderly," the clerk behind the desk greeted me. I couldn't quite remember the man's name but I returned his warm greeting. "What can we help you with today?"

"I have some questions about a loan my father took out. Who should we talk to?"

"That would be Mr. Whitaker. I'll see if he's available." The clerk left his post behind the desk and walked back to an office, knocking on the door and poking his head inside. Perhaps it was just my imagination, but it seemed as though the man's friendliness had turned to a bit of concern once I mentioned the loan. It was probably just my imagination, though.

My nerves were humming when we were ushered into Mr. Whitaker's office a few moments later, however. And not even Redvers' comforting hand on my back could calm them.

"Mrs. Wunderly," Mr. Whitaker greeted me and cast a pointed look at my companion.

"This is Mr. Redvers, my fiancé," I said. I caught a smile on Redvers' face from the corner of my eye—it was the first time I'd introduced him as such. And it seemed to do as intended, which was to set Mr. Whitaker's mind at ease.

"Ah, excellent. A pleasure, Mr. Redvers."

The men exchanged handshakes and then we sat down in the wooden chairs opposite the man's desk. It was a utilitarian office, an old map of the city framed and hanging on the wall but little else. Whitaker's hands were folded on top of his tidy desk and he regarded me steadily. "I suppose you're here about the loan your father took out."

"I am indeed. I just returned home and this was the first I'd heard of it." I hadn't met Whitaker before, but it was well-known at the bank that I took care of most of the household affairs. I was hoping Whitaker would already be up to speed as far as that went. "It would appear that we are in arrears?"

Whitaker nodded sadly. "I'm afraid Professor Wunderly failed to make any efforts toward repayment, so we are now forced to either collect the entire sum or take control of your home. Which he used as collateral."

"What is the exact sum that Professor Wunderly took out?" Redvers asked.

"Nearly ninety thousand dollars."

I gasped. I'd known it was a large sum, but that was astronomical. No wonder the bank was going to take back the row house.

"Is there anything that can be done?" I asked. I could hear the desperation in my own voice. We had nowhere near that sum of money, and I didn't want to lose the row house. It was not only where I'd grown up but also where all the memories I had left of my mother were centered.

Mr. Whitaker shook his head. I could tell that he didn't like giving me this news, which was small comfort. "I'm afraid not. I can give you an extra week perhaps, but that's about all I can do at this stage."

I tried not to panic. "So that would give us three weeks? And can we wire the money to you?" If we could locate my father, we could get the money and get it to the bank that much quicker.

"Of course."

Redvers broke in again. "Do you happen to know what Professor Wunderly wanted the money for?"

Whitaker cocked his head a bit. "I don't actually. He was quite mysterious about the whole thing." He unfolded his hands and tapped the top of his desk. I took it as a sign that we were about finished here.

"Thank you for your help, Mr. Whitaker. I do appreciate it. And I appreciate the extra time."

"I wish I could do more for you, Mrs. Wunderly, Mr. Redvers." He stood as we did the same. We left his office, and after giving the friendly clerk a wave on our way out the door, we found ourselves back on the sidewalk.

I turned to Redvers. "Three weeks. We only have three weeks to find Father, get the money back from whatever he's done with it, and wire it to the bank."

"Could you ask your aunt for the money?"

I considered that option for only a moment. I would do everything I could to solve this without asking Aunt Millie to bail us out of this trouble. She likely could find the funds to save our home, but my father would never hear the end of it, nor would I. "Let's hope it doesn't come to that."

CHAPTER THREE

Our next stop was to see Mrs. George, our housekeeper. She worked full-time for my aunt Millie, fitting us in here and there, so we went to Millie's house to find the woman. Unlike my father and me, Millie lived in the very fashionable part of Beacon Hill, and instead of a row house, she lived in a large Renaissance mansion in white limestone. The streets were still narrow here—the entire city was rather narrow when it came down to it—but the front of Millie's house faced a park that was quite beautiful in the summer and fall. The house was still close to its neighbors, but this was Boston, and that was to be expected.

It was strange arriving to Millie's knowing that she wouldn't be there. I'd never once been to Millie's when she wasn't there, and I wondered what would become of the house now that Millie was engaged to Lord Hughes. Would they reside permanently in England? Would Millie keep the house?

My thoughts were interrupted by the butler answering the door. He was surprised to see me, although the only evidence of that was the tiniest raising of his eyebrow. "Mrs. Stanley isn't at home, Miss Jane." He opened the door all the same, letting us past him into the large foyer.

I'd long ago insisted that the man call me Jane, and I had managed to get him to the point where he'd conceded to

"Miss Jane." Close enough. "I do know that, Sullivan. I'm actually here to see Mrs. George."

Sullivan nodded once. "She is in the kitchen. I'll have her meet you in the sitting room."

Redvers followed me past the grand staircase down a small corridor into a reasonably comfortable sitting room. My aunt liked things pristine, but at least here the furniture was relatively comfortable to sit on. That wasn't the case in her drawing room where she received more formal guests. Or in the dining room either, for that matter. My posterior had gone to sleep during more than one formal dinner at my aunt's table.

Mrs. George bustled into the room, an absolute dumpling of a woman with her frizzy gray hair pulled into a bun, and a warm smile. I nearly leapt from my seat to greet her, bending down to give her a hard hug.

"It's so good to see you, Jane, my dear," she said. "And who is your gentleman friend?" Her hands were clasped in front of her and she had a gleam in her eye.

"This is Mr. Redvers," I said as the man in question came forward and offered Mrs. George his hand. "We're engaged to be married."

The housekeeper's reaction was a large smile and a knowing look at me. After my own mother died, Mrs. George had offered me a great deal of warmth and a patient ear, both of which were appreciated and necessary. I would never forget her kindness to me.

"Welcome to the family, Mr. Redvers. I knew Jane wouldn't stay unmarried for too long."

I didn't argue with the woman on that score, much as I wanted to, since she was technically correct. I was remarrying despite the terrible experiences I'd had the first time around the altar.

Brushing those thoughts aside, I led Mrs. George to a seat, taking one opposite her. Before I could speak, however, she interrupted me.

"You're here about your father." Her voice was matter-of-fact.

"We are."

"That foolish man, always haring off to places without more than a moment's notice."

She wasn't wrong there. My father was both absentminded and impulsive, especially when chasing down an academic interest of his. "How long ago did he leave? It's hard to tell."

"A few weeks ago, now. He told me not to bother with anything at the house this time since he didn't know when he would be back—or you." She beamed. "But now that you're back home, Jane, I can start taking care of things again."

"I hate to inform you, but I don't think we'll be staying." I was starting to suspect that my visit home was going to be short indeed. "Do you know where he went this time?"

Mrs. George shrugged. "Back to Constantinople, I imagine."

"I was afraid of that," I muttered. "And the notices on his desk from the bank?"

"Now you know I don't look at his mail," she said primly, but a raised eyebrow from me had her conceding a breath later. "But yes, I did notice that there were more letters from the bank than usual."

"Did he seem upset by them?"

"Your father never really seems upset about much," Mrs. George told us. "And you know how he is about the mail."

"I do," I murmured. Normally I took care of everything, and had set things up before I left so that everything would run smoothly in my absence. I hadn't anticipated him taking out an enormous loan and disappearing to parts unknown, however.

*   *   *

We finished chatting with Mrs. George, learning nothing new but filling her in on how my aunt Millie was faring. She was pleased to hear about the engagement, seemingly not at all concerned that Millie would sell the house and stay there permanently. We took our leave, opting for a stroll back to my father's house. It was growing dark, and the streets were a bit spooky in the lamplight with the bare branches of the trees reaching up into the dark sky.

"Your father wouldn't have left you a note?" Redvers asked. He'd been relatively quiet at Millie's house.

"Frankly I'm surprised he didn't." I gave that a moment's thought. "There's a few more places I could check, though."

"Why wouldn't he leave it somewhere obvious?"

"It simply might not have occurred to him. He lives a bit in his own little world." I had already started wondering how we could get to Istanbul and was feeling some dread at the thought of getting on another ship, when Redvers interrupted me.

"Much like you are right now." His voice was teasing, but concerned.

"Guilty as charged. I'm just worried that we need to go to Constantinople."

"I don't think it's come to that yet. We can simply send him a telegraph and ask him to sort out how to wire the money to the bank before we head to Istanbul."

I paused. "Istanbul?"

"It's the local name," Redvers said. "What most Turks call it."

I would try to use that moving forward. "But why take out that much money? And then disappear to Istanbul with it?"

"Those are reasonable questions," Redvers conceded. "But there has to be a reasonable explanation."

When we arrived back at my own home, I couldn't help but compare the little brick row house to my aunt's stately home. I had never minded how small it seemed in comparison, though. I found our home to be quaint and cozy. I couldn't imagine losing it.

So I would do everything in my power not to.

Chapter Four

We had barely gotten back in the door when I turned to Redvers. "I think we should do a thorough search of the entire house."

Redvers smiled at me. "I was thinking the very same thing. We need to make sure your father didn't squirrel that money away somewhere here."

We decided to start on the top floor and work our way down. The bathroom held nothing of interest and was quickly searched, so we started in on the three bedrooms on that floor. The guest room was quickly eliminated as having anything of interest, so we moved on to my room. It was strange to be standing back in my bedroom, the same one I'd had since childhood. So very much had happened since I'd last been in this room—I took a moment to reflect on that. Redvers was already looking under my mattress but stopped when he saw me standing there.

"Are you simply going to supervise?"

I wrinkled my nose at him. "No, I was just thinking about how much has changed recently." I stepped forward and began searching my wardrobe. "I was also thinking it's unlikely that my father hid anything in here. Not to mention how strange it is to be searching my own things—it's usually someone else's that we're going through."

"An excellent point." Redvers looked thoughtful, but said

nothing more until we'd finished my room. There was, as expected, nothing to be found.

That left my father's room. It was the largest of the bedrooms and wasn't off-limits to me by any means, but I very rarely went in here. It was simply furnished, with a four-poster bed and wardrobe, although there was a second wardrobe that had once belonged to my mother. There was also a dressing table that still had her things on it—a hairbrush, a nearly empty bottle of perfume, and an old jewelry box. Redvers began searching my father's wardrobe and I took a seat at the dressing table and absently looked through the drawers. Nothing but bits and bobs from both my father and my mother. I ran my hands over her hairbrush and unstopped the perfume, taking a whiff. It smelled exactly as I remembered her smelling. Although whether that was due to my actual memories or just my habit of periodically doing exactly this, it was difficult to say.

"Your father kept her things," Redvers said as he opened the second wardrobe. I turned to look at him. He had yet to touch anything, instead standing with hands on hips, regarding the wardrobe full of out-of-date dresses and other pieces of clothing that were showing their age and the ravages of time.

"It's been nearly twenty years," I said. "I asked Father about it once, and he said he just couldn't bear to part with anything that belonged to her. I never asked again." I got up and went to stand beside him, and Redvers took my hand, threading his fingers through mine. It was a comforting gesture. "The memories I have of her are fading."

"You were young when she died."

I was quiet for a few seconds. "I still remember the smell of her perfume, but I can't remember the sound of her voice anymore." Admitting that made my heart ache in a way that it hadn't in a long time.

"I think that happens to everyone," Redvers said gently.

I didn't reply but gave his fingers a squeeze. After another moment I was able to gather my resolve and I released his hand, stepping forward and continuing our search.

But here too was futile. I was unsurprised—it would have been shocking for my father to hide something here, although perhaps he may have counted on that. With nowhere else to look, we trudged back downstairs and continued our search on the first floor. My father's office took the longest amount of time since it was by far the messiest room, and I straightened and examined all his papers and academic detritus as we went. None of it meant anything to me—as far as I could tell, it was nothing but student work and historical research. Very typical of what might be found on my father's desk. I'd already found what was new—the letters from the bank.

Discouraged, we finished the first floor, ending in the kitchen. Redvers sat at the small table while I eyed the icebox. "I'm a little nervous to look in here."

"You don't think Mrs. George would have cleared it out before she left?" Redvers asked.

"I think she would have, but who knows what Father might have put in there after he dismissed her." I mentally prepared myself for some kind of horrific smell once I opened the door.

"Maybe you'll find a huge stack of money," Redvers suggested.

That thought was enough to push me forward and swing open the door. I was surprised and relieved that there was nothing in the refrigerated compartment that had gone bad. Just a single stick of butter that had seen better days, but everything else had been cleared out.

All but the envelope with my name on it, sitting on the top shelf. I plucked it out and closed the door, sitting heavily in the chair opposite Redvers.

"Not where I would have expected to find that," Redvers mused.

I shook my head, my fingers already slicing open the back flap. "I'm not surprised. I've found plenty of things in the icebox over the years, including his reading glasses. Frankly, it's the first place I should have looked."

I pulled the letter from its envelope and Redvers came to stand behind me so he could read over my shoulder.

> *My dear Jane,*
> *I don't know when you'll get this letter, but we will most likely be ships passing in the night. I hope you and my sister are well and that you haven't abandoned her on the side of the road just yet. We both know how she can be. I've told Mrs. George not to bother herself with the house until you return.*
> *I believe I have had a breakthrough with my work, or that I will soon. I have also had a bit of trouble, but nothing to concern yourself with. It will all be taken care of, hopefully before you even see this. I must go. Constantinople calls.*
> *Your loving father,*
> *Henry*

Redvers sat back in his seat, his eyes meeting mine. "So he has gone to Istanbul."

"So it would seem," I said.

"Why wouldn't he tell you what kind of trouble he's found?" Redvers asked. "You took care of the accounts, so why hide whatever type of trouble he's found from you?"

I thought about that for a moment, trying to figure out how best to explain this complicated bit of our relationship. "I take care of the accounts, yes. But in other ways he still sees me very much as his child. I think he sometimes forgets I'm a full-grown woman, and a widow at that." I gazed at the letter for a moment. "I can't explain what the distinction is in his

mind between my taking care of the accounts and getting involved in thornier family affairs, but there you have it."

Redvers was quiet, mulling that over before asking his
next question, a very pragmatic one. "Do you know where
he would stay in Istanbul? So that we can telegraph him and
see what can be done."

I sighed. "I do. He's been there several times in the past
and he stays at the same place. But you're not going to like
what I say next."

It was Redvers' turn to sigh. "I already know what it is.
And no, I'm not going to like it."

We needed to go to Istanbul.

CHAPTER FIVE

That was how I found myself standing on the deck of yet another vessel, only days after disembarking the last one. But this small ship was currently cutting through the heavy currents of the Bosphorus Strait as we sailed toward the mystical city of Istanbul.

I ran my fingers over the envelope in my coat pocket once again, worrying at the paper's edges while the contents continued to worry at my heart. Father's letter had been cryptic to be sure, but also disquieting, especially the part about how he'd found "some trouble." Just the fact that he'd mentioned it at all meant that it was much more than "some."

Was the trouble simply to do with the loan he'd taken out against the house? None of that money was in the house, which meant he'd most likely taken it with him. My father appeared to be loaded down with an enormous sum of money and had set off to a foreign country. He was an adult, but his absentmindedness and general amiability made me incredibly nervous. Would he trust the wrong person and be robbed of that money? Would he leave it in his hotel room only for it to be discovered and stolen?

We now had less than two weeks to pay the money back or the row house would be repossessed. I was cursing the time this trip had ticked away from that looming deadline, days that would have been better spent looking for my father instead of riding various trains and ships. But there was no quicker way to get to where we needed to go. We'd sent telegraphs ahead of ourselves, and now there was nothing to be done until we arrived back on solid land.

A hand settled onto my back and I looked up at Redvers, his eyes creased in concern, as he pressed a kiss to the side of my head. I pressed into his side for a moment to show my appreciation for his concern even though I was certain it was more for me and my state of mind than it was for my father. Not that he wasn't concerned about my father, but I could tell that he thought nothing was terribly amiss.

"I'm certain your father is just buried in the archives. We'll find him in no time and get the money wired back to the bank. All will be well."

This was the same reassurance the man had been giving me the entire trip, although he'd had no good answers about the loan and what on earth my father could have needed that much money for. And while I appreciated the sentiment and wanted nothing more than for it to be true, my instincts told me things weren't as simple as that.

I decided to distract us both. "We must be getting close." The number of wooden fishing boats had increased exponentially as had the calls of the seabirds overhead.

"We are." Redvers took my hand and led me toward the front of the vessel where the few other travelers on our small ship had gathered to watch our approach into the city. The early-morning mist was just beginning to break up and I could see the city stretched out on either side of the port, a literal link between the East and the West. The waterway bustled with staggering numbers of small wooden boats alongside the numerous ferries ushering passengers from one side of the city to the other, and fishermen inspecting nets calling to each other in their native tongue. All this was compelling, but my eyes were immediately drawn to the large domes and spiky minarets of an enormous mosque on a hill that seemed to tower above everything. The rest of the city was laid out on rolling hills all around, minarets of numerous other mosques piercing the curtain of sky sweeping down to the sea. The view was so breathtaking that I nearly forgot the reason we were there in the first place.

Nearly. Concern for my father's "trouble" was never far from my mind and had been my constant companion since we'd left Boston.

I was anxious to head directly to the archives and find my father, but Redvers insisted we head to the hotel and freshen up first. I knew he was right and I did my best to tamp down my impatience. I was mostly successful, but I felt another precious day slipping away as we disembarked from our ship, located our luggage, and had it directed to a ferry headed for the other side of the city. I calmed myself by remembering that even though we had less than two weeks to get matters sorted out, it should still be enough time.

"It's incredible to me that the city is split in two by the sea," I said to Redvers. Right now, I found it mostly inconvenient since it added an extra step to our journey, but I knew that I would find it interesting later, possibly even charming.

"It really is a unique place. Not only is the Asian side divided from the European side by the Bosphorus, but the European side is also split by the Golden Horn."

"Lots of ferries then."

"Lots of ferries and boats," Redvers agreed.

A yawn cracked my face and I reluctantly admitted— although not out loud—that since we were dropping off our bags and freshening up at the hotel, a cup of the famous Turkish coffee wouldn't be remiss. I had slept quite poorly on the journey and had been up before the sun that morning—I could certainly use a boost.

Unloaded from the ferry and reloaded into a taxi with our luggage, I turned my attention to the street. Cars and buffalo-driven carts jockeyed for position on the streets with an electric tram and plenty of pedestrians.

We were heading into the Pera district of the city, that much I knew. There were wide boulevards lined with multistory buildings adorned with numerous arched windows. Off the main thoroughfare I saw winding narrow streets with wooden homes built shoulder to shoulder and children playing on the cobblestones. Still, I was surprised by how Western the city seemed, with its wide boulevards and electric trams. I mentioned this to Redvers.

"Don't worry, the older parts of the city are much like what you'd expect. The Pera neighborhood had a large fire within the last few decades and built these boulevards. But even the streets around the hotel are as narrow as you would expect."

I nodded. Of course, he'd been to Istanbul before. I idly wondered for a moment where the man *hadn't* been. Antarctica perhaps? If I asked the question, he'd most likely produce a photo of himself with a penguin.

The taxi deposited us at the Pera Palace, a once-grand hotel that was showing signs of aging, but was still quite beautiful. The hotel was a large multistory stone square on the corner of Grande Rue and Graveyard Street. Our taxi driver drove down a narrow street to the side of the hotel where porters waited for guests beneath a glass-and-iron overhang attached to the side of the building by cables. Balconies with elegantly sculpted ironwork lined the windows above us, and scrolled marble carvings added flourishes to the hotel's otherwise squared-off facade. A well-dressed porter came out and took charge of our luggage as we entered the hotel and I paused for a moment to take in the décor.

The front desk was just inside the doors of the surprisingly small lobby with its gray-and-pink checked marble floors. Redvers and I headed straight to the desk, my thoughts on getting our bags sorted and a quick stop in the restaurant for some coffee before heading to the archives. Redvers got us quickly checked in, directing our bags to our room so we could stop in the grand salon for that quick cup of coffee.

Unlike the lobby, the grand salon seemed to stretch on forever, stone and pink marble alternating in a striped pattern along the tops of the windows and entryways that reminded me of the Mena House hotel in Egypt. Between stone columns lining the room were numerous windows, outlined with delicately carved wood, making the space feel bright and airy. The space was further lit by two elegant chandeliers; looking up I could see six domes in the ceiling decorated with small circles of blue glass—they appeared to glow blue above us. The long red curtains and plush upholstered red chairs were beginning to show signs of wear, but the space was still stunning and I was immediately charmed. But before we could make it even partway across the room, a familiar voice stopped us short.

"Jane, I cannot *believe* this is where you've decided to stay." Aunt Millie's voice boomed in the open space—she may as well have been making an announcement to the hotel at large.

CHAPTER SIX

I couldn't stop the sigh that escaped—luckily, we were far enough away that Millie didn't hear it. A quick glance at Redvers' face told me he was quite bemused by this turn of events and I wished that I felt the same. With some reluctance, we crossed over to my aunt and her fiancé, Lord Hughes, a genial member of the British aristocracy who had a remarkable ability to ignore my aunt's rough edges. They'd taken up residency in a small grouping of the plush chairs, a tea service on the table in front of them. Lord Hughes stood as we approached, but my aunt stayed firmly seated where she was.

"Aunt Millie. When I sent you that telegraph, I didn't expect that you would actually join us here." My aunt had been included in the flurry of telegraphs we'd sent before getting on board the ship.

Millie huffed. "You can't imagine that I would stay at home while my only brother appears to have gone missing."

I could feel the crease between my eyebrows deepening. I'd let her know that Father had come to Istanbul, but I hadn't mentioned anything about the loan against the house in the message I'd sent. "He hasn't gone missing—" I started to say, but was quickly interrupted.

"Edward has already spoken to the front desk, and your father left several days ago without checking out." Millie did manage to drop her voice here, a small mercy. "Edward took care of the charges."

"It was no trouble," Lord Hughes said.

"I appreciate that." I said absently, trying to process this information. "Why would Father have left already?" Did he receive our telegraph and leave? Or had he never received it at all? "And surely he just forgot to check out—you know how he is."

Millie shook her head. "He left his trunk behind, and all his clothing was left hanging in the wardrobe. Lucky for us they held on to everything in case Henry returned." Despite Millie's blustering, I could tell that she was genuinely worried, which did nothing for the anxiety I now felt creeping back up. Even though my instincts had warned me something was wrong since finding my father's note, I'd actually begun to accept Redvers' reassurances that we'd find Father and the money and all would be well.

But there was no good explanation for my father leaving the hotel without his luggage that I could think of. Even at his most absentminded he would have taken his things with him. Was this part of the "trouble"? And had that trouble found him here? It left me wondering where he could have gone, and with such a large sum of money in his possession.

Unless the money had been left behind? This was some wishful thinking and I sincerely doubted we would find it among his things. Even my father wasn't *that* trusting.

I was still determined to stick to my original plan of keeping the information about the loan and the bank to ourselves, however. Not only would it amplify Millie's worry, but she would immediately try to take care of things before we could find Father and the money. I didn't want to be in her financial debt. Hers or Lord Hughes.

Redvers broke in. "Where is the luggage now?"

Hughes tipped his head toward the front desk. "They have it in the back. I asked them to hold it until you arrived."

Redvers nodded his appreciation at Hughes and the men shook hands. Redvers turned to me. "I'll sort it out." I smiled wanly as Hughes volunteered to accompany him and decide where to have my father's luggage sent.

A new worry flickered at the back of my mind and I squashed it before it could even fully form, turning to Millie instead. "You got here quickly."

"We did. Are you going to stand there hovering or are you going to take a seat?" I did as instructed and took a seat in the chair opposite my aunt as she looked pointedly at my left hand. "I see you still haven't managed to secure Mr. Redvers."

Despite my worry, obstinance reared its head and I refused to tell Millie that Redvers had recently proposed to me and I'd actually accepted. If I told her that the reason we'd gone to Boston in the first place was so that Redvers could meet my father before we decided on a wedding date, she would take it as a personal victory, and that stuck in my craw too much to let the words pass my lips.

And truth be told, I was in no great hurry to rush into another marriage. I was determined to take things slowly this time, and so far, Redvers was amenable to my setting the pace—a slow one.

I changed the subject instead. "Where are you and Lord Hughes staying?"

Millie sniffed. "We have a room at the Tokatlıyan. Frankly, this whole neighborhood has seen better days—it really went downhill during the war, I'm told, but the accommodations there are acceptable." She brushed at something invisible on her skirt. "We are going to tour Topkapi Palace this afternoon."

"An excellent plan," I said. That would at least keep her occupied while Redvers and I went to the national archives where my father worked whenever he visited. As a professor of history, with a specialized interest in the Ottoman Empire, my father had spent a lot of time in archives over the years, both at home and abroad, and I'd become accustomed to tracking him down amidst stacks of dusty papers. I just worried it wouldn't be that simple this time.

Lord Hughes and Redvers returned and my aunt and her fiancé took their leave of us with a promise to meet up again later in the afternoon.

"I suppose we can meet you here, if it's more convenient. At least they had a decent tea service," Millie said.

"That would be wonderful." I hoped I at least *sounded* sincere even if it didn't feel it.

Millie took Lord Hughes' arm and I watched as they exited the hotel. I waited until they were well out of earshot before I spoke. "I hope you can get alcohol in this city. Because I'm going to need a drink when they return."

CHAPTER SEVEN

Redvers chuckled. "Even though alcohol is technically banned by the Muslim religion, it's still widely available here. There's a lovely bar called the Orient on this floor."

"That's the first good news I've had all day." I rubbed at my temple and then dropped my hand. I really wanted that cup of coffee, but now we had other things to attend to. "Shall we inspect Father's things first?"

Redvers nodded. "Precisely what I was going to suggest." He held out a piece of paper. "And here's the telegraph you sent. It's unopened."

I sighed. At least that meant my father hadn't heard that we were coming and fled. But it didn't help me determine what may have driven him from the hotel.

The ornate ironwork-and-wood elevator was in use, so we opted for the stairs, walking up several flights of marble steps covered in rich red runners with a gold Oriental design. We let ourselves into our quarters and I took a quick look around. It was only one room, but a large one, with a brass four-poster bed at one end and a dark wood desk at the other with a grouping of low, upholstered wood chairs near the windows. I barely registered that the view was one of the water before turning my attention to the familiar battered leather trunk. I'd tried to buy him a new one for Christmas several years ago, but he'd insisted that he couldn't part with this particular piece since my mother had purchased it for him the first year they were married. The porter had placed it on a suitcase stand, and I stood and looked at it for a moment before popping the locks and flipping the top open.

"The porter brought it up so we could have some privacy while we looked through his things." Redvers came to stand beside me. "The clerk said that the staff packed this, since his clothes were still hanging in the wardrobe." I looked at him, worry shining from my eyes. That was nothing new, but this time I could see that Redvers was also concerned, and not just for me.

"Even though we went through his things at home, I still have no idea what he packed, so I can't say whether anything is missing or not."

"But you might be able to tell if there's something here that is new," Redvers countered.

That was an excellent point. I began extracting the neatly folded items from the trunk one by one. This alone was proof that my father hadn't packed this trunk since he could never be bothered with this level of tidiness—the hotel staff had obviously taken more care with his things than he ever would have. I removed everything from the trunk, then stood aside to appraise the contents. A number of pants, a suit coat, and numerous shirts sat beside stacks of socks—some of which I could see were beyond repair and needed to be disposed of— a shaving kit, and other necessities.

"Is there anything that doesn't seem to belong?" Redvers asked.

I shook my head. "But I'll tell you what's strange. The man always had stacks of papers with him. He didn't keep a journal or anything like that, but he had papers stuck everywhere—you saw what his office is like. And he carried a leather satchel that was always bursting at the seams. That appears to be missing as well."

Redvers bent down and began searching through the pockets of the suit coat. Without a word I did the same and began searching the pants pockets. We systematically searched every item that had come from the luggage, but beyond a few spare coins and a button that needed to be reattached to an unknown item, we found nothing. Frustration warred with new anxiety.

"Whatever happened to him, it seems he took all his papers at least." I made a *hmm*-ing noise. "And there is no stack of money." This wasn't surprising to me.

Redvers put a hand on my shoulder. "We don't know for certain that anything happened to him. He might have simply left, thinking he would be back soon to collect his things."

"And the money?" I asked. Redvers' only reply was the furrowing of his brow.

My father believing he would be back soon to collect his luggage was the best-case scenario, but I knew it was an unlikely one. This luggage had been sitting here for a week already. Six days to be precise, and it had taken two full days for the hotel to miss my father and pack his things.

It meant we were eight days behind Henry Wunderly, wherever he had gone. And we had less than two weeks before the bank went into action against our home.

We repacked my father's trunk, quickly freshened up, and headed for the Turkish National Archives, which was, of course, on the other side of the Golden Horn. We made our way down to the harbor and onto another ferry before hailing a taxi to the archives. We were indeed close to the heart of the old town now, and the streets were as narrow and crowded as I'd expected them to be for an ancient city, winding up and over the city's hills. Men hunched over with heavy loads on their backs wove past others with donkey carts carrying large metal containers of water. I saw several men hurrying through the crowded sidewalks swinging brass containers, and I made a note to ask Redvers later what they were carrying. For now, however, it seemed we had arrived.

An enormous brick wall stretched all along the road and out of sight around the corner. The corner was dominated by a rounded guard tower with elaborate gold filigree windows and a decorative roof coming to a peak. I cocked my head at the wall. "Is this where we're going?" It looked like something that would be more at home surrounding a castle than a national archive.

Redvers shook his head as he paid the driver. "That's part of the old city wall." He pointed across the street to the gate that stood opposite us in yet another wall. "It's through there—the Sublime Port, it's called."

I wasn't certain it was sublime, but the gate certainly was striking. A curved, patinated brass overhang with ornate painting on the underside outlined the main entrance, its dark wood doors bordered by ornate gray-and-white marble. Two matching curved overhangs on each side covered large gray marble façades with small gold spigots in each.

Beyond the gate lay a small warren of buildings, and Redvers led us off to the left, pushing through wooden doors to enter a rather nondescript building. The second person we spoke to vaguely remembered a recent American visitor and directed us to the office of Ziya Bey. But knocking on the unmarked door we were pointed to got no response.

I counted doors again. "We're sure it's this one?" The man had been helpful, but difficult to understand. Redvers nodded, and we were just turning to leave when a man in a gray tweed suit came down the long hall toward us.

"Are you looking for me?" He had a large rectangular head with bushy eyebrows—honestly, the dark caterpillar-like eyebrows were the focal point of his entire face, detracting attention from the intelligence in his dark eyes.

"Are you Ziya Bey?" Redvers asked.

"I am," the man said as he came to a stop before us, squinting slightly as he scrutinized me. I flushed a bit at the unexpected inspection.

"You must be Jane," Ziya said. "You look very much like Professor Wunderly."

My momentary discomfort was replaced with relief that this man obviously knew my father.

Bey opened his office door and ushered us into the small room. It was meticulously tidy and devoid of any personal touches except for the slightly worn prayer rug beneath the window. Redvers and I each took a seat.

"Can I get you some tea?"

I opened my mouth to tell him we didn't have time to take tea, but Redvers put a hand on my arm. "We would love some," Redvers said.

I was nearly vibrating with impatience, but we made small talk with Bey while we waited for the tea service to arrive. A young boy who couldn't have been more than ten years of age brought an elaborate set with small tulip-shaped cups. At Bey's nod, the boy placed a small strainer over the top of a delicate cup, then lifted the silver teapot and poured tea through it before moving the strainer to the next in order to fill it. Once this was done, the young man put the strainer aside and picked up a small pair of tongs, looking again to Bey.

"You will want two lumps," the archivist said, nodding again at the boy to continue. The child put two lumps of sugar into each cup before passing us each a small cup on an equally small saucer with a tiny silver spoon. Bey and Redvers picked up their spoons and soon the sound of gentle tinkling filled the air, spoons rattling against tea-filled cups. I followed suit, even though I dislike sugar in my beverages.

I took a sip, finding I was actually quite glad of the sugar. The tea was very unlike British tea—this was dark and very bitter. I would have found it nearly undrinkable without the added sugar cubes. But the two balanced each other well and it was actually quite tasty. "Have you seen my father? We're looking for him." I finally asked, hoping enough small talk had been made to meet the necessary requirements for politeness.

Ziya shook his head. "He has not been here for nearly a week."

This coincided with what we'd learned from the hotel.

"He came here almost three weeks ago; he was very excited about a possible discovery. We were searching through documents from the early Ottoman Empire—his Turkish was good, but not quite good enough to make translations from Suleiman's time, so I was assisting him."

My father had often talked about what he was working on, and I hated to admit that sometimes I only listened with one ear. Especially since he was prone to repeating himself quite often. Guilt threatened to overwhelm me—right now I wanted nothing more than to hear one of his stories for the tenth or eleventh time.

"I am glad you came here. If you had not, I would have sent for you, I think." Bey seemed troubled for the first time since we'd begun speaking. "The professor had been very excited about the last few items we translated, although he couldn't tell me exactly why."

Couldn't or wouldn't tell you flashed across my mind for no reason that I could discern, and I gave myself a quick mental shake.

"And then he went for lunch and didn't return. I expected to see him that afternoon, but he still did not return. I thought to myself that he would come back soon, since we have worked together for many years. He would sometimes go off for a day or so, usually to walk about the city and think, but he always came back here. I did not become concerned until I had not seen him for several days. I checked at his hotel and they told me he was not there." Bey's eyes were concerned as they met mine. "It seems strange that he would leave without his luggage."

It also seemed strange that Bey would know my father had left without his trunk, and I wondered why the hotel would have been so free with information about one of their guests. Did Bey or the hotel also know about the large amount of money he'd been carrying?

As if sensing my suspicion, Bey continued. "My cousin works at the front desk. That is how I know this."

I wasn't sure that made things any better, and I felt Redvers shift in his seat beside me. I nodded for Bey to continue, but Redvers broke in with a question of his own.

"Do you have any idea what Professor Wunderly thought he'd found?"

Bey cocked his head and thought for a moment. "I do not know the significance of the document we translated, but I do know that he felt he was close to finally locating the sultan's heart."

CHAPTER EIGHT

It sounded like an impressive pronouncement, but I was reserving judgment. "He's thought that he was close a time or two before this as well."

"That is true," Bey acknowledged. "But this time felt different. I cannot explain how, but we both felt it."

Redvers looked from Ziya Bey to me. "What is the sultan's heart?"

I knew a great deal of the story, since my father had been interested in this piece of history for as long as I could remember. In fact, it had been something of a long-standing joke between my mother and my father, although his obsession with actually finding the heart had grown much stronger after she'd died. But I decided to let Bey tell the story—I wanted to see if his explanation matched my memory, so I gestured for him to go ahead.

"Suleiman the Magnificent was a great ruler of the Ottoman Empire, one of the greatest in history. During a campaign in Hungary to expand our borders he became ill and died; the year was 1566. On the battlefield, you understand." We nodded to show that we understood Suleiman died heroically. Satisfied, Bey sat back in his chair, lacing his hands together over his gray wool vest. "His death was kept from the soldiers for some time so they would not be discouraged in battle—they were laying siege to the city of Szigetvár at the time, and could not afford to lose their resolve, so Suleiman's body was quietly prepared for burial. To do this, they removed his heart and placed it in a golden box, which was then buried."

Redvers eyebrows rose a bit, but I knew we weren't even to the good part of the legend yet. I had a question before we continued, though.

"Was only his heart removed? In Egypt they remove all the internal organs for burial."

Bey inclined his head slightly. "You are correct. Here too they removed all of the emperor's organs in order to preserve the body. They were all buried in the same place, but it is the heart that everyone is most concerned with." Bey paused for a beat and then continued with the story. "The body was kept there for forty-eight days before his son could come and claim the throne. After that time, Suleiman's body was returned here to Istanbul and properly buried."

"But the heart remained buried where it was," I said.

"This is true. It has never been found."

Redvers frowned a bit. "This is a fascinating story, but why the interest in finding the man's heart and not any of the other organs? Is it the gold box people are after?"

Bey leaned forward and shook his head. "It is not the box at all, sir. You see, legend has it that whoever possesses the sultan's heart possesses all the power of the sultan himself. He was a very powerful man—it could be dangerous if such a thing fell into the wrong hands."

I could tell that Redvers was doing his level best to hold back a chuckle at this superstitious story. I didn't believe that the sultan's heart held mystical powers myself, nor did my father, I was certain of that. Well, nearly certain. But that didn't mean there weren't others out there who believed the legend. And my guess was that they would do nearly anything to get their hands on such an artifact. Either for power, money—or both.

And while Ziya Bey may have thought it was the heart that seekers were after, I disagreed. When Suleiman was at the height of his power, the Ottoman Empire was fantastically wealthy. They had carved emerald boxes to hold other emeralds, for heaven's sake. There was every chance that the gold box itself was encrusted with priceless jewels—making it worth finding regardless of what was buried inside it.

We all sat in silence for a moment, digesting what Bey had told us about the legend. I knew Redvers would come to the same conclusion that I had—while the heart didn't have powers, individuals out there certainly would want the box. But I was curious about what Ziya believed.

"Do you think there is any truth to the legend?" I asked.

To his credit, Ziya appeared to give the matter careful thought before answering. "I think there are many things that are beyond our understanding. So while I personally do not believe such things, nor would I seek them out, I also cannot rule out the possibility that the heart is more valuable than a mere curiosity."

Silence descended again, but this time it was broken by Redvers, practical as usual. "Can we see what you were working on with the professor before he left?"

"Certainly." Ziya stood from his chair. "Let us go to the research room. I have kept the papers aside that we were working on." He glanced sideways at me. "I thought you might come and would want to see them."

We followed Bey through several dim and cramped hallways, bringing us to the reading room. Despite the domed ceilings, the lighting here was also quite dim—surprising for a place where scholars came to research and read. We settled in at a long table and Ziya brought us a small stack of ancient papers and what looked to be bound notebooks.

Ziya indicated the papers. "These are *evrak,* or papers that are not bound." He then pointed to the books. "And these are *defter*s. Now, your father and I were working with these *defters,* and translated much from them. But this *evrak* here is the last item I translated for your father," Ziya said. "It is a letter from one of the viziers that attended Suleiman the Magnificent."

Ziya gently placed the paper before us. It was yellow with age and browning at the edges—it seemed a miracle that the thing still existed at all. But it was obvious from the amount of writing on the ancient paper that this was a very short letter—there wasn't much here to work with, and he gave us a quick translation.

"It says here, 'We returned with our great ruler so that he may be buried in his tomb. Now he is with his beloved Roxelana.' Then it goes on to describe how they transported the body. Your father was excited at this part here." Ziya pointed at a place near the end of the script.

I frowned. "Is that the correct translation? 'They left his heart buried far from his heart? The key may be found nearby?'"

"It doesn't make a great deal of sense to me either, but that is nearly word for word." His eyebrows drew together as he considered the paper. "I don't know what your father liked about this phrase, but he seemed to think it was important."

Bey set the letter aside and showed us the rest of the papers. From what the man said, it seemed that my father hadn't been nearly as enthusiastic about anything else they had worked on. Which left us with the cryptic riddle from the vizier's letter.

Redvers had been fairly quiet to this point, digesting everything. And when he did speak, I fully expected him to ask about the papers. But I was wrong.

"Thank you so much for your help." Redvers put a hand on my back as though ready to usher me away. I felt a twinge of annoyance at being shepherded, especially since there had to be something else here pointing to where my father had hared off to. There *had* to be.

Ziya cocked his head. "You are most welcome. I think you will need a translator while you are here, will you not?" He nodded his head in affirmation of his own observation. "I am happy to provide this service."

"That is a very kind offer, but I'm not—" Redvers started to say, but Bey held up both hands.

"I insist. Truly." Bey looked at me, his brown eyes soft. "Your father would have wanted it."

I didn't believe for a moment that my father would have wanted an archivist to forgo his academic work to serve as my personal translator, but I kept that to myself. And this seemed like a way for Bey to insert himself into our search for my father, but what were his motivations? It could be that he was legitimately concerned about Father's welfare, or it could be something else entirely—like the prospect of finding a golden box or a stack of cold hard American cash, taken out against my family home.

Then I chided myself for being overly suspicious. It was entirely possible that Bey was just trying to help. But Redvers' hand hadn't moved from its place on my back and I could feel him tense slightly at the man's suggestion. It seemed neither of us was excited about Bey's offer.

"Very well, we accept. Would you be able to meet us at our hotel later this afternoon?" Redvers said, and I jerked a bit in surprise that Redvers had agreed—I'd fully expected him to come up with an excuse to turn Bey down.

"I can come with you now, if you like. I just need to secure these papers." The archivist was already gathering together all the papers and notebooks he'd spread on the table. Carefully, in deference to their age, of course.

"Later this afternoon would be better." Redvers' voice was affable and slightly apologetic, but I could tell it was forced. "After our journey I think we could use some time to lie down and rest."

"Of course, of course," Bey said. "I will meet you there this afternoon. You are at the Pera Palace as well, then?"

Redvers confirmed this and we exchanged final pleasantries before taking our leave. We made it onto the pavement outside before I spoke.

"I want to trust him, but I'm not entirely sure we should."

Redvers shook his head. "Not yet, anyway."

CHAPTER NINE

We set off uphill in the direction of the tram stop, weaving in and out of the sea of people on the street, mostly men wearing suits or shirts with vests and loose, traditional pants. Only one or two women were wearing dark veils, accompanied by a man. We passed several places that looked like cafés with tables out front but no one sitting at them; when I peered inside, I could see men—both old and middle aged—gathered at tables, some of them smoking tall glass pipes on the tables. I was fascinated, but there was a conspicuous lack of women in them. I also noticed that the men of the city weren't wearing the traditional fez, which I had expected to see, especially after my trip to Egypt where they wore a very similar head covering.

"What happened to the fez?" I asked Redvers. While the majority of men wore what Redvers did—wool suits and coats—some of the local men wore billowing Turkish outfits, which seemed completely at odds with the fedoras they sported. It was a rather jarring sight.

"They were outlawed in 1925. Just last year."

This caught my attention. As did the fact that I didn't actually know much about the city of Istanbul. I felt a pang of regret that I hadn't spent my time on the lengthy voyage here learning something about the culture and the city, but I'd had little ability to concentrate.

But now it was time for a quick history lesson. "Why were they outlawed?"

"The new Turkish republic is led by a man named Atatürk. He's . . . well, rather forcibly trying to move the country into modern times, and apparently the fez had too much connection to their Ottoman past."

Looking around, I realized I'd also expected to see the women wearing veils. Instead, they were dressed much as I was, bundled up against the chilly air in long coats and stylish hats, although there were fewer women out on the streets than men.

"Atatürk is trying to modernize the country, make it less fundamentally Muslim, so the women are no longer required to wear them. Many of the women you see are also Russian, I believe." He tipped his head at a small group of people in disheveled clothes begging for money from passersby. "A lot of Russians fled here after the war—White Russians who opposed the revolution there."

This wasn't our first run-in with White Russians, so I wasn't terribly surprised that there had been an influx of them into Istanbul, close as it was to Russia. And while it was all very interesting, my mind had other, more pressing questions. "Do you think he was translating correctly?" I also assumed, correctly, that Redvers would be able to follow my abrupt change of course.

Redvers looked behind us, never slowing his pace, before answering me. "It's hard to say. I don't speak enough Turkish, and certainly can't read it. Even the modern stuff. But it's unlikely that Bey would give us a bad translation."

"Why do you say that?"

"Because your father most likely made notes—you said he always had a lot of papers with him. It's entirely possible that he would have left you those notes, or sent them to you. Bey has no way of knowing whether or not that is the case, and it would be safer for him to assume he would be caught giving us bad information."

I mulled that over for a moment. "Unless the hotel actually let him look at my father's things. Then he might know there weren't any papers or notes to be had."

Redvers turned his head toward me, glancing slightly behind us. "It's possible. Especially since his cousin works at the desk."

I tried to remember just what I had told Bey. I'd mentioned that my father had left me a letter—but I hadn't told him what was in it or where my father had left it. Although with a cousin working at the front desk, the archivist probably knew a lot, including that my father hadn't left me a message at the hotel. And from that, Bey might be able to guess that the one piece of correspondence my father did leave for me had been left well before my father disappeared—and without any information from the translated letter.

Unfortunately, there was no way to know if my father had told Bey about the money he was carrying without asking Bey outright what he knew. I couldn't imagine why my father would have mentioned it, though. Unless it was to ask Bey about where he should keep it, such as in a local reputable bank.

It was a lot of guessing about who knew what, and the mental gymnastics only added to my frustration that we had nothing solid to go on other than a cryptic riddle. And no matter how many times I ran the riddle through my head, I couldn't make sense of it.

"What next?" I asked as we neared the tram stop. One was just pulling up, and I estimated that if we hurried across the street, we might be able to catch it.

Redvers took my hand and abruptly changed course, hailing a taxi and quickly ushering me into the back seat before hopping in beside me. "The Grand Bazaar, please," he told the driver.

"This is an odd time for a shopping trip," I said drolly. I was not oblivious to the fact that Redvers had noticed something—

he'd been on guard ever since we'd stepped back on to the street, and had taken several opportunities to glance behind us. I just had no idea what it was he'd seen.

And I wasn't going to get an immediate answer either since our Turkish taxi driver was proving to be incredibly friendly, attempting to make conversation with Redvers in broken English despite the very short trip. Under normal circumstances I would have been charmed, but today I was merely anxious to get to a place where I could interrogate Redvers about what we appeared to be hiding from.

While the men chatted, I idly wondered if there would ever come a time again when I didn't feel gnawing anxiety. And how on earth were we going to find my father when we were already so far behind him?

The taxi left us on a street corner, and despite the crowds, I looked around in confusion. "Where is the bazaar?"

Redvers smiled and gestured past the stalls on the sidewalks selling goods to the building before us. "It's indoors."

"Oh!" I'd expected the bazaar to be out in the open air, as it was in Cairo. Despite my burning desire to talk with Redvers about whatever it was that he'd spotted, I found that I *was* curious about Istanbul's famous market.

We entered the sprawling brick building through a large arched entrance, immediately thrusting ourselves into the chaos of the market. People and goods stretched as far as I could see in multiple directions beneath domed ceilings painted yellow and blue. The only natural light seemed to come from small windows near the roofline. It was utterly overwhelming and I said as much.

Redvers glanced behind us. "I believe there are more than three thousand shops here. If we can't lose him here, we won't be able to lose him at all."

"Lose who?"

"The man who's been following us."

The pieces fell into place—Redvers' attention to something on the streets behind us and his sudden desire to head here. I found myself feeling irritated instead of afraid—I didn't need another thing to worry about just now.

I had yet to catch sight of the man, but I didn't need to see him to believe that he was there, so I let Redvers lead the way. We moved with purpose down the first corridor, passing a dizzying number of goods. Leather shoes in a rainbow of colors, leather bags and belts, beautifully painted ceramics and plates. Another corridor held more treasures, textiles in gorgeous and vibrant colors. I was now truly sorry that we didn't have a chance to stop and look around. Every so often amidst the crowds I could see a customer was sitting on a stool outside a merchant's store enjoying a cup of tea, or even coffee with the proprietor. It was becoming more and more apparent that the people of Turkey took their tea very seriously.

"Are you certain he's still behind us?" The smell of strong Turkish coffee had just hit my nose and I was more than a little tempted to stop for a cup.

Redvers gave me a wry look over his shoulder as he continued to move. We entered a corridor that looked to offer predominantly rugs, and I nearly *oooh*ed aloud at the detailed designs and craftsmanship we were rushing past. I was thinking about how I really wanted to get my fingers in the plush pile, when Redvers suddenly stopped ahead of me.

"In here." He gently directed me past a shopkeeper who nodded at Redvers and into the man's rug shop. Everywhere one looked there were either stacks or rolls of carpets in a multitude of colors. We quickly crouched behind an enormous pile of Oriental rugs toward the back of the store. Pleased with our hiding place, I reached out and rubbed my fingers on the rugs before me, impressed with the fine weaving. Redvers was on full alert and I felt badly that I couldn't assist him, but I had no idea what the man who'd been following us looked like.

A second shopkeeper, a handsome man with dark hair and amber eyes, moved over to our stack. I fully expected him to ask us why we were hiding behind a pile of rugs, but instead, he pretended to rearrange the top rug without ever once looking at us.

"You know them, don't you?" I whispered quietly to Redvers.

Redvers didn't answer, but the shopkeeper glanced down at me and winked.

I gave my head a little shake. Of course, he did.

A few minutes later the man standing next to the door joined his friend at our stack. "I think you are in the clear," he said.

Redvers stood, brushing off his pants. "Thank you, Mehmed, Orhan," he said to each man in turn. "A pleasure to see you as always."

"Likewise, my friend. Reminds me of the last time you were in town actually." Orhan's amber eyes were alight with amusement. "Can you stay for some tea?"

"I'm afraid not this trip. But I promise to come back soon."

Mehmed chimed in. "And you'll introduce your lovely friend to us then?"

"Jane Wunderly," I said, holding out my hand. Mehmed took it and gave it a shake and Orhan followed suit. No one needed to introduce me—I was perfectly capable of doing it myself, although I was now dying to know what had happened the "last time" Redvers was in town. It took all I had not to ask these charming rug merchants to relate the story.

"Your rugs are beautiful," I told them instead. "I hope next time we can see more of them."

Orhan's eyes lit up. "I would love to show you all the rugs that your heart desires."

We took our leave, winding our way back in the general direction we'd come from. My senses were still overwhelmed by the vast and colorful displays of goods for sale, despite the dim lighting, and it took some effort to force my mind back to our immediate concerns. "You're certain he's gone?"

"I'm fairly certain. I saw him go by and he didn't return. And we'll wind around a bit so that it's unlikely he'll be able to find us."

"Excellent," I said. When Orhan had mentioned my heart's desire, it had struck up a memory that I hadn't thought of in many years but could mention now that we were moving at a rate of speed closer to normal. "You know, when I was a child and my father talked about the sultan's heart, I always pictured it as an enormous jewel in the shape of a heart. Like a ruby." We had taken a new turn into an area where there was nothing but jewelers as far as the eye could see, and I glanced around, seeing nothing like what I was describing. "It wasn't until I was older that I realized he was talking about an actual human heart. Probably mummified by now."

"Yes, a jewel would be much more romantic," Redvers agreed. "And is that what you would like? An enormous ruby in the shape of a heart?"

I laughed. "No, Redvers. It is not." I knew he was referring to an engagement ring and was also teasing me, but I thought I detected a bit of a serious question there. He hadn't given me a ring yet, and I wondered what he had in mind, although I didn't want to ask.

"Good to know." He gave me a sly smile, and I wondered just what he *did* have in mind.

CHAPTER TEN

Outside the bazaar we hailed a taxi instead of taking a tram, and made our way back to our hotel. Redvers kept one eye out the back of the vehicle, but didn't see anyone following us—we had apparently been successful in losing whoever it was. I was waiting until we were alone to interrogate Redvers about the man he'd seen, but instead of heading to our room, Redvers headed straight for the front desk. I followed with a frown.

"We are in need of some lunch," Redvers told the clerk behind the desk, a young man in a black suit who looked to be no older than twenty. I was going to argue that we didn't have time to stop and eat when my stomach growled. Rather loudly. Redvers smirked and the clerk politely pretended not to notice. Instead, the young man nodded, his eyes flicking to me before returning to Redvers. "Madam's father had a *meyhane* that was his particular favorite. Perhaps you would like to go there?"

Redvers told the young man that would be ideal, and while he collected the name of the place—I assumed a *meyhane* was a type of restaurant—I reeled a bit. Did everyone in the hotel know that I was Henry Wunderly's daughter? And more importantly, why hadn't I thought to ask the staff if they knew anything about my father and his habits?

We stepped back onto the street where Redvers took a moment to inspect the pedestrians in either direction before we set out.

"I didn't even think about asking the staff if they knew anything about where Father liked to frequent," I said glumly.

"That's why you have me along," Redvers said lightly, offering me his arm.

I accepted, linking my arm with his. "It's true." I matched his light tone. "You're fairly useless otherwise."

Redvers grinned wolfishly at me, then snuck in a quick kiss, and for a moment I felt ever so slightly better.

We arrived at the *meyhane* within minutes and were quickly seated since we were the only ones in the restaurant. The exterior was unassuming, as was the inside. A brick ceiling and wood paneling along the bottom half of the walls added some charm to the small space that was otherwise filled with simple wood tables and chairs.

Once the waiter had gone with instructions to bring a tea for Redvers and some coffee for me, I turned to my companion. "So, in addition to everything else, we're being followed."

"We are," Redvers confirmed.

I sighed. It had not once occurred to me that might be the case, and I was glad once again that Redvers' instincts were so well honed. It almost certainly came from his profession, whatever that was. In my mind I'd simply started thinking of him as a spy; I wondered if he would disagree with that generalization.

"First of all, why would anyone be following us?" I asked. "And secondly, how would they know who we are?"

Redvers looked chagrined. It was unusual for him—he was normally entirely confident. "There was a bit of an . . . incident . . . last time I was in town."

I could feel my eyebrows raise. Despite everything, I found myself quite amused. "What type of 'incident'?"

Redvers blew out some air. He was obviously not thrilled to relate this story, and I felt myself leaning forward, anticipating whatever it was he was about to tell me. "I was here several years ago for . . . reasons that aren't important."

One of my eyebrows dropped and I was now crooking just the one in question. "Oh, really?"

"Yes, really. It was because of political interests and the influx of emigrés . . ."

I held up a hand. He was right, I wasn't interested in the reason. "But something happened." It was more of a statement than a question.

"I was recognized and my cover was blown. News spread quickly across the city by interested parties and someone else had to be sent in to gather the information that I was supposed to."

"Who recognized you?" I had my chin in my palm, gazing at him intently.

Redvers paused and sighed again. "A Russian woman who was nobility back in Russia, but at the time was working in a nightclub here. She'd pawned all her furs and jewels and had taken to the stage when her money ran out."

"She sounds fascinating. Was she a decent singer at least? Or was it dancer?" Now I was teasing him—I wasn't worried about the woman, but it was fun to be the one giving him a hard time for once.

"Katerina Semenov. She was quite a good singer, actually. And you're having entirely too much fun." This was delivered as our waiter returned with our beverages and set them carefully on the table. It was enough time for me to become serious again.

"The man who was following us . . . you didn't recognize him."

Redvers shook his head. "I didn't, but that doesn't mean much. I could have been recognized by any number of people. He's probably just the one assigned to us for today."

I took a drink of my coffee, savoring the robust bitter flavor. "He's probably out of a job now since we lost him this afternoon."

"They'll send another one."

I tipped my head in acknowledgment. "Any idea what they want?"

Redvers gave a shrug. "Probably to see what I'm doing here, whether there's anything they should know about. My guess is I've caused a bit of a stir in some circles."

I put my chin back in my cupped hand. "Well, just one more complication I suppose. But since it probably has nothing to do with Father, there's not much use worrying about it, is there?"

I was about to ask another question when a woman in an intricately embroidered top and a long dark skirt belted at the waist approached our table. She was more than a decade older than me, probably closer to two, but her large hazel eyes were warm and her hair only beginning to show the first signs of graying. "Pardon me," she said. "I don't mean to interrupt, but you are Jane? Jane Wunderly?"

Surprise unquestionably showed on my face. Did everyone in this city know who I was already? First Ziya Bey, then the clerk at the hotel, and now this woman.

The woman continued speaking. "You see, I know your father."

Chapter Eleven

It wasn't terribly surprising that this woman would know my father if she worked in the restaurant he frequented. It was strange that she would recognize me, however.

"Your father, he spoke of you often." The woman was perfectly composed, hands resting on the back of an empty chair. Redvers gestured for her to join us, and she did, settling herself easily into the chair. The waiter returned just then and she quickly barked something at him in Turkish and the young man scurried off.

Redvers raised his eyebrows—I'm not sure precisely what my face was doing, but the woman chuckled. "I asked him to bring a platter of appetizers so you may eat while we talk. You must be hungry."

"Can we know your name?" I asked.

"My apologies. My name is Maral Aslanyan. My father owns this *meyhane*," Maral said. "Professor Wunderly had been coming here for years and he always had updates on how his little girl was doing. He carried a picture of you in his wallet, always."

I found this to be quite touching. "That's lovely. Have you known him long?"

Maral spread her hands. "My family had to leave the city for some time. We are Armenian, and were forced to leave, as so many of my people were. Your father was kind enough to keep in touch, and when we returned to Istanbul, he came back to our restaurant again."

I nodded, about to ask more about why her family had been forced to leave the city, but when I looked over at Redvers, I saw he had a speculative look in his eyes. "You were perhaps quite *close* with the professor?" Redvers asked.

It was an ordinary question, but the way he asked it implied something that never would have occurred to me. I sat back in my seat, stunned. Was he suggesting what I thought he was suggesting?

Maral's face colored, a flush creeping prettily up her neck to her cheeks, her quiet composure finally broken.

I opened my mouth but nothing came out. In fact, I wasn't sure I would know what to say ever again. My father had a . . . romantic interest? Girlfriend? I was desperate to know what exactly their relationship was—within reason—but I was also terrified to find out. Henry Wunderly spoke often about how much he'd loved my mother. And while she'd passed away many years ago, she had been the driving force behind my father's mounting obsession with finally finding the sultan's heart—or at least that was what I'd been told. I'd never once considered that he might meet someone else. It had never seemed that he was *interested* in meeting someone else.

And just how many times had he visited Istanbul over the years? I could remember a few trips, although now it made sense why my father always insisted on taking those trips alone. The regular letters that had arrived at our home with exotic stamps and foreign postmarks over the years also made a great deal more sense now, too.

Maral's composure had returned and she and Redvers were both sitting quietly, watching me. My first instinct was to lash out, but I tamped that down. If my father cared about this woman, then I should do my best to get to know her, regardless of my feelings. Or at least learn everything she knew.

Because right now, we needed all the information we could gather if we wanted to find my father and the money.

"It's a pleasure to meet you, Maral," I finally forced out. Her face broke into a warm smile, which I returned. At least, I hoped that was what my face was doing. Judging by the look on Redvers' face, the result was perhaps not entirely successful.

I breathed a sigh of relief when Redvers jumped in, giving me a chance to regroup. "Do you know where Professor Wunderly might have gone?"

Maral shook her head, worry evident in her eyes. "It is very unlike him to leave without saying goodbye. He did not return for several days and I asked at Pera Palace but they would tell me nothing."

That had probably been quite frustrating for her, but I was relieved that the hotel staff weren't giving out information about their guests to just anyone off the street. Hopefully it was true that the only reason Ziya Bey was able to find out about my father was because his cousin worked at the hotel. Which reminded me.

"We spoke to Ziya Bey this afternoon. He showed us the documents my father was working on before he disappeared," I said.

At the mention of Bey's name, Maral's face darkened. She opened her mouth to say something, but just then the kitchen began giving up its bounty, and dish after dish of delicious-smelling food arrived at our table. The waiter explained that these were *mezes*, or Turkish appetizers, and pointed out what some of them were: dolmas, grilled eggplant with yogurt, chili tomato paste, pinto beans, and a mint yogurt dip with bread on the side. My stomach growled again and once the last dish had been arranged on our table, I started fixing myself a plate.

But even the arrival of food didn't mean I would forget what we were discussing. "You don't like Bey?"

Maral shook her head. "I do not trust that man."

Redvers and I looked at her expectantly. She paused, gathering her thoughts.

"Your father trusted him, and I met him many times, especially during this trip. Bey always seemed to be at your father's side." Voice sour, lips pressed together, Maral's feeling about Bey were quite clear. "There was also something about an expedition that your father was quite upset about, but he would not tell me more."

That was intriguing. Was it his current expedition to find the sultan's heart? Or something else entirely? I was beginning to curse the fact that my father didn't keep a journal of some sort.

I also wondered if Maral's dislike of the archivist stemmed from Bey's simple presence, most likely interrupting her time alone with my father. Could her judgment be clouded when it came to Bey because she wanted Henry Wunderly to herself?

"Has he given you any other reason to mistrust him? Do you think he was translating correctly?"

Maral shrugged. "I have no reason to think that he wasn't. Henry was pleased with the translation work Bey was doing and I saw no reason to mention my dislike of the man."

I ignored the fact that she was using my father's given name so casually, and instead changed course slightly. "Did my father mention anything about the ancient papers they'd been working on?"

A small fond smile crept over Maral's face. As uncomfortable as I was with the situation as a whole, I could see that her affection for my father was genuine. "He did. He was quite excited. It was a cryptic riddle. I did not think it meant anything, but Henry was convinced that he knew what it meant." She shook her head. "I am sorry to say that he did not explain it to me fully. He wanted to wait until he was sure he was correct."

Hope had built for a moment before crashing back down. This must have been reflected in my face, because Maral reached over and put her hand on my arm. "I am sorry I do not know more." She sat back in her chair. "You saw the papers today? Bey showed them to you?" I nodded and she continued. "You are very like your father, and you will figure it out also."

I appreciated the sentiment, although I wasn't at all sure she was correct. Nor was I at all certain that I was that much like my father. What I did know was that I didn't like her making the comparison as though she knew both of us well enough to do so—it struck me as overfamiliar and gave me a bit of a sour taste in my stomach. I covered it by taking a bite of bread smothered in eggplant.

Maral looked at Redvers; then her dark eyes met mine once more. "There is something else you should know. Your father was worried that he was being followed."

Chapter Twelve

A glance at Redvers' face and I could tell that he thought Maral should have led with that information. I put my bread down and focused my attention back on the issue at hand.

"Do you know by whom?" Redvers asked.

Maral shook her head. "I only know that Henry felt there was at least one man, perhaps more."

"Why would someone have been following my father?" Henry Wunderly was a quiet academic, his nose and mind firmly buried in the ancient past. He wasn't even an archaeologist, just a professor of history who happened to have developed an obsession with a particular artifact. And while there were clearly hidden depths to the man—as evidenced by the woman seated beside me—why would people be following him? The only thing I could think was that it had to do with the sultan's heart. But how would they—whoever it was—have known that my father thought he was finally close to finding it?

That also brought up a different issue. If someone had been following my father, was it the same person now following us? Could it have nothing to do with Redvers and his previous visits to the city? And how on earth would we even begin to figure that out? I stifled a groan of frustration—this was the first time that Redvers' work for the British government had become a hindrance rather than a help, and it couldn't have come at a worse time.

The small worrying thought I'd previously managed to squash resurfaced with a vengeance. What if my father hadn't merely disappeared? What if he'd been taken? Of course, why would the person be following us now, too? If he had my father and his money, he wouldn't need us. So perhaps the man following us was related to Redvers and it was just a coincidence that Father had been followed as well.

Except that I found it difficult to believe in such coincidences.

"We don't know anything yet, Jane." Redvers was obviously reading the fear on my face.

I wanted to believe him, but it was impossible to keep my worry from growing exponentially. Father was being followed, and then he disappeared without his luggage and without telling anyone where he was going. Any appetite I'd had was quickly replaced by fear for my father's safety—I was losing any ability for rational thought, as my mind pinged frantically about. What should we do next? How could we find him? What would we do about repaying the bank?

"Remember your breathing." Redvers' voice was quiet and penetrated my panic. I nodded and forced myself to do the counted breathing exercises I'd been taught by a psychoanalyst years ago.

While I managed my breathing, Redvers took over the conversation. "Is there anything else you can remember that the professor said to you that might be useful? Any places he liked to go?"

Maral was doing her best to remember, frustration tightening her posture. Then her shoulders dropped back down. "Henry loved listening to live music and frequently took me to Maxim's." Maral glanced at me in concern, then back at Redvers. "Even when I couldn't accompany him, I think he liked to spend time there."

"That's very helpful, thank you," Redvers said.

I still hadn't fully pulled myself together when we excused ourselves, all offers to pay for the food waved aside. Redvers assured Maral that we would see her again soon, and I managed a half smile and a nod in agreement. The woman wrapped me in a strong hug that I returned half-heartedly before she sent us on our way.

There was an overwhelming amount of information to digest. I was swimming in emotion—fear for my father and also some hurt and betrayal that he had replaced my mother in his affections. I needed some time to process what that meant for me. My memories of my mother had faded over the years, and it was probably the same for my father, although that was hard for me to acknowledge. I assumed it to be part of the reason why he was so focused on finding the sultan's heart. But how could I reconcile his dedication to my mother's memory with his having a new woman in his life?

I knew that my judgment was clouded when it came to Maral, but I didn't trust the woman. I mentally argued that I didn't trust Ziya Bey either—it was just good sense not to trust anyone until we could rule out their involvement in whatever had happened to my father.

I was quiet all the way back to the hotel, letting my internal arguments rage, finally stopping Redvers on the sidewalk before we went inside. "I know that Ziya is most likely waiting for us, but I don't think I can tolerate any company just now. Even though I know we need to ask about the expedition Maral was referring to."

Redvers studied my face, one hand on my shoulder. "Why don't you head up to the room and I'll talk to him about it before I make our excuses to him for the rest of the evening. Send him on his way."

I nodded. "Will you follow him then?" I knew we needed to investigate the archivist and decide whether or not he could be trusted, but I was too overwhelmed to do our usual song and dance where I insisted on accompanying him and he argued with me.

"Of course." Redvers braced himself for an argument that wasn't coming.

I simply nodded again. "Be careful."

He looked at me with concern before squeezing my shoulder and opening the door for me to enter the hotel. I went straight to the elevator, giving the operator the barest amount of information before finding myself on our floor. I let myself into our suite and curled up in a chair next to the window and simply stared out at the water—it was busy with fishing vessels and ferries transporting human cargo from one side of the city to the other. I hadn't come to any conclusions even after the sun had set, but I decided I should get into bed. I crawled beneath the covers with no idea how I was going to sleep. Surely my churning brain wouldn't allow it.

But as soon as my head hit my pillow, I was gone.

The next morning my eyes were puffy with sleep, but my head felt much clearer. I lay in bed for many minutes, finally able to take in all the information we'd been given the day before and look at each piece objectively. Well, maybe not entirely objectively, since I was still reeling from the news that my father had an international romantic partner, but the rest of the pieces were easier to examine.

Redvers was already in the sitting room, fully dressed and waiting for me when I wandered in wearing a silk robe belted over my nightclothes. His warm eyes crinkled at the sight of me. "I'm glad you slept so well."

"How do you know I slept well?" I challenged.

He raised one elegant eyebrow and my face colored. I needed to remember to save the verbal sparring until after I'd had my coffee. Not that anything romantic had taken place last night, but we *were* sharing the same bed. I wondered if my aunt would discover that bit of information—she'd likely be horrified. But ever since our transatlantic cruise on the *Olympic* where we'd posed as man and wife, Redvers had taken to registering us as precisely that. In his mind, it was merely a technicality that we weren't legally wed yet. I, of course, was still skittish about the idea of actually tying the knot. Not because of the man before me, but because marriage had not been kind to me in the past.

I was making much better decisions this time around, however.

"Your aunt and her fiancé are meeting us for breakfast."

Or perhaps I wasn't. "There wasn't a way around that?" I sighed as Redvers' lips quirked in amusement. "I know, I know. We barely spent any time with them yesterday." I headed back toward the bedroom. "Although I'm not sure how much help they'll be," I grumbled. If anything, Millie usually ended up being a hindrance. But I freshened up in a very short amount of time and presented myself again, this time dressed for the day.

But Redvers wasn't quite ready to go yet—he was still seated in one of the upholstered chairs and he motioned for me to join him in the chair opposite him.

"I need coffee," I said. Brilliant ideas wouldn't be flowing until I'd primed my brain with a couple cups of thick Turkish coffee. My mouth nearly watered at the thought.

"It won't take a minute. I would rather talk here without your aunt present."

I sighed and sat down, starting with a question of my own. "Did you ask Bey about the expedition last night?"

Redvers nodded. "I did. He denied knowing anything about it, but there's little chance that's true. Based on his reaction."

"And now we need to figure out how to get the truth from

him." I shook my head. "Add that to the list of things we need to worry about." It was becoming quite a long list. "Did you follow him then?"

"I did, for quite a while actually. I didn't learn anything about your father, but I did learn quite a bit about Ziya Bey. For such a devoutly religious man, as Bey claims to be, he has some . . . interesting habits."

This piqued my interest. "Such as?"

"I followed him to a section of town known for its vices. If I had to guess, I would say our archivist is either a fan of opium or women."

"Maybe both," I suggested cheerfully.

Redvers smiled at my enthusiasm. "I didn't risk going inside to find out—the place was too small and he would have spotted me immediately." His smile faded and he looked me over. "How are you taking the news from yesterday?"

I could have pretended that I didn't know what he was referring to, but there was little point. Besides, this conversation stood between me and coffee so best to get it over with as quickly as possible. "It was a shock to learn that father has a . . . romantic interest." I still wasn't certain what to call the woman. "I don't know what to make of it."

"Isn't it natural that your father would meet someone? How long ago did your mother pass away?"

"She died when I was quite young, so it's well over twenty years ago now." I didn't want to figure out the actual number. The larger the number of years between us became, the more depressing I found it since my memories of her grew weaker with every passing year. "It's just that the sultan's heart . . . it was a sort of joke between them." I cast my mind back for the fleeting images of my mother giving my father a hard time—good-naturedly, of course. Father had a good sense of humor but was often too buried in his studies to deploy it. My mother had teased it out of him, and he had called her his heart of hearts. "She'd loved to say that the sultan's heart was his true love and they would argue about it—but not in a serious way." I smiled a little at the memory, but then my smile faded. "After she died, finding the heart became an obsession for him. A way to keep her memory alive, I suppose."

"But now that he has someone new . . ." Redvers said.

"I suppose I'm left wondering why he's still trying to find the heart. Has he put his memories of my mother away? And why would he take out the money against the house?" What I didn't say was that I wondered what would become of my father—and myself—if he lost the money and our row house. I didn't want to have to depend on anyone for a place to live, but it was easier to know that I had a home to go back to, even if it was technically my father's. What if that was taken from us?

Redvers was quiet for a moment. "I see what you're getting at." He held out his hand and I stood, taking it. He pulled me into his lap and wrapped his arms around me for a moment.

"We'll find him," Redvers said against my shoulder. I couldn't say anything, but for a moment, with his arms wrapped around me, I felt assured that we would. I was also reminded that I had agreed to make a home with this man, and I felt a little less unsettled.

Then he stood, nearly dumping me out of his lap. "Time for breakfast."

We made our way to the lobby, where Millie and Lord Hughes were already waiting. I braced myself for a dressing down about how long I'd slept or how tired I still looked, but Millie just looked me over, rolled her eyes, and herded our small group to the little restaurant attached to the lobby of our hotel. Redvers took my hand and squeezed it. I looked up at the twinkle in his eyes—he'd known precisely what I'd expected from Millie, and I gave his hand a squeeze in return along with the first genuine smile I'd mustered in days.

After all, if the two of us could survive Aunt Millie, we were certain to be able to track down my father. What couldn't we do together?

Breakfast was served in a brightly lit room just beyond the grand salon—one entire wall was made up of a bank of windows broken up by thick white pillars. The space was crowded with tables covered in white tablecloths, and the tall palmlike plants sprinkled about added some needed warmth. The attentive waiter showed us to our table and waited for us to make a decision about what we wanted to eat before hurrying off. Millie and Lord Hughes demurred, ordering only tea, claiming that they'd eaten earlier. I ordered some eggs in addition to a traditional Turkish breakfast and Redvers followed suit. I liked to try the local cuisine and eat the way the locals did at least once during a trip.

As soon as we placed our order, Millie started in. "Topkapi Palace is quite beautiful in its own way, although almost scandalously ornate. I think the tiles were hand-painted. And you should see the room where they have gold and jewels on display—it's quite something to see."

I wasn't able to pay much attention to my aunt's lecture about what they had taken in the day before until I had my Turkish coffee in hand—mercifully, it was delivered quickly. It was thick and dark and exactly what I needed to jumpstart my brain, although it was tiny. The waiter raised an eyebrow when I almost immediately ordered a second cup but he fetched me one all the same.

Redvers watched the fellow go. "Your coffee intake is going to scandalize the nation." This was whispered as an aside since my aunt was still describing the palace grounds in detail. She hadn't even gotten to the building itself yet.

"They're tiny cups," I whispered back. "It would take four of those to equal one cup—"

"Jane. Are you listening to me?"

I wondered how it was that I always seemed to get in trouble for these whispered conversations but Redvers never got caught. He was taking another sip of his tea and looking entirely innocent. I might have accidentally kicked his leg under the table before answering my aunt.

"I am, Aunt Millie. You were talking about the sultan."

"Yes, I was. Suleiman the Magnificent."

I was momentarily saved from a further lecture by the delivery of our breakfasts. The eggs looked good, but the rest of the plates outshone them by far. Sliced cheeses and crusty bread, a tomato paste along with olives, fresh cucumbers and tomatoes, each in their own bowls looking fresh and delicious. I tucked in immediately, and Redvers did the same.

Millie paused only long enough for us to fix our plates before she started back in. "You know, I find the entire idea of harems to be quite shocking, but this sultan was apparently different. He had one, of course he did, but do you know, after a time anyway, that he was quite in love with only one woman. Edward, what was her name?"

Lord Hughes cleared his throat. "Roxelana, I believe it was. Or sometimes Hurrem Sultan."

Millie made a noise of agreement. "That sounds correct. In any case, he was quite enamored of her, even though she was a slave and he had an entire harem of women to choose from. Apparently, he eventually married her. It sounds as though it was quite the love story—they wrote poetry to one another while he was away." She dug in her satchel for a moment. "We had a tour guide and he recited a bit of poetry that the sultan wrote for her. I made him write it down for me." She paused long enough to shoot Lord Hughes a secret smile and he returned it. I could do nothing but blink at the two of them—it was still jarring to see Millie's softer side. After a moment she resumed her search, finally pulling out a piece of paper.

"Here it is. The sultan wrote under a pseudonym you know, Muhibbi. Anyway, this is what he wrote to her:

"Throne of my lonely niche, my wealth, my love, my
   moonlight.
My most sincere friend, my confidant, my very
   existence, my Sultan, my one and only love.
The most beautiful among the beautiful . . .
My springtime, my merry faced love, my daytime,
   my sweetheart, laughing leaf . . .
My plants, my sweet, my rose, the one only who
   does not distress me in this world . . .
My Istanbul, my Caraman, the earth of my Anatolia
My Badakhshan, my Baghdad and Khorasan
My woman of the beautiful hair, my love of the
   slanted brow, my love of eyes full of mischief . . .
I'll sing your praises always
I, lover of the tormented heart, Muhibbi of the eyes
   full of tears, I am happy."

Millie read the poem with feeling, and we all listened quietly. It was lovely as far as poems went, but it shook something else loose for me. The sultan's love for this woman was
evident and he called her many things—springtime, rose,
moonlight. Was it possible that he would also sometimes
refer to her as his heart? And wasn't the sultan's heart precisely what had gotten us here? The riddle rattled around in
my mind for a moment. The heart far from the heart, but
the key . . .

"I think I know where we need to look," I said slowly.

My three tablemates went quiet. "Where?" Redvers asked.

"Wherever Roxelana is buried."

Chapter Thirteen

"Whatever are you talking about?" Millie was obviously miffed that I'd interrupted her lecture on Topkapi Palace and the love story between the emperor and his wife, the former slave. It was clear her lecture had continued after I'd stopped listening and started thinking.

But now I was busy watching Redvers put together the same pieces I had. He nodded slowly, sitting back in his chair. "I think you may have something there."

"Especially since his viziers would have known about his devotion to her."

"What are you two talking about?" Millie's voice was a shade louder this time, and I knew we would have to give an explanation before the entire restaurant was given a detailed account of Millie's frustration with us.

Redvers cleared his throat and gave Lord Hughes and my aunt a brief sketch of things, leaving out any mention of my father being followed or the fact that we were as well. I wondered if this was wise, since it occurred to me that my aunt and Lord Hughes could also have someone following them, but sensing there was a reason for Redvers to leave out this salient detail, I kept quiet.

Millie grudgingly seemed to accept that I might be right about where the cryptic clue was leading us. "We should go there immediately," she announced, and raised her hand to signal our waiter.

I could see Redvers was thinking fast, so I leaned back in my chair and simply watched the spectacle.

"You know," Redvers said slowly, "I think we should *not* go there together. In fact, I think it would be wise if we broke into two groups."

"Whatever for?" Lord Hughes asked.

Redvers paused for a moment and I struggled to dampen my amusement. "We will be able to cover more ground if we split up. In case Jane isn't correct. It would be helpful to take a look anywhere else the sultan's wife spent time." As the idea solidified, he began speaking more quickly. I could tell he'd warmed to his own idea, which he'd been making up as he went along—I wasn't even annoyed at his suggestion that my guess was incorrect. I was far too entertained by his verbal tap dancing. "Lord Hughes, I think you and Mrs. Stanley . . ."

Here my aunt interrupted him. "Millie," she said, her tone brooking no arguments.

I couldn't stop my eyebrows from disappearing somewhere into my hairline, but no one was paying me the slightest mind. I went back to my little cup of Turkish coffee—I had come toward the bottom of the cup where the coffee was more like sludge. Most people stopped drinking it, but I kept going, relishing the grit against my teeth.

Redvers shot my aunt a warm smile. "Millie, then." He continued on with the plan he'd pulled from thin air. "I think the two of you should return to the palace grounds and inspect the harem. It's quite likely that's where the next clue is, and we'll need your sharp eyes to inspect that large of an area."

Millie pressed her lips together, then nodded firmly. "That is a capital idea."

I had to admit I was impressed. My aunt would never have agreed to this plan if I'd been the one to suggest it. Although I was a little surprised that she hadn't seen through his obvious flattery.

"Come, Edward. We have work to do." My aunt stood with no further ceremony and began bustling out of the restaurant.

Hughes gave us a warm smile. I suspected he knew precisely what Redvers had been up to, getting the two of them out of the way, but he wasn't bothered by it. "See you both later this afternoon, then." He ambled out after Millie, catching up with her when she impatiently turned to see why he wasn't with her.

Redvers and I waited a few moments before standing as well.

"Nicely done," I said.

"Thank you. I'm pleased that went as well as it did."

"Are we heading directly to the grave?" I asked.

"I believe Roxelana is buried in a mausoleum on the grounds of the Süleymaniye Mosque. But that's not what we're doing first."

Frustration bubbled. We needed to find my father, and as far as I could see, solving this riddle was our best bet for doing that.

But before I could open my mouth to speak, Redvers put a hand on my shoulder, his eyes never leaving Millie and Lord Hughes. "First we're going to find out if they're being followed as well."

I deflated, my frustration replaced with gratitude that Redvers was keeping his head while mine compelled me to steam around the city with no thought for who I might be leading around. I took a deep breath. We would find my father. We just needed to be smart about how we went about it.

I forced my body to still as we stood partially concealed by a large pillar at one end of the lobby.

Hughes and Millie were already entering a taxi when a man dressed in a gray suit stood up from one of the plush red couches. He was short but otherwise completely nondescript, and I could see how he would easily blend in with other natives of the country. The giveaway was that he moved quite deliberately after Millie and Lord Hughes, striding across the lobby and quickly hailing a cab of his own.

"I believe that answers that question," Redvers said.

"Do you recognize him from yesterday?"

Redvers shook his head. "He isn't the same man that followed us yesterday."

I looked around the lobby, wondering if I could pick out anyone else that looked suspicious. Because if someone was following my aunt, surely there was someone here to follow us as well.

Redvers gave me his arm and led me across the lobby as though we were returning to our room. We entered the elevator and gave the operator polite smiles as he closed the doors, lifting us to the level of our room. Everything was perfectly normal until the elevator doors closed once again and began descending.

"Quick." Redvers pulled me in the opposite direction from our room. "We'll go down this way." He opened a nondescript door that appeared to be used only by hotel staff. As the door closed behind us, I could hear the sound of the elevator stopping on our floor again.

We hurried down the stairs and out a lesser-used entrance of the hotel, which deposited us onto a narrow and crowded street, ideal for our purposes. I realized after a moment that it was raining, and I was glad that I'd thought to bring my wool coat with us to breakfast. Redvers only had the suit jacket he was wearing, and I hoped he would be warm enough.

"That little trick will only work once," Redvers said as we hurried to the next cross street, splashing through the water collecting on the cobblestones. "We'll have to be even more clever in the future to lose them."

At the intersection Redvers quickly found a cab and we climbed in. For the next several blocks he watched behind us to see if any other conveyance was following, but it appeared we had managed to get away unseen.

This time, anyway.

CHAPTER FOURTEEN

"Do you think they're here because of you? Or because of Father?"

"I'm leaning toward your father since Hughes and your aunt are being followed as well." Redvers' voice was low. "But it's hard to say for certain. And now they know that we're aware of them."

That was certainly true. By giving them the slip so deliberately—whoever they were—we were essentially announcing we knew they were there and that they were following us. I hoped Redvers had some ideas for how to lose them in the future as well as for figuring out why we were being followed in the first place—and by whom.

But a public taxi was not the place to ask those questions. The Süleymaniye Mosque was back on the other side of the Golden Horn not far from where we had been the day before. The mosque, however, was on the highest hill in the city, making it easily visible even from our side of the city once we neared the water. The taxi sailed across the bridge and through the narrow streets, letting us out near the mosque.

The complex was sprawling, the stone mosque with its numerous domes surrounding one large dome and towering minarets dominating the area. Despite the anxiety and frustration that had dogged my every step in Istanbul so far, I couldn't help but take a moment to be awed by the stunning architecture of the complex before me.

"This is enormous."

"It is," Redvers agreed. "In addition to the mosque itself, there are several schools, a bathhouse, and several other buildings on the grounds as well."

We entered at the front of the complex, passing between what Redvers thought were the religious schools attached to the mosque. They looked like small complexes of their own. We then found ourselves in a large courtyard and made our way to the front entrance of the mosque, where we removed our shoes, carrying them in our hands. "We may as well peek inside—Roxelana's grave is behind the mosque. You'll need to keep your head covered, though."

I wished I'd brought along a scarf to cover my head in deference to their beliefs, but I hoped my wool cloche would suffice.

We entered and kept to the sides of the cavernous room, and no one commented on my headwear or my presence. I'd stopped worrying about it as soon as we walked through the door, however, because the interior was so stunning. It was light and airy, with enormous round chandeliers hanging low from the ceiling. The dominant feature of the marble interior was the arches—large arches framed with alternating pink-and-white marble, and multitudes of arched windows reaching up to the large dome painted in gold and green overhead. I realized I was nearly gaping, and I was momentarily glad that I wasn't letting my impatience for the task at hand ruin my appreciation for the sights we were seeing on our way to Roxelana's final resting place. We continued along the side of the room passing columns and arches until we reached an exit toward the rear and passed into another, much smaller courtyard.

Once we arrived in the courtyard and I caught sight of the

mausoleums, however, I became all business. There were two—
one was noticeably larger with a colonnaded walkway all
around it, decorated with arches and the distinctive dome on
top. Redvers tipped his head towards the smaller of the two.

"That's Roxelana's," he said.

Without discussion, we moved straight to the octagonal
building. There was a small foyer area—more modest than
the sultan's by far—and Redvers pulled open the doors so
that we could pass through and move into the space beyond.
The tile work throughout the complex had been beautiful,
but what was in this room was nothing short of jaw-dropping.
The tiles were painted in patterns reminiscent of feathers in
shades of blue and teal and the colors stretched from the
floor to the ceiling. There were also larger tiles with beautifully painted script above each of the windows that could be
shuttered with elaborately carved wood. The windows,
bathing the space in light despite the gloomy day, alternated
with small alcoves decorated with the same tile. I'd seen some
beautiful tiling in Egypt, but it couldn't quite compare to the
exquisite work I saw here.

But what I didn't see was a place to hide something. "There's
not really anywhere to hide a scroll," I whispered. Unfortunately, the rain seemed to bring out more people rather than
keep them away, and the grounds were fairly teeming with
other tourists.

Looking around, I realized that in addition to the extra
people, we didn't really know exactly what we were looking
for. In my mind I'd pictured an ancient piece of paper, rolled
up and neatly tied with a ribbon, but that wasn't realistic. In
fact, it was downright implausible.

There were three stone graves in the center of the room
with steepled roofs. Intricately carved wooden fences about
waist high encircled the largest tomb, which belonged to
Roxelana. I nudged Redvers. "You don't think . . ." I tipped

my head toward the graves. It would be a bit of a feat to get over the fence and then into the tomb itself without being seen.

He shook his head. "Roxelana did die some years before the sultan, but it's unlikely they would have disturbed the bodies," he whispered close to my ear. I had to admit some relief—I wasn't particularly looking forward to doing any grave robbing today. Even though I was willing to do whatever it took to find my father, I was glad it hadn't come to that quite yet.

Redvers inspected the first of the alcoves as I began slowly walking the perimeter, studying the Oriental patterns. Swirling colors and tiny details started to make my eyes cross, but I kept at it, all while other people moved in a current past me, feet squelching slightly on the marble floor. I spent a little extra time admiring the painted feathers above the windows.

Behind me I could sense that Redvers had stopped moving but I didn't dare take my eyes from their inspection. Even when yet another couple passed through, bumping my arm as they went by, I continued on, never taking my eyes from the walls.

Eventually I found what I was looking for. I would have loved to crow in victory, but the other couple was finally making their way from the room and I didn't want to draw even more attention to myself—the woman who stared at the walls. Once the pair had circled back around and exited, I gestured to Redvers.

"There." I pointed at a spot dead center of the wall I was facing where the pattern was disturbed by one tile facing in the wrong direction.

Redvers glanced at me. "Do you want to do it?"

I stared at the tile for a moment longer, walking closer to it. My father must have come here and seen the same thing, then somehow replaced the tile. As I drew nearer, I could see that the thin line of mortar surrounding this tile was broken and missing.

"It looks like it shouldn't be hard to remove again," I said, still not touching the tile itself.

"Why don't you keep watch and see if anyone is coming. I would prefer not to end up in a Turkish prison."

"I'd prefer neither of us did."

Redvers pulled his lock-picking set from his inner jacket pocket and selected a thin metal tool. "It shouldn't take much since it looks like he already removed it," Redvers muttered to himself. While he went to work, I took up my post in the doorway, casually leaning against the doorframe, gazing out into the courtyard beyond, but keenly aware of what was happening behind me. I hoped he would be quick since it wouldn't be long before someone else came along— this small mausoleum was surprisingly popular with tourists. I supposed it was because of the love story between the famous sultan and his wife.

The gentle scraping sounds coming from behind me were not at all conspicuous but made my shoulders tense and begin creeping toward my ears all the same. I reminded myself that we were simply following in my father's footsteps, doing what was necessary. Hopefully we'd be able to put the tile back later—maybe even before it was missed. Although I knew that was wishful thinking.

It was only a few more moments before Redvers touched my arm as he passed through the doorway.

"Let's go."

We took a different route out of the complex, dodging umbrellas and hoping that no one had seen us near that particular part of the complex. Our pace was unhurried, so as not to draw attention to ourselves, but we still moved toward the exit with purpose. My nerves were strung entirely too tight to enjoy the surroundings this time, although I did have a pang of regret that I was unlikely to visit these beautiful buildings ever again. It would be especially nice to see it on a sunny day so we could enjoy the view of the Golden Horn and the city laid out all around it.

Once we were back on the street and splashing quickly in the opposite direction of the Süleymaniye Mosque, the call to prayer sounded. It was a beautiful and distinctive sound, a man's voice singing what might have been words, but it was difficult to tell. The sound reverberated around the streets, coming from each of the numerous mosques in the city.

With the call echoing around us I finally braved the question.

"Did you get it?"

Redvers shot me a quick, cocky grin. "Of course, I did."

CHAPTER FIFTEEN

We found an out-of-the-way *meyhane* where I ordered another coffee and Redvers requested a cup of tea. I stripped off my wet wool coat and hung it on the back of my chair, and Redvers did the same with his suit jacket. Our table was tucked into the dark interior, back in a corner, just as Redvers had requested. When he was certain our waiter was entirely occupied elsewhere, Redvers reached back into his coat pocket and pulled out the tile he'd extracted from the wall, along with a fair amount of dust. He held it out to me before looking at it himself, which warmed my heart even as I began my close inspection.

The front of the tile was simply the featherlike design in blue and teal that had repeated all over the wall of the mausoleum, but the back had what looked like Arabic writing scratched into it. I was relieved that I'd been correct about the piece of tile being the clue—heaven help us if we needed to return to the scene to do even more vandalism. Unfortunately, neither of us read Arabic script, let alone ancient Turkish language written in Arabic script.

I could feel my brows pulling together and I mentally smoothed them back out as I passed the tile back to Redvers. "We need a translator."

He gave it a brief once-over before securing it back in his pocket. "We do."

Our waiter arrived bearing hot beverages, and we took a moment to gather our thoughts while the table was laid out for us.

Once the waiter had disappeared again, I said aloud what I'd been thinking over. "The obvious choice is for us to ask Ziya to translate this. My father trusted him to do his translation work while he was here."

"And yet Maral does not," Redvers said.

"It's hard to say precisely why that is, though."

Redvers nodded his agreement, then considered for a moment before continuing. "I don't see how we have any other choice than to take it to Bey. We don't want to risk showing it to a stranger who might realize what it is and either report us for vandalism or follow the clue themselves."

I grimaced. I still felt terrible about defacing such a beautiful and ancient site, but circumstances being what they were, I felt as though we didn't really have a choice. And I vowed that we would return the tile as soon as we had a chance to do so.

"Do you think Ziya will turn us in?" I asked.

Redvers shrugged. "It's a possibility, of course. But I think he's less likely to than someone who is totally unfamiliar with us."

"Can we even be certain that my father found this clue? Did he disappear before he had a chance to look for it?" I had no idea how my father would have pried the thing from the wall without anyone noticing. He was an academic, not an international spy. I also wondered how he could have translated it right there—he was able to do a little bit of translation, but I doubted his abilities stretched to this. Was it possible that we'd been the first to find the thing?

Redvers shook his head. "There was a bit of sticking paste in each corner, and then it looked as though someone applied a cheap mortar in the cracks. It didn't take much scraping for me to get the tile out, which means someone else had been there before."

In that case we had to hope that it had been my father, or this entire search for the sultan's heart would be fruitless.

Redvers gave a little shrug, oblivious to the arguments raging inside my head. "If it was someone else and they went ahead and found the heart, I think your father or the black-market community would have gotten wind of it. Which means it was most likely your father who uncovered this tile—after all, he's the one who found the document and the riddle."

If that was the case, had Father taken the tile, had it translated, and then returned it to its place? Without anyone seeing him coming or going? For the translating he would have taken it to Ziya Bey, but I couldn't imagine the archivist would have neglected to tell us that. It was rather an important detail—my father bringing this tile to him.

Or had Bey left that out on purpose? Was it possible that Maral was right about not trusting the man? I wanted to scream in frustration.

"What if Maral is right and we shouldn't trust Bey? He's hiding something, but what if it's something more than just a penchant for women?" For simplicity's sake, I boiled down my internal discussion down to the essentials.

"I've thought of that." Redvers took a sip of his tea, grimaced slightly, and added another sugar cube, stirring it in. "We don't need to tell him where the tile came from, obviously. And we'll simply have to keep the man close so that we can keep an eye on him."

"Keep your friends close," I said on a sigh.

"And your enemies closer," Redvers finished.

We went to the archives in order to find Bey, but we were told by one of his colleagues that Bey hadn't come in that

day. The man mused that Bey had left quite early the day before as well, which was right after we'd visited him. He'd been
waiting at our hotel late in the afternoon, but it left quite a
few hours of his time unaccounted for. This did not make me
feel better about trusting Ziya Bey.

"I don't like it," I told Redvers once we were back on the
street.

Redvers' face was dark. "I don't either, to be honest." He
looked around. "If we head back to the hotel, we're sure to
be followed again. But I think that's our best bet for the moment; we need to regroup."

I agreed and we took a tram to the port and then grabbed
a ferry to the other side of the Golden Horn where we were
staying. The inclement weather made the crossing less than
ideal, and my stomach revolted a bit at the rocky trip. I was
glad when we were on the other side—and by the time we
found a taxi to take us to the hotel, my stomach had righted
itself.

We trudged into the lobby—well, I trudged. Redvers had
an irritating tendency to stride elegantly wherever he went.
We hadn't made it far when someone in my peripheral vision
stood quite quickly and I stopped to look.

It was none other than Ziya Bey.

"Mr. Redvers! Mrs. Redvers. I was wondering when to expect you."

I nearly corrected the man that not only was my last name
Wunderly, but Redvers wasn't even *his* last name. It was his
given name. But the explanation of why Redvers avoided
using his surname and the fact that we weren't actually married yet . . . well, I didn't have the energy for any of it. If Ziya
Bey wanted to call me Mrs. Redvers, that was fine. I was certain it wouldn't be the last time it happened, either. People
loved to make assumptions.

Redvers and I stepped out of the path of foot traffic in the lobby while Bey joined us. I danced from foot to foot, impatient to get out of my wet things.

"I hope you haven't been waiting long," Redvers said. "I'm sorry we weren't able to meet with you yesterday."

With everything else that had happened, I'd nearly forgotten that Bey had intended to meet us at the hotel the previous afternoon, or that Redvers had followed him the night before and found out some rather unsavory things about the man. I wondered if Maral somehow knew about whatever vice Bey was involved in and that was why the woman didn't trust him. I made a mental note to ask her about it later.

"I understand how exhausting travel can be." He smiled. "I hope you are well rested today."

"We are, thank you." Redvers paused, studying the man for a moment. I could tell he was trying to figure out whether we should still go with our original plan of asking Bey to assist us with our translation. Since the man was waiting for us here, it *did* make sense that he hadn't gone to work at the archives. So perhaps there was no reason to be suspicious of him. Well, no additional reasons.

Ziya gestured to the restaurant off the lobby. "Perhaps we can take some tea?"

"I think that's a capital idea." Redvers glanced around the lobby. "But let's have it sent to our room."

If Bey was scandalized by Redvers' suggestion, he did an admirable job of concealing it. And while Bey might not understand the reason for going to our room, I certainly did. We had to assume at all times that we were being watched—so pulling this pilfered tile out of a pocket and analyzing it in a hotel restaurant was not the wisest course of action.

We stopped by the front desk and requested that a Turkish tea service be sent up to our room immediately before heading to the elevator. Bey and Redvers made small talk while I continued second-guessing the wisdom of trusting this man.

But we'd already set ourselves on a course of action, so I kept silent. Bringing in an outsider at this point was simply far too dangerous.

Once inside our room, we divested ourselves of our wet coats, hanging them to dry, before we settled into the array of upholstered chairs in the sitting area. We didn't have to wait more than five minutes before there was a knock on the door.

I stood, grateful for something to do other than continue making idle conversation. "I'll get that."

Unfortunately, it was not our tea. It was Millie.

Chapter Sixteen

Millie was pushing through the door before I had it opened all the way and was moving past me before I could fully register who I was seeing. Lord Hughes was standing behind her and gave me a kind, conspiratorial wink before following Millie into the room. I stuck my head into the hallway, checking both ways for a waiter bearing a tea tray, before slowly closing the door again. I closed my eyes for a moment, bracing myself, then joined the others.

"I have to say that I feel as though we're wasting time here," Millie was saying as I took a seat. She and Edward had taken the small love seat on the far side of the room. "It doesn't feel as though we're making any progress toward finding my brother. Edward and I searched the harem quite thoroughly and we didn't find anything useful."

I was about to explain to her that we had in fact made some progress when she continued. "I also find it shocking that you two are not married but are sharing this room."

Redvers' mouth quirked in amusement, but I could feel my face flaming with heat. I wondered if there were a way I could crawl beneath my chair and die quietly without anyone noticing.

Ziya Bey's face registered absolute shock. "You are not married? The hotel would never permit an unmarried couple to register in the same room. Despite the changes Atatürk has made, this is still a very religious country, very conservative." He cocked his head, considering. "Although the city is less so, that is true. But all the same . . ."

"Well, it's just a matter of when, really. We are engaged to be married," Redvers said casually, crossing one leg over the other. "I was supposed to be speaking with Jane's father about that very matter when we discovered that he'd come here to Istanbul."

I closed my eyes and pinched the bridge of my nose. This was definitely not how I wanted to tell my aunt that I was getting remarried. It somehow felt as though she'd won and she'd be nothing short of unbearable from here on out.

Millie clapped her hands together. "This is wonderful news! Jane, we'll have to start sorting out your trousseau. You'll need new dresses, of course. You have a few that are acceptable, but not many." She continued rattling on for a moment before I stopped her with a raised hand.

"First of all, I don't need a 'trousseau.'" This wasn't the Victorian age, after all, but I held my tongue there. "And second of all, we really need to focus on finding Father before anything else."

This sobered Millie quickly. "Of course." She paused, looking repentant for once in her life. "I got carried away for a moment."

Quiet, glorious quiet, descended for a few beats before Redvers took over once more. "Bey, we have a rather delicate matter we need to discuss with you. Something we need translated."

Bey spread his hands. "I am at your disposal."

"But what we discuss here cannot leave this room. Are we agreed?" Redvers looked around the room, making eye contact with everyone seated there. They each gave him a nod, and his dark eyes finally settled on mine. I held his gaze, communicating silently that whatever he decided in that moment, I was with him. He gave a tiny nod, then pulled the tile from his jacket pocket.

"We found this, and we need to know what the inscription on the back says." Redvers handed the tile to Ziya first, which compelled my aunt to push up from the couch and stand over the man's shoulder to see what we had found. I was a little surprised she didn't snatch it from his hands.

"Where did you find this?" Ziya held the tile carefully in his hands, looking incredulous.

Redvers shook his head. "That's not important."

The archivist looked as though he wanted to argue but then thought better of it. We watched him read the text several times. "I'm not sure it makes sense, what I am reading here."

Just then there was a knock at the door and Millie huffed impatiently from her position behind Bey. I stood and went to the door once again, letting in the waiter with the tea service. We all watched in silence as the man set things on the low table, occasionally glancing around at the group, especially at my aunt who continued standing awkwardly at Bey's shoulder while everyone else sat. He could no doubt sense the tension in the air, especially since no one was saying a word and everyone was avoiding making eye contact. Flashing a quick look at Bey, I noticed that he was no longer holding the tile, and I was glad he'd thought to obscure it.

"Will that be all?" The waiter was still looking around at us curiously, so I ushered him to the door with an assurance that it certainly was.

Once the man had left, I bolted the door and returned to my seat.

"There aren't enough cups here, Jane," Millie commented.

I just looked at her for a long moment and she gave a little huff. "I suppose we'll make do without."

Bey had retrieved the tile from wherever he'd hid it and was looking at it once more. Millie was no longer hovering over his shoulder and was now fixing herself a cup of tea.

"You said it doesn't make sense. But what do you think it says?" Redvers asked.

"Some of these words are difficult to make out," Bey said slowly. "But it seems to be referring to a map." The archivist's eyebrows pulled together as he read it again, his mouth moving as he read the words again to himself. "And that it can be found . . . beneath the city. Where water collects and the monsters keep watch." He read it again and then shrugged. "That is as close as I can come."

"A map to what?" Millie demanded as she crossed to the love seat and settled herself back down. I noticed she didn't bother touching the cup of tea she had just prepared. Lord Hughes reached over and began drinking it instead even though I knew he took his with less sugar than my aunt.

"Well," Redvers began reluctantly. Our eyes met and after a moment I gave a small shrug, leaving it up to him just how much we revealed. "It's most likely a map to the sultan's heart."

"What are we talking about here? A large gemstone?" Millie asked. "Of course, I can't see Henry being interested in jewels."

I shook my head. "It's quite literally the sultan's heart. Mummified, I would guess, and buried in a gold box."

Millie pressed her lips together in disgust. "So the gold box is what is valuable."

"No, madam," Ziya said. "It is believed that the heart gives mystical powers to those who possess it."

Millie stared at Bey for a long moment. "That's ridiculous."

Bey was utterly unfazed by my aunt's dismissal and gave a small shrug before leaning forward to prepare himself a cup of tea. "You may think so, but there are many who would not agree. And those are the ones we must concern ourselves with."

I hid a smile at how efficiently the man had shut my aunt down.

Lord Hughes broke in. "How will we figure out where this clue is directing us?"

"I think I already know what it's referring to," Redvers replied. "One of the cisterns beneath the city."

Bey nodded. "That is what I was thinking also. It is just a matter of which one—there are several hundred."

Redvers considered for a moment. "We could try the Basilica Cistern, since it's the largest and most well-known." Bey inclined his head in agreement.

Millie stood, hands on ample hips. "Well, let's go there now." She looked around impatiently at the rest of us who remained in our seats.

"We will head there, but not right at this moment," Redvers said. "The trouble is that all of us are being followed."

Millie's mouth gaped open at this announcement and she slowly sank back into her seat next to her fiancé. Despite everything, I found I was rather enjoying the show my aunt was inadvertently putting on.

"Are you certain?" Hughes asked.

Redvers and I both nodded. We still weren't sure if our shadows were because of Redvers or Father, but it didn't seem necessary to get into that with the others.

"We've seen the men following us, as well as the both of you." I indicated Millie and Lord Hughes.

Redvers continued. "It means we need to have a solid plan before we march over there. We don't want to lead anyone else there with us."

"Do we know who they are?" Hughes looked concerned.

Redvers shook his head. "Not yet." He didn't elaborate, although I knew he was working up some sort of scheme to figure out this piece of the mystery.

I looked at Bey's face and it hadn't changed expression—it was still completely neutral. I'd been watching him during Redvers' announcement; Ziya had betrayed no surprise that we were being followed, nor when I clarified that Millie and Lord Hughes were as well. Was he simply good at hiding his emotions, or did he already know?

The tea had long gone cold and our group still hadn't come up with a plan that satisfied everyone. This was not really a surprise since Millie was involved and loathe to miss out on any of what she considered "the action." I sincerely regretted letting her in on the search, although knowing her the way I did, I wasn't sure there was any way to keep her out of it short of slipping her a sleeping draft or leaving her tied up in her hotel room. Tempting though those options were.

But at the moment, my real concern was keeping Bey close since he knew not only exactly where we were headed but what we were looking for as well. I didn't want to let him out of my sight. Truthfully, I'd have been happier shackled to the man just to ensure he couldn't slip away.

"I think our best bet is to wait until tomorrow. Perhaps even the evening," Redvers said. I didn't like this one bit, since it left Bey open to contact . . . well, anyone . . . once we'd retired for the evening. What if he turned us in to the authorities or, worse yet, went to the cistern alone to retrieve whatever was there? But I needed to wait until I had a moment alone with Redvers to bring these points up. I knew he'd already considered the issues—I just wanted to know what plan he'd cooked up to overcome them.

"For tonight I think we should split up." Redvers was already raising a hand to stifle Millie's easily anticipated protests, which it did, allowing him to continue uninterrupted. It was a neat trick, although one I could never get away with.

"We should spend time in the places that Professor Wunderly did before he left."

"Disappeared, you mean." Millie needed to get at least two cents in. She sat back in her seat, looking satisfied that she'd had at least that much say in what was going on.

"Very well. I suppose we should acknowledge it. It does seem as though Professor Wunderly has disappeared."

I couldn't help the shiver that ran up my arms. Redvers noticed and shot me a look of concern, but I gave my head a little shake and motioned for him to continue.

"We should ask discreet questions. See if anyone remembers what Professor Wunderly did or who he spoke to in the days leading up to his disappearance." Redvers looked around the group, who nodded their agreement back at him.

"Bey, you'll be with us," Redvers said, and I nearly sighed with relief. We'd be keeping an eye on the archivist without having to trust anyone else to do it for us. "Millie and Lord Hughes, I think you should head to the *meyhane* where the professor took his meals. Talk to the people who work there and see what you can learn."

Millie made a noise of protest. "But where will you be going?" I could tell she was upset at the prospect of having to eat in a small local establishment. Upscale and expensive were far more comfortable for my aunt.

"You don't actually have to eat there," I offered. "You could go after your meal and just have tea." I hid another smile as I said it, although I did feel the slightest bit sorry for Maral since my aunt was about to be unleashed on the unsuspecting woman. I also had to wonder why Redvers was sending them there since we'd already spoken with Maral about my father.

Redvers was undeterred by Millie's protest and turned to Ziya and me. "We will be heading to Maxim's."

"And what is Maxim's?" Millie asked.

"It's a nightclub," Ziya volunteered. "It is quite popular these days—they have live jazz bands and dancing."

Millie made a noise of disgust. But in the end, she grudgingly agreed to their assigned task since she had even less desire to set foot in a nightclub. "Who knows what sort of riffraff they'll be subjected to," Millie muttered to Lord Hughes as they left our room.

Which left the three of us. I was desperate to get Redvers alone to discuss my concerns with him, but there was no way I was leaving Bey by himself.

Redvers checked his watch. "We have some time before Maxim's will be busy. Should we grab a bite to eat first?"

Bey paused. "Yes, but I will meet you downstairs in a few minutes."

I opened my mouth to tell him we would all go together when Redvers beat me to it. "We'll see you down there."

I gave him my most incredulous look as we watched Bey leave the room, the door closing softly behind him.

"Who knows who he might contact now!" I hissed.

"Exactly," Redvers said. He quickly opened the door and poked his head into the corridor. "Let's see who that might be."

Bey had already gotten into the elevator, and the numbers were ticking down when we passed the machine on our way to the stairs. Just as we were taking the first few steps down, I could hear that the elevator had stopped, but well before the bottom floor. I assumed they were picking up another guest, despite the fact that there was barely room for three people in the small machine.

"What happens if we get to the bottom floor first?"

"If we hurry, we should be able to hide—there's a corridor off to the right we should be able to use and not be seen."

I was always impressed with the man's ability to mentally map a location without ever seeming like he was doing it.

When we reached the ground floor, it appeared that the elevator had only descended one more floor and then stopped moving altogether.

"That's strange," Redvers muttered.

I danced from foot to foot, impatient for something to happen while Redvers made a decision about our next move. I was surprised when that move turned out to be pushing the call button for the elevator—it was normally operated by a live staff member, but there was still a mechanism to bring the elevator down. The machine ground back into motion, and even before it had come to a stop on the ground floor, I could see through the windows of the wooden door that there was a crumpled heap of clothing on the floor of the cage. Unfortunately, it looked like there was a human in that clothing and no elevator operator to be seen.

Redvers managed to unlock the outer iron gate and pushed inside the door, blocking my view of the small space, but I suspected that I already knew who it was.

"It's Ziya Bey," Redvers said. "And he's dead."

CHAPTER SEVENTEEN

We only had a few moments before another guest or staff member came along—we were lucky that the elevator and stairs were as quiet as they were right now. Of course, the murderer had gotten lucky that way as well.

Redvers quickly rifled the archivist's pockets before he sent me back up the stairs to our room. I waited for him impatiently—the carpet in our room really was getting quite the workout as I paced the floors again. I was fine with waiting upstairs though since I didn't relish the idea of meeting any Turkish police, so I was happy to let Redvers field that issue. It was nearly half an hour, but he let himself into our room and came straight to me, wrapping me in a hug before releasing me and taking a seat.

I didn't even say anything; I just stared at him until he started talking.

"He was stabbed. Several times, but very efficiently for all that."

"By the elevator operator?" It sounded silly, but I wasn't making a joke. I was in complete earnest.

"It would appear so. I asked and there was a mix-up with which young man was supposed to be working the lift this evening. One of them was unable to come into work because he's ill and another was supposed to fill in but didn't show, and no one could remember who was actually working."

"Damn," I said. "I didn't get a look at who took us up to our room."

Redvers shook his head. "I didn't either. If I think about it, it seemed he was keeping his face obscured. Probably on purpose, in retrospect."

"A lucky break for him that Bey went down by himself."

"Indeed. Unless he was simply going to follow him afterward and take care of the man elsewhere in the hotel." Redvers ran a hand down his face. "As we know, a hotel uniform is an effective disguise." We'd had occasion to use such disguises and he was correct—people tended to overlook the staff in uniform. Just as we just had. "I found it discarded in a trash can near the rear exit."

"Of course." I knew he would have looked for it to be certain his assumptions were correct about how this was carried out. "What did you tell the police?"

"Nothing. They've been called, obviously, but I simply reported to the desk that there was a man in the lift who appeared to have passed out. I told them that I didn't know him, so they let me leave."

"What happened next?"

"The clerk went to look at him and then ran to the phone." Redvers shrugged. "I assume they called the police."

"What took you so long then?"

"I asked some questions among other members of the staff. They were shocked enough that they were happy to answer—and spread a bit of gossip. Nothing else useful unfortunately."

"Poor Ziya." I was perched on the edge of my own chair and now sat back heavily. "Whatever his sins, he didn't deserve this."

Redvers agreed. "And it leaves us in something of a pickle. We know that he was helping your father with the translations. And that he was involved with some kind of expedition with your father—based on his reaction earlier I would say it was something other than the sultan's heart. But it's going to be even more difficult to figure out what that was."

"And it's going to be difficult to figure out why he was killed."

"It has to be related to this, though," Redvers said. "I can't imagine there's anything else he was involved in that would get him stabbed in an elevator immediately after meeting with us."

That was true. He'd most likely been stabbed because of our business with the sultan's heart.

We waited for a bit, but the police didn't come knocking on our door, and we decided to go ahead with our original plan for the evening. I was sad for the archivist, but we also couldn't afford to lose any time—my internal clock was still ticking down to when the bank would take our home.

We entered Maxim's, a typical nightclub with dim lighting, tables packed together, and a dance floor near where the band was setting up. At first glance, the crowd seemed to be an eclectic one—locals mixed with foreigners and tourists. I was surprised we had the good fortune to be almost immediately shown to a table—it was still early in the evening, but the place was already busy. The proprietor himself, a black man named Thomas, showed us to our table.

Once he left, Redvers leaned forward. "He is originally from America but emigrated to Russia."

"Yes, I gathered that from his accent," I said. "Why is he here now?"

"He came here with the rest of the White Russians," Redvers said. "The dancers there are probably Russian as well. Most of the women who perform in these clubs are."

"Interesting," I said, taking in the line of women in short fringed skirts dancing to the band, but thinking about the owner of this establishment. Since Thomas was black, I was only a little bit surprised to see that tonight's band was also black—and from what I could tell, American as well. Back home, a black jazz band playing for a mixed crowd would be quite shocking, but here it seemed to be taken in stride. I appreciated the attitude as well as the music—they'd started to play while we took our seats, and they were excellent.

A member of the staff came to take our drink orders—I asked for a gin rickey and Redvers for a Scotch on the rocks.

The number the band was playing ended and the lights came down even further. I looked around, wondering what was happening, when a spotlight lit up the stage. A moment later the band picked up again, this time a slower song, and the curtains parted, revealing a woman in a heavily beaded and scandalously short green dress.

I heard Redvers make a noise and looked over at him. He looked resigned, and I leaned over to whisper a question. "Your friend Katerina?"

"One and the same."

This made our evening at Maxim's significantly more interesting. She was a very good singer, with a low smoky voice and a commanding stage presence. All eyes in the place were glued to her, and I could see that she not only knew that—she enjoyed it. Which meant that she and I could not be more different.

I sipped at my drink slowly, savoring it. It would be easy to down the thing, since it was top-notch quality and went down smoothly, but I didn't want my faculties compromised in any way, and I noticed that Redvers was doing the same. I had been thinking that we needed to blend in while keeping our wits about us, but with Katerina on the stage and a full view of the room, there was little chance of us going unnoticed. Specifically Redvers. The best we could do was keep our wits about us.

Katerina's song came to a close and she took a short bow in several directions, blowing a kiss at our table before disappearing back behind the curtain. I could almost hear Redvers' internal groan, but the band picked the tempo back up and people returned to the dance floor. If anyone had noticed the special attention she paid us, they would be quickly distracted.

I turned to Redvers. That had been a terribly familiar gesture, leading me to wonder just how well they knew each other. But I was proud of myself for pushing those thoughts away and focusing on more pressing concerns. "Since there's little hope of remaining inconspicuous now, should we ask around about my father?" It was, after all, what Redvers had said we would be doing here. Although I wasn't sure where we should start—the waitstaff? The owner? Katerina? But who was likely to remember one unremarkable man in a crowd like this?

He shook his head. "I don't see that there's much point. It will be more useful to us to find out exactly who is following us—and for what reason."

While Redvers was speaking, I could see that a man wearing a thoroughly modern suit but a disreputable look was threading his way through the crowded room toward our table. If I had to pick someone to play the part of a pirate, it would have been him—dark eyes and a closely trimmed beard, but hair that was just slightly too long.

The man stopped at our table, standing close to be heard over the music and the crowd. "You are Mr. Redvers and Miss Wunderly, I believe?"

Redvers' eyes narrowed slightly. "And if we are?"

"You knew my brother," the man said.

"And who is your brother?" Redvers asked.

"Ziya Bey."

Both our faces must have registered shock because the man

nodded once before grabbing a chair from a nearby table, setting it between Redvers and I, and taking a seat before either of us could invite him to do so.

"Word got around quickly," Redvers said. "It can't have been two hours since the . . . incident."

"I'm in the business of knowing things," the man said, but didn't offer further explanation.

"Might we know your name?" I asked.

"Ekrem Bey," He smiled widely, his teeth gleaming in the low light. I didn't trust that smile or the man behind it, not for a second. I found it disconcerting that he didn't seem to be in the slightest bit upset about his brother's death, instead appearing as though we were discussing the weather.

"It's a pleasure to meet you," Redvers said. "Although I'm sorry about the circumstances."

"Indeed," Ekrem replied, his black eyes raking me over before turning back to Redvers.

I considered telling him that I was sorry about his brother's murder, but I held my tongue. I found that I didn't want to bring his attention back onto myself—there was something unnerving about his gaze.

"What do you know about my brother's death?" Without waiting for an answer, Ekrem signaled to the waiter and ordered a whiskey. "The whiskey is quite good. An imported brand. Can I get you one?" This was directed at me and said almost seductively.

I shook my head but met his eyes directly. "Thank you, but no. I'm quite fine at the moment."

Ekrem's eyes lit up with inner amusement, but he said nothing more until the waiter had left, then turned back to Redvers, his eyebrow lifted in anticipation of an answer to his earlier question.

"He was killed in the lift. That's about all we know at the moment."

100 Erica Ruth Neubauer

"Come now, you have to know more than that," Ekrem said.

Redvers regarded the man for a long moment. "Why should we share any information we have with you?"

Ekrem inclined his head. "A fair point." The waiter delivered his drink and Ekrem took a leisurely sip before continuing. "How about a trade in kind? I happen to have information you might be interested in as well."

"Such as?" Redvers asked.

"Such as what happened to Professor Wunderly's money."

CHAPTER EIGHTEEN

If it weren't for the hum of the crowd and the band playing an upbeat number, I suspect the gasp I gave would have been heard as far away as the bar. And it was impossible for me to hold my tongue now. "What do you know about the money?"

"Ahh, my fair lady. I see I have caught your interest at last."

I thought about his face catching my drink, but I restrained myself, taking a fortifying sip instead. Luckily for everyone, he stopped oozing what he most likely thought was charm and sobered ever so slightly.

"My brother was a devout Muslim. He always was a good boy, even when we were children." Ekrem saw the look on Redvers' face and paused. "You think otherwise?"

Redvers shook his head. "I saw him the other night in some, shall we say, disreputable parts of town."

Ekrem cocked his head. "He was looking for me, in a panic as usual. It is I who frequents such establishments, not my brother." Those wolfish eyes turned to me. "Only in the name of my business, you understand."

I didn't bother to acknowledge this—I wasn't going to play into his game, whatever it might be. Although it did make sense that Ziya had been looking for his brother rather than indulging in some secret vice. Everyone had secrets, that was true, but Ziya had never struck me as the type that was hiding an addiction to opium or women. It had seemed too incongruous with his personality, despite my suspicion of the man. Suspicion that now looked as though it was warranted, although not for the reasons I'd thought.

Ekrem turned back to Redvers and continued. "Ziya was also a bit naïve, and he was taken in by an associate who claimed to be setting up an expedition to Hungary to find some artifact."

"The sultan's heart?" Redvers asked.

Ekrem cocked his head. "That may well be it. In any case, there was a large buy-in, and Ziya convinced your father that he should invest since this associate promised large returns. Of course, there was no such expedition, and the man left town with the money. Quite a hefty sum, if rumors are true." Ekrem sipped at his drink and looked around the room casually before turning his intense gaze back to us.

My heart was now somewhere around my feet. Could this possibly be true? Could Father have taken out that money against our row house only to invest it in a scam? Was it possible that we'd never find the money at all?

I could tell by the troubled look on Redvers' face that he was wondering the exact same thing.

"In Ziya's defense, he had no idea this expedition was a scam. He simply knew your father had been searching for the heart for many years." Ekrem sighed. "Such a trusting man, my brother. Or was, rather. I'll have to get used to that."

His heartless tone grated at me and I shifted uncomfortably in my seat. Ekrem noticed and set his glass on the table carefully. "I am sorry my brother is dead, Miss Wunderly. But I will mourn him in my own fashion." His tone was low and warning.

I nodded in response but said nothing.

"Will you give us the name of this associate?" Redvers interrupted the tense moment.

Ekrem turned his attention back to my fiancé. "Of course, but I think you're quite unlikely to find him."

And it wasn't as though we had unlimited amounts of time in which to do so, either. Even if we could find this man, there was no guarantee that he'd have any of the money left anyway. I was devastated—it seemed we would lose our family home after all.

"My brother felt guilty for his role in all this. He told me he was going to find a way to make it up to your family, although I haven't the slightest idea how he thought he would do that." Ekrem shrugged. "And look what good that did him, anyway."

"What's your interest in this now? Why tell us all this?" Redvers asked.

"Because I will find the person responsible for my brother's death. We may not have been close, or even liked each other very much." At this, Ekrem briefly glanced at me before continuing. "But I will avenge his death. And you can help me do that."

I was unable to keep myself from taking a verbal stab at this man. "That's all very dramatic, but do you have any idea who was behind it?"

Ekrem's expression was one of vague amusement. "I do not. But I will find out."

I glanced at Redvers, but his attention had been drawn elsewhere. I followed his dark gaze and saw that he was looking at Katerina—she was standing at the edge of the room, openly watching us while a young man in a navy suit talked at her. The woman had changed into a more elegant evening gown, black, low-cut, and striking against her pale skin. Her dark hair had been let down, and I could now see that it was unfashionably long but waved beautifully around her face. So far, she hadn't made a move to come over, but it appeared that was about to change. Without a word to the young man, she stepped away, leaving him with his mouth hanging slightly open. She cut a path through the crowd, people instinctively moving out of her way.

It looked like I was going to meet Katerina Semenov whether I wanted to or not.

I set aside my feelings about Ekrem Bey and the impending loss of my family home just in time for Katerina to arrive at our table with a flourish. Ekrem stood and fetched another chair from a nearby table, holding it out for Katerina as she sat, then scooted her chair closer to Redvers'. I could feel the tension radiating from my fiancé and the amusement from Ekrem Bey.

"Redvers," Katerina cooed, her low voice full of smoke and sensuality. "It's been entirely too long."

"I wouldn't say that." Redvers took a sip of his whiskey, his eyes meeting mine over the rim of the glass. From his gaze I knew he was attempting to reassure me, which wasn't necessary even though the difference between me and this woman couldn't have been more stark. I felt more curious at the moment than anything, especially as she didn't let his brusque response trouble her in the least.

Her focused gaze turned to me but she didn't say anything.

Redvers drew her attention back to himself. "Unfortunately, we don't have time to catch up. Jane and I must be on our way."

Katerina looked amused. "And when I just got here." Then she smiled, a dazzling display revealing one small dimple in her cheek. "Is this because of the man following you? The one at the table back there?" She indicated the direction with nothing more than a small tip of her head, a gesture that would have meant nothing to an outside observer.

Redvers only sighed, finishing his drink and putting it back down on the table.

Ekrem didn't so much as move his eyes in the direction that Katerina had indicated. Which told me that the man had experience with this type of thing. Instead, he waited a few beats to turn and signal to a waiter, allowing him to take in the room behind us. "The man with the fedora on the table?" He took a sip of his drink. "Quite rude, you know. That hat should be checked." Ekrem ordered another drink from the waiter he'd called over.

Redvers tapped the side of his glass throughout this exchange, and once the waiter left again he spoke. "Do either of you know him?"

"Yes, of course I know him." Ekrem took another long pause and a drink before setting his glass down. "But I do not know who he works for. Do you, Katerina?"

She shook her head. "How on earth would I know such a thing?"

Ekrem chuckled, the wolfish grin back in place, but this time directed at the other woman. "Because we are in a very similar business, you and I."

Katerina didn't respond, simply sitting back in her chair and flashing that dimple. I didn't need to ask how these two knew each other. It was obvious they were well-known to each other, and it wasn't necessary to know how.

"But would you like me to find out for you, fair lady?" Ekrem asked, his attention now directed at me. The insinuation in his voice was just this side of polite, and I realized I much preferred when his focus was on Katerina.

I also pressed down every instinct I had to splash my drink across the man's face—the second time I'd been tempted in one evening—and instead spoke through gritted teeth. "Yes. I would very much appreciate that." I caught Redvers' eye across the table and he gave a tiny nod of encouragement. If it hadn't been for that, my drink truly would have gone flying at Ekrem's face this time.

"Oh, that won't be necessary," Katerina said, standing elegantly from her seat. "I'll take care of things." As she passed

Redvers, her hand stroked over his shoulder and the back of his neck before she sashayed across the room, bending across the table to flash what I imagined was a great deal of cleavage.

I looked at him with raised eyebrows, and he met my gaze, lips pressed together in obvious distaste before turning to Bey.

"It looks as though that's our cue to leave," Redvers said. "Ekrem, what is your plan?"

I could only hope his plan did not include us.

Ekrem gave a casual shrug. "I'll see what I can learn here." He cast a glance in Katerina's direction before looking at me, clearly amused by the woman's earlier gesture. "She appears to have things well in hand, but I would recommend leaving now."

Redvers regarded him for a moment, then stood, grabbing his overcoat. We hadn't checked them at the door for this very reason, and I followed suit, grabbing my coat and following Redvers to the dance floor.

I hoped three things. First, that Katerina could keep our shadow busy long enough for us to slip out relatively unnoticed. The second, that Ekrem wouldn't take this opportunity to follow us and would instead try to learn who the man following us worked for. And third, that I wouldn't have to actually dance.

Chapter Nineteen

Glancing behind me told me that Ekrem was still seated at our table, his eyes on Katerina and her prey, so it seemed unlikely that he was going to be following us out of the nightclub. I didn't want him to know where we were headed next, even if I only had a vague notion of where that would be. When it came down to it, I didn't want Ekrem Bey anywhere that I was, and especially not if we were tracking down clues as to my father's whereabouts and that of the sultan's heart. Our luck held further in that Katerina was still strategically blocking our shadow's view of us, and I was both grateful and suspicious of her help. This had been an eventful evening already, and there was much to discuss with Redvers later—not least her overfamiliarity with him.

I breathed a sigh of relief when my luck held out on the third item as well—there was no dancing involved as Redvers led me straight through the gyrating crowd and toward the back of the building. It would have looked strange anyway, since we were carrying our overcoats and my hat, which I'd unceremoniously stuffed into a sleeve earlier.

Redvers slipped some currency to a very surprised member of the waitstaff, who checked his palm only once before giving an enthusiastic nod and leading us through a back hallway to a storage area. Another member of the waitstaff was sitting on a low stack of boxes as we were led through and looked at us curiously but said nothing. The waiter unlocked and pushed open a door on the opposite wall and let us usher past him. With a brief wave, the door shut again and we found ourselves alone in a cramped alley.

"This way, I believe," Redvers said.

"To the Basilica Cistern?" I asked.

"Where else?" Redvers replied. He took my hand and led me away from Maxim's, down the alley, and to the left along a narrow street. I noticed that the both of us were well aware of whether or not we were being followed, keeping a close eye on our trail, but we seemed to be in the clear.

The hour had grown late and there weren't many trams running at this time of night, so we flagged down a taxi several blocks from the club. I was able to breathe a little easier the more distance we put between ourselves and our companions from the evening, finally feeling free of scrutiny by the time we were approaching the bridge.

The cistern was back on the other side of the Golden Horn, in the same neighborhood as the other historical sites we'd been to, all of which were well and truly closed for the evening. The hustle and bustle of our previous visits was gone with the sun, leaving us standing on a near-deserted street. The feeling was eerie, to say the least. Redvers had asked the car to deposit us a block away from our destination, just in case, and as we made our way to our actual destination, I tried to determine what time it might be, based on the dark sky and lack of pedestrians. I knew that a call to prayer had gone out around sunset several hours before, so I thought we must be nearing the last call for the night but couldn't say for certain.

We could see the Hagia Sophia from where we were, and we were close to the grounds of the Blue Mosque as well, which stood very close to its neighbor. But what we stood in front of now was nowhere near as grand. It was a simple building with alternating pink-and-cream brick, only one story tall. It would be easy to overlook entirely, especially given its grand neighbors just behind us. The two of us stood at the door and Redvers cocked his head at me. I nodded and came to stand in front of him, just as I'd done plenty of times before, effectively blocking anyone on the street from seeing Redvers and his sleek lock-picking kit. It was cold and I shivered in the night air beneath my coat.

Within a few minutes, Redvers was through the door and I waited until we were certain the few scattered pedestrians left on the street weren't paying us any mind before slipping through the door myself. We closed it silently behind us, and Redvers locked it from the inside.

We now stood in total darkness. I was cursing the fact that I hadn't brought a flashlight with me when Redvers flicked on his.

"Just how much do you carry in that jacket?" I asked. I also wanted to know how it never looked as though he was carrying an arsenal of burglary tools. In the glow from the flashlight, I saw Redvers give me a wink. I rolled my eyes, although it was lost on him since he was already searching the small room where we stood.

"Ah, excellent," he said. "Just what we need." A moment later a hand-held lantern was lit, casting a soft but wider glow than the flashlight. Redvers held the lamp up and passed it to me. A moment later another lantern added its own glow. Redvers held on to this one and secured his flashlight in his coat pocket.

We descended several sets of stairs with the glow from our lamps lighting our way until we came to the lowest level. On the last set of stairs, Redvers needed to duck to avoid hitting his head on the stonework above, but then we found ourselves in the main chamber where the ceilings were tall and a series of wooden boats were tied up. Redvers and I held up our lanterns, the yellow glow reflecting in the water. We couldn't see terribly far ahead of us, but what I could see showed a sea of ancient columns, their bases lost in water. Arched ceilings soared overhead, and both the space and the columns seemed to go on forever, well past the meager light our lamps cast and into the inky darkness beyond.

Redvers was already pulling a boat closer to the platform so that I could step in. I set down the lantern I was holding and stepped into the bottom of the boat, holding one of Redvers' strong hands as I got in. I moved to the front of the small craft and got myself settled before Redvers leaned forward and placed my lantern on the wooden seat. I leaned over and grabbed it, turning toward the back of the cistern, lantern held aloft. Where should we even start? We needed an idea of where to begin this search or we would be here all night—and well into tomorrow as well.

Redvers got into the small boat, and I lowered the lantern while the little craft rocked with his added weight and then settled back into the water.

"I think we should start in the back. Hiding it up here would make it entirely too easy to find," Redvers said.

"That seems like a reasonable assumption," I said.

Redvers began rowing us toward the back of the cavern. It was difficult to tell how deep the water was, but with the two of us seated in the little boat, we skimmed over it easily. I held my lantern aloft even though my arm quickly grew tired, trying to ensure he didn't row us directly into a stone column. I didn't think we would come out well in that scenario.

While Redvers rowed, I couldn't help my mind from drifting back to the things we'd discovered that evening and what they meant for us. "Even if the money is gone, we still need to find Father."

Redvers made a noise of agreement over the swooshing of the oars in the water. "Although we must keep in mind the source of that story, even if the pieces do fit."

"He's the last person in the world I want to associate with

or trust," I said. "But I also think the story rings true. Unfortunately. I should have known Father would get himself into trouble while Millie and I were abroad."

Redvers didn't have a response to that, but I wasn't looking for one.

"If he actually manages to find the heart, it might bring enough money to repay the loan," I said.

"If I were a betting man, I'd wager that is exactly what your father is thinking."

"We need to find him before he gets into more trouble. Which he may have already done since there were men following him who are now following us."

"It does all seem to be related."

"How does Katerina fit in?" I asked. I didn't think she fit in with my father's troubles, but I was curious about the tension at the table earlier between Redvers and the Russian singer—especially how she'd taken her leave of us. I found that I wasn't jealous, since clearly he didn't relish her attentions, but I was interested to know more about their history.

"I don't think that she does." Then Redvers rather abruptly changed the subject. "We should decide how best to do a systematic search of the cistern. I think we should start where it's dry. Several hundred years ago the water level was higher, and I imagine they would have tried to keep it as far above the water level as possible."

He couldn't see it, but my eyebrows were raised at this sudden torrent of information. It was obvious to me that he didn't want to talk about Katerina Semenov, and I would let it go for the time being since we had other important matters to attend to—such as discovering if something was hidden in this vast cistern. But I would not be forgetting to explore this topic in depth later.

We were now at the back corner of the cistern, not moving at all, and I felt something drip onto my head from the

curved ceiling some thirty feet over our heads. It was unpleasant, but I forced myself to study the wall—or as much
of the wall as I could see. It seemed unlikely they would have
been able to hide the map in the wall itself since it was solid
stone.

I ignored my anxiety about my father and our row house,
as well as my piqued curiosity about Katerina, and concentrated on thinking things through. Where else could Suleiman's followers have put a map? I swung my lamp to the side
to look at the pillar nearest me. There was nothing terribly
special about it—just a large stone column with some decorative elements at the top and base. I vaguely remembered
my father at one time discussing ancient methods of water-
proofing, so was it possible they weren't worried about the
waterline at all?

"Row me closer to this column, please," I said.

Redvers did as I asked. "Do you see something?"

"No, I'm simply trying to see if something could be secured in one of these." There was nothing unusual about the
pillar I was inspecting. But was that true of every pillar down
here? "Do you know if all the pillars are the same?" I wasn't
sure how much Redvers actually knew about this cistern.

He was quiet for a moment, obviously casting around in
his memory. "I think they are not. If I recall correctly, there is
one pillar that is called the Hen's Eye column. It is carved
with the eyes of a peacock tail."

I brightened. "Do you know where that column is?"

"That I can't quite recall," Redvers said. "But there are
also two columns where the bases are even more unusual.
Many of these were taken from other ancient buildings to be
used here."

I was impatient with the history lesson since I was already
well aware that people had been reusing materials since the
beginning of time. I needed to know which columns were different not how they came to be here. "Redvers," I said, add-

ing a noise in the back of my throat. I couldn't quite see the expression on his face, but he gave a little cough.

"Sorry, my dear." His voice was chagrined. "There are supposed to be two columns where the bases rest on carvings of Medusa's head."

I nearly clapped my hands together at this news. "Medusa. Like the monster in the riddle."

"Excellent point."

"And do you know where those would be?" I could feel the boat rock gently as Redvers looked around himself in the semidarkness.

"I want to say they're toward the front. Which goes against what I would have assumed, but let's take a look."

Redvers began rowing toward the opposite wall, and minutes later I spotted the first of the gorgon heads. It was upside down, water lapping at her eyes. I held my lantern up, inspecting the side we were nearest to. Redvers immediately realized what I was doing and directed our boat around the base of the column while I ran my hand over the stone. Nothing. We came back around to Medusa's face, and I looked at her eyes, then turned my head to see where her sightless gaze led me.

"Over there." I pointed at the column opposite.

"Brilliant, Jane. You might be on to something here." I couldn't see Redvers' face, but I could hear the admiration in his tone clearly enough. I didn't respond, keeping my hand moving over the base of the column, testing the stone, but I did allow myself a small smile.

But there was nothing to be found, although it took me a few long minutes to admit it. "Nothing." I was disappointed, but we still had another Medusa to go.

Redvers paddled us over to the other column with a Medusa base. This pillar rested on the side of her face, the column pressing into one cheek and the floor into the other. I did the same routine as I had done with the last head, checking the base of the column and running my hands over the stone as far as I could reach without capsizing the boat, but I found nothing unusual. Once again, I turned my own head to follow the gorgon's gaze and found myself looking at another column precisely like the majority of its neighbors, but this one had a brick enclosure around its base.

This was entirely more hopeful.

I ran my hands over the bricks, pushing gently at each one. "Here," I said. I found a brick that looked slightly less aged than the others and moved ever so slightly when pushed against.

"Can you get it out?" Redvers asked.

I worked at it for a moment, but it was wedged in tightly. I bent a fingernail back in my efforts to get the brick free and I shook out my hand before deciding to turn it over to Redvers. "You try it."

Redvers maneuvered the boat so that he was now nearest the low brick wall. I held my lantern high so that Redvers could see what he was doing while also keeping an eye on the level of the boat. I didn't want us to accidentally tip into the water in the course of pulling at those bricks. Especially since I didn't know how long we would last in what could only be frigid water, nor did I have any sense of how deep the water beneath us actually was. Staying safely in the boat was the best course of action.

The loud scrape of brick echoed through the chamber and a shiver ran down my spine, although I couldn't say exactly why. I watched as Redvers carefully removed the brick, pausing to ensure that the integrity of the little wall was sound and wouldn't come tumbling down, then peered into the hole behind.

"Jane, could you hand me the torch?"

I carefully leaned forward and located the flashlight in the pocket of his coat, which he'd dumped in the bottom of the boat, cognizant of the little boat's rocking while I did so. I stayed in that position and let the boat settle again before passing it to Redvers as he'd asked. Redvers shone the flash-light into the space left by the brick, grunted, and put his hand inside, coming back out with a small black package. My heart raced—I had to admit it was thrilling to follow a clue and actually find something at the other end of it.

Redvers sat back and unwrapped the oilskin, pulling out a piece of paper and shining a light on it. "It's a note."

I huffed impatiently. Of course, it was a note.

Redvers looked up at me. "It's for you."

My heart did a stutter step. That it was for me personally could only mean one thing—my father had already been here and taken the map, leaving a note for me in its place.

Redvers leaned forward and passed it to me. It was a fresh piece of paper, not the ancient artifact I'd been hoping to find.

> *"Dearest Jane,*
> *I expect you have made it this far, since you've always been such a clever girl. I myself made it this far only with a great deal of luck and found the map that has been hidden here for centuries. What a find, my girl! After all these years, I might finally have the location of the heart. It is near the city where I thought it would be, but of course I would never have found it without this map. I'm heading to Hungary."*

I smiled at my father's enthusiasm. But my smile quickly faded.

> *"I don't want to worry you, my dear, but I do fear that I'm being followed. That is partly why I'm leaving you this note. Don't come after me—I'm certain I will be fine, and I'll be in touch once I have cleared things up. Love to you. Henry"*

I made a noise of frustration. I already knew the "trouble" he thought he was going to clear up, although of course he wasn't aware that I knew about the scam and the lost money. Still, I wished I could simply talk to him and help him figure out how we were going to resolve this mess. We still had about a week and a half before I thought we would have to use our last resort, Aunt Millie, and part of me was holding out hope that there was yet another way out. But it was diffi-cult to decide what that way out might be when we were spending our time trying to figure out where the man had gone.

At least we had a country now, and I thought I also knew the city that he was referring to. It was another step in the right direction, even if it wasn't fast enough for me.

I slipped the note and the oilskin pouch into my coat pocket as Redvers pushed the brick back into place. Once he was relatively certain no one could tell it had been disturbed, he took his lantern back from where he'd placed it. Redvers opened his mouth to say something, but at that moment we heard the distinct sound of footsteps coming down the stairs at the end of the cistern.

CHAPTER TWENTY

My panicked eyes met Redvers' in the dim light and he motioned for us to extinguish our lanterns, which we did as quickly and as quietly as we could, stowing them in the bottom of the boat. I could feel our boat dip slightly and I assumed that Redvers had reached out to pull our rowboat a little closer to the nearest pillar since we were now nestled up to it. The person had been moving slowly—you could tell that whoever it was, they were attempting to stay quiet, but hadn't thought to remove their footwear, and it was nearly impossible to remain completely silent on the stone floors wearing soled shoes.

The footsteps were now making their way down the final flight of stairs. I barely dared to breathe and I silently prayed neither of us would suddenly have to sneeze—it would echo in the chamber, and even though it would be difficult to pinpoint exactly where we were, it would give us away. Our rowboat was a fair distance from the stairs, so it was unlikely that a light would be able to reach us, but my heart beat wildly in my chest while I wondered who this might be. I'd felt fairly confident that we'd made it here without being followed, so who would be creeping down the cistern stairs this late at night? A night watchman? Redvers had thought that the cistern wasn't guarded at night. Could we have been followed despite Katerina's efforts—or was it Ekrem himself?

We heard the distant sound of shuffling, followed by what sounded like a lantern being placed on the ground—the small clang of metal on stone. A little rustling of clothes, and then nothing. What on earth was going on? It sounded as though this person was settling in to wait us out. Silence stretched out as minutes ticked by.

We appeared to have reached a standoff.

I don't know how long we sat there in the dark, but it was long enough that my posterior fell asleep. Not to mention the chill I had from sitting in the damp without moving for an extended period of time—it had begun to seep beneath my clothes and deep into my skin. At least we weren't sitting on the cold stone stairs as our mysterious visitor was. In fact, I was beginning to think that whoever it was had to be made of stone themselves since we'd heard no sounds from them since they took a seat.

I hugged my arms across myself, desperately wanting to go back to solid ground, but what options did we have? Moving would only expose us, and there was no real way to get an advantage over whoever had set up on the other side of the cistern. We couldn't even see each other enough to try to work out a plan now that the lanterns had been extinguished, and I didn't dare whisper with the acoustics in this place. Not even directly into Redvers' ear, if I could get to it. Changing position in the little boat was too much of a risk, especially in the dark. Capsizing now would be a disaster.

I'd begun to shiver with real enthusiasm and hoped we weren't settling in for the entire night when a voice finally cut through the darkness.

"Jane? Are you down here?"

I nearly keeled over with relief. "Maral? Is that you?"

"Yes, of course."

I had an impolite reply to the "of course," but my thought

was interrupted by Redvers flicking the flashlight back on. He held it as I leaned down and retrieved my lantern, relighting it. I held the light steady as Redvers grabbed the oars and maneuvered us around the column and then rowed us back toward the stairs at the front of the cistern.

As we drew near the staircase, I could see that it was indeed Maral. She was dressed warmly, now holding her own lantern aloft. I could also see the amused expression in her eyes, which did nothing to improve my temper since I wasn't nearly as amused, although I was relieved that it was no one more nefarious.

"I wasn't entirely certain it was you, though I suspected," Maral said as we stepped carefully from the boat.

"If you thought it was us and you knew where we were, why didn't you say something sooner?" I didn't bother hiding the temper in my voice.

She gave a casual shrug. "I could tell that one of the boats was missing. But what if it *wasn't* you? There are some unsavory people with an interest in what your father was doing. Or so it would seem."

Redvers made a noise of irritation, and I mentally agreed. What was the use of us sitting in the dark and damp for so long? It wasn't as though we could have snuck up on the woman from a rowboat. I'd already been struggling with my feelings toward Maral, and nothing about this was helping her cause. Despite her explanation, I felt more than a spark of anger.

"Did you find what you were looking for?" Maral asked, one eyebrow raised.

I would have bet a fair sum of money that Maral knew exactly what we'd found down here. "We found a note." I heard my own voice and it wasn't friendly.

"As I suspected." Maral nodded once. "Shall we retire to somewhere more comfortable?"

*   *   *

We made our way back up to the cistern's entrance, the call to prayer echoing through the streets, all the louder near the two mosques standing only a few hundred yards away. I checked my watch with the flashlight I still held—it was only 10 P.M., but it felt much later. I wouldn't have been surprised to learn it was the wee hours of the morning.

One by one our little group slipped out of the entrance door, and we began making our way back across the city. I assumed Maral had a specific destination in mind and I was right—we went back to her *meyhane*. It was closed now, but she pulled a key from her pocket and unlocked the door.

"Sit yourselves down. I will get us something to drink. You need something to warm you up, I think." Maral moved gracefully through the small cluster of empty tables, returning moments later with an unlabeled bottle in her hands and three cups. She set them down on the table, uncorked the bottle, and poured a liberal amount into each cup.

Maral passed me my cup and I sniffed at it experimentally, the strong alcohol nearly burning the inside of my nose. I jerked back and Maral laughed. "It tastes better than it smells," she assured me.

With a shake of my head, I shot back a long draft, then coughed a fit as the liquor burned a path through my insides. It had a strong taste of black licorice, which I had never enjoyed, not to mention the burn. But she was right about one thing—it warmed me up. "What is this stuff?" I managed to ask. I wanted to know so that I could avoid it in the future.

"Raki," she said. "My father makes it right here in the back."

That certainly explained some things.

I was gratified to see that it also made Redvers cough and his eyes water before he got a handle on himself. Maral drank it as if it was nothing more than lemonade on a hot summer's day.

Maral waited until we'd finished coughing to ask her question. "You found your father's note?"

I nodded. "How did you know it was there?"

She smiled. "How do you think he got down there in the first place with no one around to see him?" She shrugged. "A friend of mine works at the cistern. Sometimes he has the keys." Maral didn't elaborate further, but she didn't need to.

"There were some important details you left out last time we spoke." Redvers' voice was casual but I could sense he was also angry. From the outside it certainly seemed Maral was leading us on a merry chase. Why hadn't she mentioned my father visiting the cistern? Or the note he'd left for me? In fact, we could've avoided vandalizing Roxelana's mausoleum altogether if Maral had told us that my father had left me a note in the cistern. I could feel my temper rising again. Why had she let us waste so much time? We were trying to follow the clues so that we could find my father. Didn't she want us to find him?

Maral topped off our cups of raki even though I'd already had more than my fill of the lethal stuff. "He never showed me the clues, and he never told me exactly what he'd found or where." She played with her cup, a veil of sadness falling over her face. "I wanted him to trust me, but he said he didn't want me to know too much, didn't want to put me in danger." She said nothing more although I could tell there was plenty more to be said on the topic.

"You let him into the cistern—why didn't you tell us he'd hidden a note there for Jane?" Redvers asked.

"Because I did not know that he had. Henry said he had left his daughter a note, but not where he'd left it. And he told me that he'd found a map, but he never once told me where he'd found it or what it showed." She shrugged. "Henry asked for the keys to the cistern and I got them for him, but I did not ask questions. You must understand all these things transpired at different times, not all at once, so I did not put together what was where. But after I met your aunt this afternoon, I realized he must have left the note for you in the cistern."

I felt my anger deflate, but only slightly. While my aunt was quite adept at secret-keeping, there were times when her pride got the better of her and she couldn't hold her tongue. Maral was clever—it was entirely possible she'd gotten Millie to say something she shouldn't have. But because Maral was so clever, I struggled to believe that she hadn't put all the pieces together well before talking with my aunt.

This conversation had not cleared up much, although it had done one thing. Instead of simply struggling with the idea that my father had a romantic partner, for the first time I worried that perhaps we shouldn't trust this woman at all.

Chapter Twenty-one

"What did your father's note say?" Maral asked.

I looked at Redvers, unsure if I should answer. He tipped his head a bit, and I took that to mean that I may as well share the contents. Despite what she was telling us, I knew Redvers and I both thought she knew more. I waited a beat longer, then took the note and the oilskin pouch from my pocket and placed them on the table. Maral picked up the note and read it, a wistful smile coming over her face. The one thing I *did* believe about this woman was that she actually cared about my father—all evidence pointed to the fact that she did, and deeply.

"So typical of him, is it not?" Maral said, placing the note down gently before me. She sighed. "He has gone to Hungary."

"It would appear that way," Redvers said.

Even though Father's note said not to follow him, there was no way I would be taking that advice. Because while this message made it appear that he'd left under his own steam, too many questions remained. Why *had* he left his trunks? Why hadn't he checked out of the hotel or said goodbye to Maral or Ziya Bey? I now knew where the money had most likely gone—into a scammer's pocket. But why were men following him?

I watched Maral for a moment, considering. "Did Father tell you about the expedition he'd invested in?"

Maral's face betrayed nothing as she took another sip of raki. She held the bottle aloft, gesturing to both Redvers and myself. We both shook our heads and she shrugged, then poured herself a bit more of the lethal drink. It felt like a delaying tactic so she could gather her thoughts.

"When he arrived, he asked me if there was a bank where he could make a deposit. It seemed like a large sum of money, and he was nervous about leaving it in his hotel room."

It was reassuring that he'd had at least that much good sense.

"But then, perhaps a week or so later, he seemed very upset. I asked if it was to do with the money, and he became short with me." Maral cocked her head, remembering. "He apologized later for his temper, but he did not explain himself."

It was unlike Father to have a fit of temper, and I was surprised that he would have taken it out on Maral. Of course, I didn't know their relationship existed at all let alone what it was like, so I couldn't speak to their dynamic.

There was a lull in the conversation since I didn't know how much to reveal, so Redvers stepped in. "It would seem that Professor Wunderly invested in an expedition that turned out to be nothing more than a scam. He appears to have lost the money he came with."

Maral nodded slowly. "That would make sense given what I know about it. And how he reacted."

"Why wouldn't he have told you about the expedition?" I asked.

Maral raised an eyebrow at me. "I expect you know how your father was. Some things were to be shared and some things he felt he should handle alone. Many men are like this."

I couldn't disagree with her. Much like how my father trusted me with the household accounts but not with many other issues that the "man" of the house should handle. It was quite irritating, and based on even the little I knew of her, I would guess that Maral found it equally as annoying.

"I'm surprised the archivist isn't with you," Maral said.

I'd nearly forgotten that the man had been murdered earlier that evening and felt terrible. It seemed callous, although much had happened in a short period of time and I hadn't had a chance to work through any of it yet.

"He was killed," I said. "Earlier this evening."

Maral's eyes were wide and her face betrayed her shock. It appeared quite genuine—although there was no good reason for it not to be. It was unlikely that Maral had played the part of a male elevator operator and stabbed Ziya Bey. What would her motive for such an extreme action be?

"I am very sorry to hear that." Maral's voice was soft. "I did not like the man, nor did I trust him. But I did not want to see him dead."

Redvers spun his cup on the table in his hands. "Did you know it was Ziya's suggestion that Professor Wunderly invest in the false expedition?"

Maral shook her head. "I had no confirmation, but I suspected that might be the case."

"What made you suspect?" I asked.

The woman cocked her head. "Little things. After your father was so short-tempered, I saw the two of them together several times and something between them had changed. Your father was not as warm, and Bey was even more . . . deferential than before."

If Ekrem Bey's story was true, and I suspected more and more that it was, everything Maral was saying only confirmed it.

"Do you know who killed Mr. Bey?" Maral asked.

Redvers and I looked at each other and I shook my head.

"We do not," Redvers said. "But we intend to find out."

I didn't have the faintest idea how we were going to do that, especially since as far as I was concerned, we needed to be on the next train to Hungary.

Which led me to my next question. "How do we get to Hungary?" I asked Redvers.

"We'll book ourselves on the next train heading to Budapest. But from there . . . your father didn't tell us what city."

"Oh, that's easy," I said. "It's Szigetvár." Redvers raised an eyebrow and I shrugged. "Father talked about it often, how Suleiman the Magnificent died on the battlefield outside the city. Everyone knows that the heart was buried somewhere nearby, but it would be nearly impossible to search a radius several miles wide around the city. He was looking for something to narrow down the field."

"And he found it," Redvers finished for me. He leaned back in his chair. "We'll head to Budapest and then change trains to take one going to the south. I think that will be the most expedient way to get there."

"I suppose there's no way we can convince Millie to stay behind."

"I doubt it," Redvers said.

Maral had been quiet, but here she spoke up.

"I'm afraid there's no way you can convince me to stay behind either," Maral said. "I will pack my things and be ready to leave in the morning." She tossed back the rest of what was in her cup and set it down on the table with finality.

Redvers rubbed his forehead. "We'll look like a traveling circus with this many people."

I couldn't disagree, but short of the two of us fleeing the

city in the middle of the night, I didn't see any other option. "How likely is it that we would be able to get on board the train without being followed anyway?"

Redvers thought about that for a moment, then he sighed. "It would be difficult even with two of us and luggage. With five of us . . ." He shook his head. "We will just have to do our best."

We took our leave, agreeing that Maral would meet us in the morning at Pera Palace to make further plans.

What an interesting train ride this would be.

We'd left word at the Tokatlıyan Hotel for Millie and Lord Hughes, and they were already waiting for us in the morning when we came down. Millie glared at me, and I was too tired to wonder what exactly I'd done this time—I'd barely slept the night before. My brain wouldn't stop tumbling over all the questions and suspicions in my mind as well as the travel we now needed to arrange.

Redvers and I hadn't yet eaten breakfast so we headed to the restaurant, where we were promptly seated and I was promised coffee. I hoped the waiter would bring it before Millie started in on me.

But it was not my morning for luck.

"You went without us," Millie accused as soon as the waiter was out of earshot. "Did you send us on a wild-goose chase deliberately?"

I let Redvers take this one. "Not at all," he soothed. "It just worked out timing-wise and we were able to lose the man who was following us. We decided to take advantage of the situation."

"Well." Millie's feathers weren't completely smoothed, but nearly. "We did learn some interesting things at the café. What is that called?"

"A *meyhane*," Lord Hughes said.

"Yes, that." Millie smoothed down the front of her skirt. "Did you know that your father had a friend here in Istanbul?" Millie looked at me. "A *special* friend?"

I let my eyes close for just a moment. Where was that coffee?

"It hardly matters, I suppose." She continued without waiting for a response. "What did you find in the cistern?"

"A note from Father," I said. "It says he went to Hungary."

Millie was quiet for a moment, just long enough for the waiter to return with my Turkish coffee.

"Can you keep them coming?" I whispered. I must have sounded a bit desperate because the waiter smiled kindly and gave me a wink. I sank back in my chair in relief, tiny cup of caffeine held close.

Further interruption arrived in the form of Maral who arrived at the same time as my second cup of coffee. I sat quietly sipping the first while greetings were offered all around and the newcomer pulled up a chair to our table. It was obvious Millie didn't know what to think about Maral's appearance, and I just hoped my aunt would avoid saying anything outright rude to the other woman.

Then Redvers proceeded to get everyone caught up with where we were in regards to my father's disappearance, avoiding mention of Ziya's murder and the lost money.

"Are we still certain he disappeared? It sounds as though he simply traveled to Hungary." Millie looked at me. "And you know how your father can be. He might have left and forgot to tell anyone."

I blinked at her for a moment. This was a complete turnaround from her insistence just yesterday that my father had disappeared. True, I wasn't entirely certain myself what to think about my father's actions, but I thought that the term "disappeared" was too strong. That didn't stop me from arguing with my aunt, however. "That's true, although the fact remains that he left all his things behind. And there's the issue of the men who are following us, and were following him as well." I was still surprised that my father figured that out, since he *was* terribly oblivious. Of course, he'd have been increasingly more careful the closer he came to the map. Or at least I would hope that to be the case.

I considered telling Millie the last bit of information I'd held back from her about the loan and the ticking clock against Father losing the row house, but Redvers stepped in with a bomb of his own.

"And Ziya Bey was killed yesterday. In the lift as he left our meeting."

Millie gasped, and even the unflappable Lord Hughes looked shocked at this news. "That had to be only minutes after we left," Hughes said.

Redvers agreed quietly.

I expected a similar outburst from my aunt about the danger they'd nearly faced, but I was surprised yet again. Millie simply sat quietly for a long moment before nodding once. "The four of us need to get to Hungary, then. We need to find your father."

Maral both broke in and renewed her argument for coming along on our trip, and I listened, mixed feelings swirling. I didn't trust her, but I didn't see how we could avoid her joining us, either.

Maral's concern for my father was evident, but there was quite a lot about my father's activities that she'd neglected to mention. Not to mention letting us sit anxiously in a dark cistern before revealing herself. No, Maral had not done a lot to endear herself—quite the opposite, in fact. And I'd already been struggling with my feelings about her relationship with my father and what that meant for his memories of my mother—and my own.

There was nothing I could do about these concerns at the moment, so I tuned out and enjoyed my coffee while my tablemates argued about who was going where. When they finally ran out of things to quarrel about, we sat quietly for a moment. It was an uneasy silence, but silence nonetheless and I savored it. Until the peace was broken by Lord Hughes.

"Very well. We are all going. But when do we leave?"

Chapter Twenty-two

Another argument ensued. Millie insisted on taking the *Orient Express*, which left from Istanbul only twice a week—we would have to leave the following evening if there were berths available. I didn't even want to know how much such a trip would cost or who would cover the expense. Maral argued for a cheaper alternative, but the *Orient Express* was also an express train and thus the fastest way to get us to Budapest, despite leaving the following day.

Millie looked smug as Redvers and Lord Hughes went to make the train reservations. Maral also excused herself, agreeing to meet us at the train station the following day. I was relieved that we would be free of all of them for at least the next day and a half, even though it meant we would be at loose ends for that long.

On our way back to the room, the desk clerk hurried up the short flight of stairs to intercept us before we could get into the elevator. "Mrs. Wunderly," he said. "There is a message for you."

I thanked the man and frowned at the note in my hand, wondering who on earth it could be from. Everyone I knew in Constantinople . . . er, Istanbul, had been at breakfast with us, with the exception of Ekrem Bey, and any day we went without having contact with that man I considered a win. I slid the note into the pocket of my green wool dress, where it burned a hole until we were back in the room.

"Who is it from?" Redvers asked.

I opened it and my eyes went to the signature at the bottom. "It looks like it is from your friend Katerina Semenov."

Redvers' eyebrows shot up for a brief moment. "I should have known the woman wouldn't let us leave without seeing her again."

"She wants me to meet her at the Cağaloğlu Hamam tonight. I know I'm not pronouncing that correctly." I looked up at him. "What is that, and where?"

Redvers sighed. "It's a Turkish bath. And you do not have to meet with her. Especially not at a bath if you're uncomfortable with everything it entails."

I thought about that for a moment. The note insinuated that Katerina had information for me, and while it was entirely possible that was a lie, I found that I was curious enough to risk a meeting—including subjecting myself to whatever the baths had in store. I handed the note to Redvers while I talked it through aloud. "I'd rather take the chance that she has nothing for us and meet with her anyway. Because what if she does have some information? She did help us last night by distracting the man who was following us."

"She did, but I'm sure she had an ulterior motive for that. The woman does nothing without reason."

I looked at him for a moment. "Just how well do you know Katerina?" I hadn't forgotten the tension at the table the night before, Katerina's fingers on his neck and Redvers' obvious ploy to avoid discussing it later.

Redvers shook his head and avoided my eyes. "Well enough to know that she can't be trusted."

I shrugged. "At this point, who can?" But there was a deeper point he was missing, purposely if my guess was correct. "Was there something between the two of you?"

This time Redvers met my eyes directly. "Not on my part."

That was interesting, but I decided to let it go because I truly did believe him. Even if I was curious about the bigger story.

Meeting Katerina that evening left us with quite a lot of time to kill between now and then. I surveyed our things. It would be very short work to pack up since both Redvers and I were fairly efficient travelers. What were we going to do with an entire day? Movement helped me think so I began walking back and forth across the sitting area again.

"Get your coat."

I stopped in my path to look at him. "Where are we going?"

"We'd best go see some of the city. You can't pace around this room all day," Redvers said.

"Why not?"

"Because we can't afford to replace the rug." His tone was wry.

I sighed and conceded that perhaps he was correct. Not about the rug, but that we should see some of the city and attempt to take my mind off things. Because my mind was absolutely swirling—worry about my father and our home, concern that we shouldn't trust Maral, sadness over Ziya's murder and wondering who was responsible, frustration over the men following us, and now a meeting with this Russian woman . . . There was a lot to sort through and keep track of. Pacing the room wouldn't help me make sense of things, but perhaps getting out and moving around the city would.

"Maybe we'll be followed," I suggested, finding the idea strangely appealing for once. Especially since we weren't planning to do anything of interest. I liked the idea of taking our shadow on a pointless tour of the city.

Redvers just shook his head at me.

We left the hotel on foot, debating where we should go. We eliminated crossing the Golden Horn since we'd done so much back and forth already. Redvers suggested the Dolma-bahçe Palace, but I found that I wasn't terribly interested in touring any more royal grounds. I had no doubt that it was beautiful, but it wasn't appealing at the moment—I didn't think I would be able to truly appreciate the sights.

In the end we simply hiked up and down the hills of the city, around the Pera neighborhood and into the ones nearby, despite the chilly weather—at least it wasn't raining today. The exercise was a good way for us to keep warm and for me to burn off nervous energy. It also let my mind work through the knotty problems we were faced with while sporadically tossing ideas and questions at my patient companion.

We passed numerous little shops as we went, and I stopped to look at some beautifully painted ceramics in a window. The shopkeeper came out and immediately began telling me about how each was hand-painted by an artisan, the floral designs in blues and reds, but I listened with only one ear because I had finally picked up on the man following us—I could see him now in the reflection of the window, waiting across the street for us to start moving again. I wanted to crow in delight, but instead I nudged Redvers and we continued on our way, much to the shopkeeper's disappointment. I felt a little badly, but I also was in no need of any ceramics, painted or otherwise.

"I finally spotted him!" I murmured to Redvers a minute later.

"Are you certain? It could have been just another tourist."

I gave Redvers a dark look and he chuckled. But just to be certain that I was correct, I tried the same tactic a few more times, stopping somewhere to look at something, and found the man nearly every time—now that I'd spotted him once, it was much easier to find the same face in the crowd. I gave myself a mental pat on the back for my success. It had taken several days, but I'd finally gotten there.

We had lunch at a small café on the way back to our hotel.

Our shadow stopped down the street from us, waiting in the shadow of a building. They were fairly good at their job, these minders—if Redvers hadn't first noticed that we were being followed, I might never have realized. Although watching the man now I was tempted to march over and ask him who he worked for and what he wanted, but it wouldn't have gotten us anywhere. By the time we could even cross the street, the man would disappear—I had no doubts about that.

Seeing where my attention had wandered off to, Redvers read my mind. "I've thought about approaching him. But I think the best place to corner him will be at the nightclub tonight."

"Oh, are we going to a nightclub tonight?" I asked, amused.

Redvers smiled. "We are. After your date at the hammam."

I made a rude noise. "Thank you for letting me know. I'd hate to actually be involved in deciding what we do with our time."

Redvers' smile became a full-fledged grin, his dark eyes crinkling at the corners in a very charming manner. He knew I was teasing him. This was the first time in several days that Redvers and I had been truly alone—our shadow notwithstanding. And our conversation so far had been mostly centered on our upcoming train trip and what we might find once we got to Budapest, not what we might do that evening.

We were dealing with an awful lot of unknowns, not least who was responsible for Ziya Bey's murder. Both of us assumed that the stabbing had been carried out by the elevator operator, but most likely on someone else's order, which seemed to be the larger issue. Who was behind everything? It was someone who was taking my father's search seriously if the men following us and Bey's murder were any indication.

But there was little to be done until that evening. I was harboring a small hope that I might be able to learn something from Katerina—after all, she seemed to know Ekrem

Bey well. Perhaps she could tell me something to help clear up even one of the mysteries surrounding us. And because there was nothing to be done for the time being, I let myself enjoy time alone with my fiancé.

It was strange to think of him that way—I didn't have a ring yet, and even though I didn't feel it was necessary, Redvers insisted on speaking to my father. Regardless of who spoke to whom, the fact remained that I'd agreed to marry the man. At some point. In the distant future.

Until we found my father and figured out how to save my family home, it was an issue for another day.

Chapter Twenty-three

After finishing our lunch, Redvers and I continued meandering around the neighborhood, Redvers taking the opportunity to teach me a few things about following someone. Mostly he pointed out the ways our shadow was being successful and the ways in which he was not. It was a useful exercise, and I was pleased that we were making the most of our circumstances. Especially since we were up to our necks in complications, none of which seemed to be resolving themselves anytime soon.

We wasted several hours until it was time to head back to our hotel and change for the evening. I was certain that our shadow was relieved, but I didn't feel the slightest bit bad for keeping him on his feet and moving all day.

I needed to get ready to meet Katerina Semenov, both practically and mentally. And since we were heading to Maxim's afterward, I needed an outfit that would be appropriate for both places. I dithered for a bit before I finally settled on a pair of wide-leg black trousers and a white silk blouse, adding a long, beaded necklace.

"Trousers?" Redvers asked.

"Trousers," I replied. "I feel as though I need to be prepared for anything."

He came over and gave me a kiss that made me want to reconsider leaving our hotel room at all. "You'll cause a stir, but I expect nothing less."

Redvers wasn't wrong. I got more than a few stares and outright looks of disgust from passersby on our way to the hamam, but after a bit I stopped paying them any mind. I had too many other things to worry about.

We arrived at the Cağaloğlu Hamam a few minutes early. It was tucked into a row of shops on a nondescript street, the only thing marking its presence a large brass sign hanging over the door. Leaving Redvers on the narrow sidewalk, I pushed through the wooden doors and stepped down a few marble stairs and through another set of doors into the reception room. A wooden desk stood before a large marble fountain dominating the rest of the room. The reception room was empty except for one middle-aged woman who looked up when I entered. "Jane Wunderly?" She gave my trousers a long look, but the friendly expression on her face didn't change.

"Yes," I said. "I'm supposed to meet someone here. . . ."

The woman smiled. "She already wait."

It figured that no matter how early I arrived, Katerina would have arrived even earlier. There was no way she was going to give up the upper hand.

"Follow me please." The woman beckoned with her hand, leading me down a hallway decorated with potted palms and through a narrow wooden door. The walls of this circular room were lined with more wooden doors leading to private changing rooms. Looking up, I could see there was a second level above with a wooden railing at waist height. I appeared to be the only person in the room—I wondered what it must be like at busier times if they needed that many changing rooms for patrons. The woman pointed me into the room directly in front of us, a brass number six affixed to the door.

"There is towel for you. Take everything off and wrap towel around you. Someone come get you."

I nodded, uncomfortable with both the instructions to remove everything I was wearing and the fact that there was no one else in sight, including my Russian hostess. But I did as I was instructed, removing all my clothing and wrapping the soft cotton towel around myself. I was very aware of the scars on my back—a souvenir of my first marriage, but I pushed thoughts of them aside. A pair of wooden slippers had also been provided and I put them on, then opened the door and cautiously put my head outside. Someone had indeed come to fetch me.

A woman also wrapped in a towel stood waiting for me. She had kind brown eyes and her long dark hair was bundled into a large bun at her neck. "Jane?" she asked.

I nodded again, and she gestured for me to follow her. We crossed the marble floor and pushed through two narrow doors leading into a room that was significantly warmer than the outside chambers. Here too the floor was marble—in fact, nearly everything was. An enormous seven-sided gray-and-white marble pedestal about three feet tall took up most of the center of the room. Columns with decorative tops held the arches framing the white dome soaring overhead. Along the walls were fountains, also of the now-familiar marble in gray-and-white. But my guide continued through this room, ducking through a small passage in the marble. I followed her and found myself in a very small chamber. Here the marble went about three-quarters of the way up the walls. Beyond the marble it was red brick to the high domed ceiling above. The dome was painted white here as well, and the cutouts—stars and circles—let natural light into the chamber. The benches were of marble and I could hear steam hissing out of the vent in the wall to my left.

I was also no longer alone.

"Katerina. A pleasure to see you again."

She smiled, a distinctly feline smile, and inclined her head. The attendant left us and I sat on the marble bench across from Katerina. I wondered how long she had been there before me—it couldn't have been terribly long since she wasn't sweating. And it was warm enough in this little room that any healthy person would be sweating in no time. I could already feel moisture beading up on my face, and I'd only been in the room for a few moments.

I'd seen the woman up close the night before, but here in the brighter light I was once again reminded what a striking woman Katerina was, not necessarily beautiful, but her features were arresting. Her dark hair was tied back, highlighting her high cheekbones, and her hazel eyes were large and wide set.

"Thank you for joining me here." She gestured with one delicate hand to the walls of the room. "This is one of my favorite places to relax."

"Of course," I said. No doubt she did enjoy relaxing here, but I was also well aware that she'd asked to meet me at a bathhouse in order to keep me off-balance and make me uncomfortable. Especially since I suspected the next room involved getting completely naked in front of strangers. It was a rather savvy way to get information out of an opponent, really.

But she didn't know me.

"Does Redvers still blame me for the last time he was in town?" Katerina's gaze was direct and amused.

"He does, actually." If she could be blunt, then so could I.

"Silly man. It wasn't me that ratted him out, although I did know he was an agent of the Crown, of course." She gave a practiced shrug, drawing attention to her small shoulders. I felt like a bit of a behemoth compared to her small size, somehow more obvious to me with both of us having so little on. "It's important to know who all the players are."

"You're in the habit of keeping track of the players?"

She cocked her head at me. "I like to gather information. I find it useful."

I could just bet that she did.

"I was sorry that he wasn't interested in catching up on old times last night, however." From the tone of her voice, it was obvious what I was supposed to insinuate about "old times." "I suppose that has to do with you."

I met her gaze steadily. "I have no objections to him catching up with you." It wasn't true, but I hoped I sounded convincing. I added a casual shrug hoping it had the desired effect, but it was difficult to say whether it did.

"Hmm," she said. "Still, I suspect he will not meet with me because of you, all the same." She sighed dramatically. "I am sorry to see *old friends* go." Her emphasis was unmistakable.

I decided to change the subject and try for the upper hand. "What other kinds of information do you collect? Anything about Ekrem Bey or his brother's murder?"

Katerina cocked her head. "More like how I know that your father was in town until recently."

CHAPTER TWENTY-FOUR

I felt my blood run hot and then cold. I didn't like this woman mentioning my father—it made my skin crawl for reasons I couldn't pinpoint. Redvers had said the woman couldn't be trusted, and I wouldn't have done so even without his warning. But was this a threat rather than a simple observation?

I did my best to keep my face entirely neutral while all this ran through my mind. "He was, actually. He enjoys Istanbul and visits somewhat regularly."

She smiled again, her dimple flashing. "He and his girlfriend came into Maxim's several times. I recognized his lady from the restaurant down the street."

I felt my shoulders relax a bit. Perhaps I was overreacting. Yes, this woman liked to collect information about people, but she'd just told me that outright, so it wasn't exactly a secret. And she knew about my father because he'd come into the nightclub where she worked. Something I already knew—it had been confirmed by several other people that Father enjoyed spending time at Maxim's.

I was saved from having to reply by the attendant returning for us. I was glad for the opportunity to gather my thoughts and prepare myself for the next inevitable onslaught. I suspected Katerina wanted something from me, I just wasn't sure what that was.

There were two attendants waiting in the room, one for

each of us. "Don't worry," Katerina called to me. "They don't speak English."

I didn't bother responding to that. My attendant smiled at me and led me to the marble pedestal where she gestured for me to remove my towel. I hesitated, thinking of the scars on my back, but did as she asked, standing naked while she spread the soft cotton towel on the marble. I closed my eyes, hoping that Katerina wouldn't take this opportunity to look at me—those were questions I most certainly would *not* be answering. Mercifully, she stayed silent, keeping any further questions to herself for the time being.

My attendant didn't ask either. She simply motioned for me to kick off my wooden sandals, then took me by the hand and led me over to a fountain on the wall. She smiled and picked up a metal dish out of the bubbling water, then reached up to pour the water over my shoulder. She repeated this action several times, dousing me with warm water everywhere. That finished, she led me back to the marble pedestal.

"Down," she said, indicating the towel. Out of the corner of my eye I could see that Katerina was being walked through the same steps, and I had a flash of jealousy that the woman seemed entirely comfortable in her body with all its sensuous curves, whereas I was always conscious of mine and the scars it bore.

I lay down on my towel, the marble warm beneath me. I had a moment's relief that even though I was as naked as the day I was born, those scars were now hidden. For the moment, anyway. My attendant put on a rough cotton glove and began rubbing me vigorously with it, starting with my arms and neck and then working her way down.

"Will you and Redvers be staying long?" Katerina asked from her position somewhere past my feet.

"Only a few days," I told her.

"That's a shame," she said. "And your father?"

Did she know what my father was looking for? Or about

the money that he'd invested so poorly that we might lose our home? I had to be careful here—I didn't want to give her any information that she didn't already have. But the question made it seem as though she didn't know that my father had already left the city.

"About the same," I said, glad that I didn't have to make eye contact with the woman while lying outright. "And now I have a question for you; how do you know Ekrem Bey?"

"It's difficult not to know Ekrem when one works at Maxim's," Katerina said.

That was hardly an answer. "And have you heard anything about his brother's murder?"

"Nothing interesting," she replied.

I nearly sighed out loud at her evasive non-answers, but just closed my eyes instead. "Was there something that you wanted to tell me? A reason you had me come here?" I was tired of this game already, and finding that I wanted to enjoy the treatment I was receiving instead of verbally sparring with this woman. My attendant was currently rubbing me down vigorously with the glove, exfoliating my entire body. It verged on painful, but at the same time felt wonderful. She had me flip over and only paused for a moment before giving my back the same treatment. I tensed, but she was extra gentle where the scars were concentrated, so I let my muscles relax again.

Katerina chuckled. "Oh, yes. I wanted to tell you and Redvers that I'm looking into who is following you, or rather who ordered it. I can tell that it's been bothersome to you, so I have decided to ask around on your behalf."

"And you'll let us know when you find out?"

"Certainly, I will."

"In exchange for what?" I asked. "My firstborn?"

She laughed her smoky laugh. "Nothing so serious as that. But I am certain there will come a time when I could use help from you in return."

If I could see her, I imagined she would be giving me her catlike smile. And if she could see me, she would have seen me roll my eyes. "So you collect favors in addition to information?" I asked.

There was a pause where I imagined she was thinking that over. "Yes, that is true. I find both helpful to a woman in my position."

I suspected she wanted me to ask about her "position," so I changed direction instead. "You didn't learn anything from the man last night?"

Katerina sighed audibly. "He was a mere pawn. Does not even know who he is working for."

I didn't bother asking how she acquired that information. I had no doubts that her methods of interrogation were persuasive. Instead, I stayed silent while my attendant doused me with warm water from a metal pail, washing away the dead skin. Next, she took what looked like a large pillowcase, dipped it into another metal pail, then waved the cloth bag back and forth a few times while holding the top open. She gathered the end up, stood close to me, and ran her hand down the fabric, squeezing an incredible number of bubbles onto my body. In seconds I was covered from head to toe with warm soapy bubbles. I felt like I was floating in a cloud. Then she began rubbing me down once again with surprisingly strong hands from head to toe. I was going to be the cleanest I'd ever been in my life.

I was flipped over and covered in another round of bubbles before Katerina spoke again.

"It is too bad that your father is no longer in town," Katerina said. Her voice echoed a bit in the large chamber, bouncing off all that marble. I was looking up at the large dome overhead, this one also painted white with decorative cutouts to let in natural light, and my body tensed at the mention of my father again.

"Yes, it is." I wasn't sure what she thought she was going

to get out of me, information wise. Because even naked and covered in bubbles I wasn't going to tell her anything.

"I haven't seen him at the club in some days," Katerina said. "I was hoping you would all come hear me sing again before you left town."

"I suppose just the two of us will have to do."

"I suppose so." Her voice was musical, low and smoky, just as she'd sounded when we'd heard her sing the night before. "I will not bother asking if Redvers would be willing to come alone."

I was tired of her interest in getting my fiancé alone. Even if she did, I trusted Redvers fully—nothing would happen between him and this woman. But she was becoming tiresome with her obvious disappointment. She behaved as though I'd taken away her toy, and not even her favorite one. Katerina simply didn't want anyone else to have something that she didn't.

"Do you miss Russia?" I figured I might as well try to get in a parting shot.

Her laugh filled the space. "Oh, no. What a dreadful place with terrible cuisine. I miss having money, of course. And a title. But the rest?" She made a noise that sounded like *pshaw*. "Besides, Istanbul is a good place for someone like me."

I almost asked what she meant by that, but I didn't. Once again it seemed like she wanted me to ask about her and I didn't want to give her the satisfaction. And also, because it was unlikely that anything she said would be the truth anyway. At least, not the entire truth. I had no doubt that she hid plenty behind her seemingly blunt manner.

My attendant had me sit up, and she led me back to the fountain on the wall. I stood as she once again doused me with warm water, shoveled elegantly with the metal bowl. Then she wrapped a soft cotton towel around me.

"It was a pleasure, Jane Wunderly." Katerina's voice came from behind me. "Until the next time we meet."

I whipped my head around to see her, but she had already gone. My woman led me back to the changing room, which felt cold now by comparison, and I shivered. I looked around but didn't see Katerina or her attendant anywhere. Where could she have gone? Did she have a private room?

It appeared the woman had disappeared into thin air.

I changed back into my clothes, which were just as I had left them—it didn't appear that my things had been searched. My attendant had left a small cup of tea and a piece of Turkish delight waiting for me outside my room, so I sat on a small upholstered stool and took a sip of the tea. I took a bite of the candy, then put it down. I kept trying to eat the stuff, thinking I might like it this time, but always finding that I didn't. It tasted entirely too floral for me, like eating a rose.

It would have been nice to stay and relax after my experience, but Katerina had disappeared and it was unsettling to be down there alone. I hurried back to the reception area, which was also deserted, and back up the stairs to the ground level.

Stepping back onto the street, I could see that Redvers was standing in the shadows of the building on the other side. I joined him, and we started walking back toward a main thoroughfare. This area was deserted—we would need a busier place this time of night to find a taxi.

"Did she tell you anything?"

"Nothing useful," I said, and related everything she'd said to me.

"Did you tell her anything?"

"No. I didn't give her anything." I poked him in the side at the mere suggestion that I would have been cracked open so easily.

"I didn't mean to insinuate that you had." Redvers' voice had a smile in it.

"You should know me better than that." Then I sighed. "I

can't imagine why she wanted to meet with me at all, except that she appeared to be sizing up the competition."

"There is no competition to be had," Redvers said somewhat stiffly.

"I know." I put my hand in the crook of his elbow, giving it a squeeze, and I could feel him relax slightly. "Although I see why she insisted on meeting me here—it is an excellent way to put someone off-balance, stripping them of their clothing."

Redvers nodded. "She is clever. And I doubt she does anything without a reason. We just may never know if there was anything more to it than her wanting to talk with my fiancé alone."

I thought about her disappearing act. "Did you see her leave?"

"I didn't see anyone leave."

I shook my head. Just one more mystery surrounding the woman.

CHAPTER TWENTY-FIVE

By the time I rejoined Redvers it had grown late, but I was starving, so we found a small *meyhane* where we could grab a late meal. After a quick dinner of kebabs, chicken for me and lamb for Redvers, with a slice of sticky sweet baklava for dessert, we headed back to Maxim's for the evening.

The nightclub was equally as crowded as the night before, if not more so. I wasn't surprised when we were informed that we would have to wait for a table, so we headed for the bar instead. I didn't mind standing for a while. We would have plenty of time to sit once we were on the train.

We slid into an open space at the long wood bar, and I surveyed the room while Redvers attempted to get the bartender's attention. The walls were covered in dark wallpaper with gold accents, and a thick smoke hung in the room, stinging my eyes a bit. I hadn't noticed it the night before, but with the extra customers came extra cigarette smoke. Turning, I could see that there were some tables toward the back that were using the tall glass smoking pipes I'd seen elsewhere in the city, adding to the general fug.

In a few minutes I had my gin rickey in hand, and I sipped at it slowly, wondering if Katerina would be making an appearance that evening. After my earlier encounter with her, I was genuinely hoping it was her night off.

"Hmm," Redvers said next to me.

The same band from the night before was playing and I pulled my attention from them to look at him. "What?"

"I see someone we should have a chat with."

It seemed Redvers was being deliberately vague. "Another spy?" I whispered dramatically.

Redvers looked amused. "This is Istanbul . . . spies and intrigue abound."

He said this as though it were common knowledge even though it was news to me. Although, when I reflected on it, it made a certain sort of sense. The city was poised at the confluence of two very different continents. Empires had risen and fallen here. It was probably a natural meeting place for spies to gather information about the other side, which was only a ferry ride away.

It also made sense given what Katerina had said to me earlier—that this was a good city for her. A woman who liked to collect information.

But I had other questions. "Just how many people in this city are you acquainted with, anyway?"

Redvers looked at me and I shrugged. "Just wondering if I need a larger address book."

His mouth quirked in a smile and he tipped his head in the direction of a table toward the back. I looked for myself and was disappointed to see it was merely Ekrem Bey.

"That was a lot of buildup for just Mr. Bey."

"I know how much you enjoy his company."

I grumbled. I wasn't excited to speak with the man again and for a moment considered letting Redvers go by himself, but only for a moment. Glasses in hand, we threaded our way through the tables as the band struck up their next song, coming upon Ekrem and a woman speaking in low voices, heads close. Without a word, Redvers pulled out an empty chair for me, then did the same for himself while I sat down.

"Hello, Ekrem," Redvers said.

He sighed. "My dear, would you excuse us for a bit? I need

to take care of some . . . business." Ekrem's young friend looked quite put out, until Ekrem assured her that he would make it up to her later. Slightly mollified, the young woman flounced to the bar, short, beaded skirt swinging.

Ekrem sighed again, watching her go. "I hope this will be worth it."

Redvers was unimpressed. "There are plenty of women here tonight."

"But none quite so desperate."

My lip curled, but I was able to rein it in before the man noticed. I was doing my best not to draw his attention to myself.

"Did you learn anything last night?" Redvers got right to the point.

"About which issue?" Ekrem cocked his head. "My brother's murder or the men who are following you?"

Redvers gave him a long look. "Either."

It seemed the man was enjoying being deliberately difficult this evening. "I have not." He turned his eyes to me and I did my best not to recoil. "Did you learn anything from your chat with Katerina?"

I wasn't surprised that he knew about that, although it did make me wonder just how well the two knew each other. And whether they worked more closely than either of them would have us know. But I also knew it wasn't worth asking about—they would never tell.

"She didn't know who he worked for. And neither did he," I said shortly.

Ekrem gave a casual shrug and turned back to Redvers. "I'll let you know when I have something." He pushed up from the table. "If you'll excuse me." The man gave me only the slightest glance—although it was plenty full of insinuation—before heading to the bar to reclaim the attention of his young friend.

We both watched him go before I turned back to Redvers.

"Well, that's one way to get a table, I suppose." I took a sip of my gin rickey. "I'd wager he knows more than he's telling."

"I always knew you were a sensible woman."

"Do you think he'll be able to find out? Who is behind . . . things?" I waved a hand vaguely at the "things" we were up against, including his own brother's murder. "And do you think he'll actually tell us?"

"That's the gamble. But I do think it's in his best interest to share with us at least some of what he learns."

I didn't bother arguing that point—I didn't see how that was the case, especially since we were leaving town. "How will he know where to send the information if he does get it? We're leaving tomorrow."

"I have no doubt he'll find us."

That was all he would say on the matter, which was just as well since the band was starting up again. The tempo was good and a vocalist took the stage—a black woman with a bold, throaty voice perfect for the genre. I breathed a sigh of relief since it looked like Katerina did in fact have the night off, although I found that I was still scanning the room for any sign of her, unable to fully relax. We ordered another round of drinks, drinking slowly so as to keep our heads, but enjoying the music.

My relief was short-lived, as I spotted Katerina against the far wall of the nightclub. Tonight she was less obvious about her observation, but I had no doubt that she was keeping an eye on us. Redvers, especially.

I didn't move my head, but indicated her location with my eyes. "Your friend is here."

"I wish that I was surprised."

As the words left his mouth, she left her post, winding her way through the smoky air hanging over the tables she passed. She arrived at our table with little ceremony, sliding elegantly into the seat Ekrem Bey had vacated.

"When I said I hoped you would come to Maxim's again,

I didn't mean so immediately," Katerina said to me. "I'm not on stage tonight." Her tight black dress had a sequined bodice and it sparkled in the dim light.

I shrugged but didn't say anything.

She turned her gaze onto Redvers. "You always did like to hear me sing. Perhaps if I talk to the band . . ."

Redvers finally turned his attention to her. "Not necessary." The words were clipped, and I reflected that it wasn't often I saw his feathers so thoroughly ruffled. What was it about this woman?

Katerina seemed to know exactly the effect she had on him, and she smiled, although her dimple didn't make an appearance this time. I believed Redvers when he said there'd been no interest on his side—I had no reason to think he would lie to me. But it was obvious that whatever had happened had left quite the impression on both of them. I both did and did not want to know the whole story.

She turned back to me, pouting slightly and behaving as though we were now friends. "He would not have been able to resist me before, in Russia, when I still had money and all the luxuries."

I made a *hmm*ing noise instead of explaining to her that Redvers was unlikely to have had a different reaction. Jewels and finery and the trappings of wealth didn't change the woman underneath. And that is what he was uninterested in.

When Redvers continued to ignore her, watching the band instead, Katerina's eyes hardened briefly before her face assumed a neutral expression, and she gave an airy wave of her hand. "I am in need of a drink, so I will leave you to your evening. Until next time, Jane, Redvers." Redvers still didn't so much as glance her way, and this time she left the table without the passing caress.

I waited a few beats before addressing it. "Well," I started to say.

Redvers shook his head. "It's not even worth the breath."

I regarded him for a moment, then let it go. We were quiet, watching the band and sipping our drinks. When the band took their next break in between sets, Redvers turned back to me.

"Did you notice our shadow?"

"I did." The man was standing at the bar, tucked behind several groups of people who were laughing and chatting, but obviously not with any of them. I recognized him from the night before, so apparently he'd been given a second chance at keeping us in sight.

"This might be a good opportunity to have a word with him," Redvers said.

"How do you propose we do that?" I wasn't sure we'd have any more success getting information from him than Katerina had, but it was worth a shot. Especially since there was nothing to say the woman hadn't been lying.

"We'll fetch our coats but head out the same way we did last night."

I nodded. That back alley was quite dark, especially this time of night.

"You'll walk ahead and chat as if I'm with you, and I'll find a place to obscure myself so that once he follows you, I can get behind him."

"And then what?"

Redvers finished his drink. "Then we'll see what happens."

We did precisely as he suggested, retrieving our coats from the coat check station and making our way back through the club toward the back instead of using the front door. The same member of the waitstaff from the night before barely raised an eyebrow when Redvers slipped him another folded bill to escort us out the back. I supposed it was fairly common-place if the city was teeming with spies and underworld characters—a quick slip out the back probably made the staff quite a few extra dollars a night.

"We're being followed," Redvers told the young man. "But bring him out the same way." The young man nodded as if this too was an everyday request. I stepped out into the alley first, pulling on my coat. Redvers handed me his.

"What am I supposed to do with this?" I asked.

"Stick to the shadows, but sort of hold it up a bit." Redvers crouched down on the other side of the door behind a pair of garbage cans that offered plenty of cover.

I immediately understood what he was getting at. If I could make it look as though two people were walking away, all the better. I moved down the alley, then did my best to hold the coat out to my right as I walked along, doing my best impression of a human coat hanger. I hoped this would go quickly since my arm wasn't going to last in the awkward position for very long.

But I didn't have long to wait. I wasn't halfway down the alley when I heard the door open and softly close again behind me—so softly that if I hadn't been listening for it, I might not have heard it at all. I began chatting with myself, hoping to lure our shadow in my direction so that Redvers could come up behind him. I heard muffled footsteps behind me as I neared the end of the alley and I shook the coat a bit, like a cloth in front of a bull.

I heard a muffled shout behind me and dropped the coat I'd been holding, my arm shaking from the strain of keeping it held up so high. I turned to see Redvers restraining the man who'd been following us—Redvers had the man's arms pinned behind him, and the men were struggling against each other. Our shadow's fedora fell to the ground.

Then I heard a gunshot come from directly behind me.

Chapter Twenty-six

The shot echoed down the alley and I immediately dropped to the ground, hitting my knees hard on the cobblestones. My palms came to the ground too as I swung my head wildly back and forth, unsure where to focus my attention first. Farther down the alley Redvers was standing in shock, staring at the man he'd been holding who was now on the ground at his feet.

"Go!" he shouted, and I slowly staggered to my feet, kicking myself into gear. I ran the few remaining yards to the street, keeping close to the brick wall of the building, and peered around the corner. I saw someone dressed all in black, head to foot, sprinting in the opposite direction. They were relatively small and slim and had already turned a corner by the time I caught sight of them.

I didn't even bother trying to follow whoever it was. They had too much of a head start.

I turned back and hurried down the alley, stopping to scoop up Redvers' overcoat from where I'd dropped it and hugging it close to my chest as I continued toward my fiancé. Redvers was already checking the man's pockets when I reached him, tucking something into the pocket of his trousers. I stood over the men in the shadowy darkness, and even without the benefit of an overhead light, I could see that the man had been shot right through the heart. Or near enough that he must have died almost instantly. I tried not to think about what might have happened if the bullet had gone through the man and into Redvers behind him.

"They were too fast," I said.

Redvers didn't respond, finishing up his task and standing quickly. He held out his hand and I handed his overcoat to him. He pulled it on and buttoned it up, fingers flying.

"We need to go."

I was shocked. Normally we waited and informed the police when we came across a dead body. "But . . ."

Redvers shook his head. "Let's go." He grabbed my hand and pulled me away, leaving the man exactly where he was. We hurried the few meters to the street, turning in the opposite direction that the shooter had gone, and continued on. We were moving with purpose, although to an outside observer it wouldn't have looked as though we were fleeing a murder scene.

At least that was what I hoped.

By the time we were several blocks from Maxim's, I started to shake quite badly.

Redvers glanced at me. "We're nearly there."

I assumed he was referring to our hotel. He was, but he didn't take us in through the lobby as I'd expected. Instead, we went around to the back where he efficiently picked the lock on a service door. We stepped inside, Redvers glancing around to ensure there was no one about before leading me through a small corridor to a staircase. We climbed the stairs to our floor, pushing out through a nondescript door into a hallway adjacent to our own. I was shaking with some vigor now, and I was relieved when we finally were on the other side of our hotel room door.

Redvers was watching me as he unbuttoned his overcoat. In doing so I could see that he had blood spattered on his suit and shirt. I was not the type of woman to swoon, but my head did feel quite light at the sight of the drying blood—I'd been trying to ignore the fact that he could have been the one who was shot, but seeing those stains really hammered the point home for me. I stood there, staring blankly at the reddish brown spots while Redvers removed my own coat and gently led me to the bathroom. He turned on the taps, running a warm bath for me.

"We were almost killed. Whoever that was could have shot you," I said through chattering teeth. "What if the bullet had gone through him?"

"But they didn't and it didn't. We're both okay." He repeated this sentiment several more times but it didn't make a dent; not for quite a while anyway. The warm bathwater had almost gone cold again before I was able to stop shaking. When I felt steady again, I let the water out of the tub, wrapped myself in a robe, and went into the sitting room.

"Feeling better?" Redvers was standing near the window in a robe of his own. I went and sat on the couch and he came and sat next to me.

"Yes," I said. There didn't seem to be need for further explanation. "Did he have identification?"

"Of course not." Redvers' brows furrowed in frustration. "I found a matchbook in his pocket, but that was it. We did learn something, though."

"What's that?"

"Whoever is behind this is willing to kill their own people to keep themselves from being found out."

I shuddered again and Redvers looked at me in concern, but I gave a little wave of my hand. "Was the matchbook from anywhere interesting?"

Redvers shook his head. "A place in the same neighborhood, with a similar setup to Maxim's. And everyone here smokes, so it likely doesn't mean much."

I thought about the quick figure in black. "Why didn't they shoot us as well? It certainly would have taken care of any problems we present."

"I've given that quite a bit of thought. The best I can come up with is that they must still need us for something."

"I don't know what that might be. Father has the map, and the money I assumed he was carrying appears to be long gone. We don't have anything, really." Something occurred to me. "Unless they think we can lead them to him."

"That's entirely possible. In fact, it would make a great deal of sense. Whoever is behind this doesn't want to be revealed, but they need us alive to figure out where your father has gone with the map." Redvers stopped talking and I could tell he'd thought of something else.

"What is it?"

He pulled me into his side, hugging me a bit before releasing me again. It was meant to be reassuring but it had the opposite effect, since I knew it meant he was actually quite concerned about what he was going to say next. "Since they were following him, we can only assume they followed him to Hungary as well. I just hope nothing happened to him, that's all."

Following his reasoning, I could see where his concerns were. If Father had been followed, he'd most likely led them right to Szigetvár, since he wasn't a trained spy able to lose a shadow. I agreed with Redvers—I hoped nothing had happened to either him or the map. But it was concerning that they seemed to need us—I could only hope it didn't mean Father had disappeared after all. Or worse, had been taken.

I did my best to push these new worries away. They wouldn't help anything, and we were headed to Hungary shortly where hopefully we could find some answers. I went back to our original issue. "How did the shooter know that we would try to corner our shadow?"

"My guess is that they didn't. Whoever it is was simply doing a bit of their own reconnaissance and saw what was about to happen. That's the best I can assume, anyway."

"And we still have no idea who that might be." Could we eliminate anyone we knew? The figure didn't look like Ziya Bey, and Katerina . . . well, the last I had seen her was at the bar talking with a pair of young men. Which wasn't to say that it couldn't have been her, but it seemed unlikely that she could have changed clothing so quickly. She also hadn't showed any interest in my father's search for the heart—it didn't seem like something she was aware of at all, although she had been aware that he'd left town. Her interest seemed to lie purely in my fiancé and his disinterest in return.

Could it have been Maral? She was about the right height and size for whoever it was. On the other hand, I didn't get a very good look at the person. And dressed all in black—well, it made it difficult to judge from a distance just what they looked like.

I was starting to doubt my own memory of the figure, and I shook my head to clear it.

I turned my thoughts to the other people we had to manage. "Both Ekrem and Katerina said they would attempt to find out who is following us. Do you think either of them will meet the same fate?" It was hard to learn things from a dead man. Or woman, as the case may be. I was a little shocked at my own callous attitude, but I was reaching the limits of my endurance. This was a beautiful city, but it was time for us to leave.

Redvers sighed. "That occurred to me as well, but both of them know how to take care of themselves. Besides, I'm sure once the body was found, the entire club heard about it within minutes. Everyone will be more cautious than they might have been before."

It also might stop them from asking questions altogether, although Ekrem claimed to have a stronger cause since he was looking for his brother's killer. Whether that motivation would be enough for him to continue his inquiries and risk getting shot, it was hard to say. And it was impossible to tell what Katerina might do, or even know for that matter.

A new thought occurred to me. "Will the police find us, do you think? We were let into the alley just before that man was shot, and I know the waiter will be able to describe us."

"I think it's best we keep a low profile until our train departs. Just to be safe."

I didn't find that answer terribly reassuring.

CHAPTER TWENTY-SEVEN

I slept a long time that night, but I couldn't say that it was restful. I woke up at least once from a nightmare in which Redvers was the one who'd been shot, and rolling over to see him sleeping soundly beside me allowed me to fall back asleep, but the bad dreams continued. I didn't remember everything I'd dreamed, but I awoke with even more anxiety about my father than I'd felt previously. Was Millie's first instinct that Father had disappeared correct after all? It was difficult not to worry about his safety with people being killed right and left. Concern about losing our row house was beginning to take a back seat to my other worries.

Redvers ordered breakfast up to our room, and I was well into my second cup of coffee before it occurred to me that my aunt might be looking for us at the breakfast table.

"Millie . . ." I started to say.

Redvers smiled. "I sent them a note letting them know that we would be indisposed this morning and would meet them at the train later today."

I breathed a sigh of relief for that, though she would probably find it quite scandalous, Redvers announcing that we were "indisposed." "Did you tell them what happened last night?"

He shook his head. "I think we should keep last night's events to ourselves."

I agreed. There was no need to wind anyone else up. It was unlikely that anything would happen to any of them in broad daylight, and by nightfall we would be on the *Orient Express*, heading away from the city.

Besides, we were the ones the police would be looking for.

Redvers did his best to distract me for the next several hours. Despite everything—the anxiety and suspicion and worry—the man could still easily set my person on fire, and he was quite successful at keeping my mind elsewhere. I was entirely grateful for the DO NOT DISTURB sign hanging on our door.

We did risk showing our faces downstairs to take a late lunch at the restaurant on site. We'd both worked up quite an appetite, and we lingered over our meal of lentil soup followed by a delectable rice pilaf loaded with vegetables, finishing off with the traditional baklava and tea. Time was a luxury we could afford since we'd already packed our things and ensured that my father's luggage would be loaded with our own.

By the time we came back through the lobby, our things were being loaded onto a cart for transport to the train station. A man in police uniform passed by us on his way to the café and I stiffened, but he paid us no mind. Redvers noticed and gave a quick nod. "It's time for us to leave."

I couldn't agree more.

Everyone else was meeting us at the Sirkeci railway station, so Redvers and I checked out of the hotel and took the taxi that was hailed for us.

"I assume we're still being followed," I murmured. "Even though they're down one person." I hadn't noticed anyone in particular, but I expected they were there all the same.

"I think we can safely assume that's the case," Redvers said quietly in my ear, his breath teasing my hair and sending a shiver up my spine. I wondered if I could ever get enough of the man. "I'm sure they'll be on the train as well, but perhaps we can use that to our advantage. Especially since they will be nervous now that one of their own has been eliminated."

I had questions about how precisely that might work, but I kept them to myself.

The Sirkeci station was on the other side of the Golden Horn, on the tip of the small peninsula where so many of Istanbul's ancient sites were located. It seemed to be a bit of a hike, and I said as much.

"Wasn't our hotel built for customers of the *Orient Express*?"

"It was," Redvers affirmed.

"Then why wasn't it built on the same side of the water as the station?"

"Space and land, I would imagine," Redvers said with a shrug.

That didn't exactly answer my question, but I let it go as we crossed over the bridge spanning the Golden Horn one last time. The taxi let us off in front of the station, a beautiful building with a large domed central atrium and two wings extending from either side. Red brick was topped with large swathes of what appeared to be pink marble, both set off by the ever-present gray marble I'd seen throughout in the city. Each wing had a series of round stained-glass windows over arched doors running the entire length of the building in both directions, giving it a very Oriental look. Redvers caught the eye of the porter who had charge of our luggage—I was glad to see it had all arrived just before us—and directed it toward the train. He and I walked up the few steps toward the intricately carved wooden doors leading into the main part of the station as passengers and family and porters bustled all around. A large, round stained-glass window dominated the space above the main doors, with stained-glass windows on either side featuring the familiar onion-dome arch at the tops. The inside of the station opened up into a bright airy space—the ceiling of the dome soared far above my head. The entire place was painted white alternating with dark brown, creating lovely, symmetrical patterns on the ceiling and all around the room. The stained-glass windows ran around the entire top, bathing the space in beautiful light. I tried not to gape, but it was difficult.

Our tickets had already been arranged for, so we moved straight through to the platform on the other side of the building where we found Millie and Lord Hughes already waiting for us.

The *Simplon Orient Express* had a large black steam engine in the front, followed by the baggage car and a series of passenger cars in navy blue with gilt lettering running along the top that read "*Compagnie Internationale des Wagons-Lits et des Grands Express Européens.*" It appeared to be nothing but first-class all the way down the train, although I was told there was a second-class sleeping berth that had been added in recent years—which was where Maral would be bunking. From all appearances it was going to be an elegant trip, and truly there was no quicker way to get from Istanbul to Budapest, where we would change trains to head south into the Hungarian countryside.

Redvers and I had our own compartment in first class and I was grateful that the men had made the arrangements. If left up to Millie, I might have found myself sharing a car with her for "propriety's sake," which was a trial at the best of times. And this was certainly not the best of times.

Although I did wonder who was paying for all this luxury—Millie and Lord Hughes? The question reminded me that we might lose our house and the clock was rapidly ticking down. I'd still been mentally keeping a tally of how many more days remained despite everything that had been happening. Concern for my father's safety had pushed thoughts of the bank repossessing our row house to the back of my mind, but it was still never far from my thoughts. Certainly it was only a building, but it had so many ties to my childhood and my mother, as well as providing a feeling of security— knowing that I would always have somewhere to go back to, no matter what happened. It had been a refuge after my first husband died, and it was difficult to imagine giving that up. I had no doubts that Redvers was entirely different from Grant, my deceased husband, and that things would be much smoother sailing, but it didn't mean I was entirely comfortable losing my safety net either.

But I tabled all this since at the moment we were being escorted to our car by a porter in a smart blue uniform with gold braid details. The hall was narrow, wide enough for one person to walk through comfortably, decorated in beautiful mahogany wood with rich carpet beneath my feet. The porter opened the door to our room, and I passed by him and settled onto the plush cushioned seat upholstered in fabric that was soft as a lamb. Redvers thanked the man and assured him that we didn't need anything at the moment.

"I know one of your favorite authors has ridden this train," Redvers said as he took the seat across from me.

"Who is that?"

"Agatha Christie."

"Oh!" I looked around at the elegant décor—all mahogany and teak paneling with inlaid designs, and thick drapes in a floral pattern that could be pulled back by gold cords. A tiny table beneath the window sported a brass lamp with a fabric-covered shade. "It's rather surprising that she hasn't set a novel on this train. A moving locale would be fun." I didn't bother asking how Redvers knew about Ms. Christie's travel history. There was bound to be some reason that he couldn't share with me.

"I'll be sure to suggest it to her," Redvers said, a distinct twinkle in his eye.

I rolled mine. I opened my mouth to reply, when there was a knock on our door. Redvers opened it to reveal a man in another blue uniform. This was the porter assigned to our car, who had come to introduce himself. I let out a little sigh of relief—I was glad it was anyone other than Millie. I needed a few more minutes to fortify myself before dealing with my aunt—there didn't seem to be any reason for her to complain about the accommodations, but you could never be quite certain with her.

But I needn't have worried. I didn't see Millie and Lord Hughes until it was time to meet them in the dining car for the evening meal. Tables for four covered in white tablecloths and set with fine silverware and china lined one side of the car, and matching tables for two lined the other, creating an aisle for passengers and waitstaff. Brass lamps at each table cast a pleasing glow, and I noticed that a vase of fresh flowers graced each tabletop as well. The walls were covered in decorative mahogany, looking well with the plush leather seats and heavy damask curtains. We were seated at a table for four, and I could see that Maral had been seated at a small table toward the back of the car where she would be dining with whatever strangers were assigned to the same table.

"We took this train into Istanbul, obviously, and I was very pleased with the service," Millie said as she settled herself in her seat. "I can only assume it will be equally as good on this trip."

One of my eyebrows threatened to pop up, but I managed to keep a neutral expression. The service must be nothing short of exceptional to earn such praise from Aunt Millie.

"Of course, it looks as though they've squeezed more seats into the dining room on this trip since there's a *second-class* car on the train right now." Her lips pressed together into a thin line.

I wasn't certain that was even true about the extra seats and was deeply tempted to reply with *heaven forbid*, but I held my tongue. Antagonizing Millie with sarcasm never went particularly well. I caught Lord Hughes' eye, however, and we shared a small smile. I was grateful that the man seemed to truly love my aunt and took her in stride. His was a quiet but comforting presence.

Dinner consisted of several courses beginning with lentil soup, followed by a mutton pilaf accompanied by sautéed potatoes and beans and finishing with cheese and fruit. Redvers and I both had a glass of wine with dinner but switched to our usual cocktails after the meal was finished. The waiter was just delivering those after-dinner drinks when I noticed that the empty seat at the table behind us had been filled. The man's back was to me, so I couldn't see who it was, but he seemed familiar.

"Who is that?" I whispered to Redvers, sending his attention in that direction with a little flick of my head.

Redvers frowned. "I'm not certain, but I have some suspicions."

Millie gave us a dark look—she didn't like being left out of anything, and especially not a conversation at her own table—but for once she didn't start an interrogation.

I was still watching when the man turned halfway in his seat toward the aisle, then twisted around fully to face me.

It was Ekrem Bey.

CHAPTER TWENTY-EIGHT

I gave the man a smile that I was certain looked much more like a grimace. "What's he doing here?" I muttered aloud as Bey stood and approached our table.

"Hello again," Ekrem said.

Millie looked him up and down. "Who the hell are you and what do you want? This is a private table." I'd forgotten that we hadn't filled my aunt in on who Ekrem was.

My mouth tipped up on one side. Millie's brusqueness could be entertaining, even useful. When it wasn't directed at me, that was.

Ekrem Bey was entirely unruffled by this reception, and I had to admit that I rather admired his self-possession. "I believe you met my brother Ziya. He was an archivist. I am his brother Ekrem," he told my aunt, ignoring her grunt in response. "I just wanted to stop by and say hello since I'm joining you on this journey." He spread his hands at this pronouncement.

"And why exactly are you joining us?" I asked.

"Because it is an adventure." Ekrem gave me a wink that caused me to physically recoil for several reasons, not least because I thought he should be less cavalier about his brother's murder, which I could only assume was the reason he was here. Bey then gave a little bow to the rest of the table before returning to his own.

"I would love to go one day without a new surprise," I said to no one in particular.

"Good luck." Millie tipped back the rest of her whiskey and signaled for another.

When we returned to our compartment, the porter had transformed the cushioned seats into a sleeping berth, which was more comfortable than I would have thought possible for train travel, although you still knew you were on a moving train. I was worried that I wouldn't be able to sleep, but the restless nights finally caught up to me and it wasn't long before the rocking of the train on the tracks lulled me to sleep.

When I woke up the next morning, Redvers was conspicuously absent. I could see that his side of the small bed had been slept in, but it was impossible to tell how long he'd been gone—I hadn't felt him get up despite our close quarters. I put on a gray wool day dress with a practical pair of flat oxford shoes and went down the hall to the bathroom. An attendant in blue uniform stood outside and pulled open the door for me. It was a much larger room than one might expect on a train, kitted out in white tile and wood paneling with brass fittings and a small shower against the back wall. I took care of my morning ablutions, splashing my face with water at the marble sink before catching sight of my face in the mirror. Even though I'd slept long and hard, the bags under my eyes should probably have been checked when we boarded. I stepped out of the room, and the attendant hurried in after me to tidy up for the next guest—I could only assume this was the reason it was spotlessly clean.

I returned to our compartment and nearly walked right into Redvers. In the few minutes I'd been down the hall, he had come back from wherever he'd disappeared to and switched things back to a sitting area.

"You startled me!" I took a breath. "Where did you go?"

"To have a chat with the conductor," Redvers said easily. "How did you sleep?"

I gestured to my face. "Contrary to these bags, I actually slept rather well."

Redvers left that alone, which was a wise decision on his part. "Speaking of bags. Someone broke into the baggage car last night."

I sighed. "Let me guess whose luggage was targeted."

"I haven't gone to look yet. I thought you might want to join me."

"You're finally learning." I'd been quite vocal in the past about how much I hated it when he left me out of investigating.

Redvers didn't respond, but I did catch the twinkle in his eye as he turned and led me back out into the hallway.

The baggage car was at the very front of the train, just behind the engine, and we passed through a few cars nearly identical to our own before we arrived. I kept my eyes open for familiar faces, such as any of the men who had been following us around Istanbul, but I didn't see any that I recognized.

"Have you seen any of the men who were following us?" I asked.

Redvers shook his head. "Not so far. But that doesn't mean one or two of them aren't here. In fact, given that our things have been searched, I would say it confirms that there is at least one on this train."

I nodded and didn't say anything else until we arrived at our destination. A man in the train's distinctive blue uniform was arguing with one of the porters at the junction, but they stopped as we approached.

The man whom I assumed was the conductor tipped his head at Redvers. "It's as I suspected. The door to the car has been damaged beyond repair. It will latch but it will not lock."

He glared at the porter, who kept his eyes on the ground. I wondered if the man would still have a job when we got to the next station.

Redvers made a noise of acknowledgment and turned to the porter. "What time did you retire?"

The young man's hands clenched at his sides. "Around midnight." His voice was barely audible.

"A reasonable time. Your charges were all in bed?"

The man nodded, still not making eye contact with anyone. I knew that there was a porter assigned to each car and responsible for the occupants of that car. Once they all retired for the evening, the porters were allowed to catch a few hours of sleep while sitting at their post, although there was a call system in case someone needed something in the middle of the night that would wake them. It had to be exhausting, frankly. I could only imagine what some of the travelers might demand at any given hour of the day. I'd traveled with my aunt Millie—I knew what it could be like.

"Has anything been disturbed?" Redvers addressed this to the conductor.

"I haven't had a chance to look yet," the man said before turning to the young porter. "Go about your business."

The poor man didn't need to be told twice and scurried away down the narrow hall. It was hardly his fault that someone had broken into the baggage car while he caught what sleep he could; I hoped he wouldn't be held responsible.

The three of us entered the baggage car, Redvers taking a moment to inspect the broken lock before entering the wide-open compartment. I glanced at the lock myself, and could immediately see that someone had done short work of it, most likely with an instrument like a hammer. Although I didn't know where someone would have gotten such a tool on a train like this one. Unless they had brought it with them.

None of the elegance of the other cars was to be found

here. This area was all utility with large shelves built along the sides and down the center to carry numerous trunks and cases on multiple tiers. The first area we looked at was where our own luggage was being stored. It took only a glance to see that both of our trunks as well as my father's had been tampered with, the locks scratched and broken beyond repair. The conductor gasped in shock at the obvious damage, but neither Redvers nor I were surprised in the slightest. "I'm sorry that your things have been damaged. This has never happened on our train before."

I wanted to tell the man that he'd never had *us* on his train before, but I held my tongue.

"We should take inventory and see if anything has been taken," the conductor said.

Redvers already had the lid on his trunk open and shook his head. "Not necessary." I was inclined to agree. We had been careful not to leave anything of interest in our trunks. The most anyone would have found was spare clothing, all of which could be replaced if there was any damage done. I peeked into my own trunk and saw that while things were messy, nothing appeared to have been harmed.

We did, however, need to see if anyone else's trunks had been searched. It took some time but we located the trunks of each of our traveling companions—Millie, Lord Hughes, and Maral—finding that each had been broken into and the contents rifled, although it was impossible to tell if anything had been taken. Ekrem Bey didn't seem to have any luggage that I could see.

"They were thorough," Redvers mused idly.

"Indeed," I said, looking around with hands on hips. "I don't see any luggage for Bey. Do you?"

Redvers glanced around. "It's possible that he didn't check any—he might have just thrown together an overnight bag to join us at the last minute."

"For a train trip to another country? He can't know how long he'll be gone—how could he manage with nothing but an overnight bag?"

Redvers just shook his head—he didn't have an answer to that.

I also couldn't help wonder how Ekrem Bey managed to secure a last-minute seat upon the *Orient Express*. We'd had a hard enough time with a day's notice—just when had Ekrem made the decision to join us?

I didn't like any of it.

Our search took longer than expected, and by the time we reached the dining car my stomach was growling in dismay and a small headache had started behind my eyes from the delayed infusion of caffeine.

"Will they still serve us?" I rubbed at my temples once we'd been seated at our table. I was relieved to see that Millie and Lord Hughes had already eaten—their place settings were being replaced as we entered, which meant they'd long since had breakfast and were gone. I was glad for the respite from my aunt's ever-critical inspection.

Within seconds my question was answered by our waiter taking our order. Another member of the waitstaff was already arriving with hot coffee for me and tea for Redvers by the time the first man had left. The service really was impeccable.

I gave a sigh of relief as I took my first sips of coffee, doctored with a bit of fresh cream. Redvers watched me in amusement for a few moments before his face grew serious. I glanced around the dining car, but we were nearly alone except for a table near the back whose occupant appeared to be lingering over their morning tea.

"Who do you think?" I asked. "I assume it has to be either someone traveling with us or one of the men assigned to follow us."

"It could be nearly anyone. Frankly, if they were smart, they would have damaged their own luggage to divert suspicion."

I nodded, unsurprised. It was precisely what I'd been thinking as well.

"What would they be looking for?" I asked.

"If it is someone outside our group, I would assume they're looking for the map. Which we don't have, since your father found it first and took it with him." Redvers looked thoughtful. "We've gone back and forth on whether your father left under his own steam, and if they're still looking for it, then it's reasonable to assume that he did leave on his own." He paused. "I think it's also reasonable to assume that if someone did have him, they would also have the map. And then what would they need us for? Or need to search our luggage?"

The thought lifted my spirits considerably. Perhaps Father had managed to escape without being followed, unlikely as it seemed.

But it still meant that someone on this train searched our things. It was a sober reminder that even though we'd left the city, we hadn't left the danger entirely behind. Ziya Bey was dead, a man had been killed outside the club, and we had no idea who was on this train with us.

"It's unlikely that it was either Maral or Ekrem since they already know that my father has the map," I said. "I doubt either of them searched our things."

"Unless there is something else they're looking for? Some other piece of the clue? Or perhaps something in regards to the money?" Redvers' eyes were intent on mine.

"If there is something else, I certainly don't know what it is. My father took all his papers with him and we know that the money is long gone. Ekrem himself told us that he was swindled and the culprit fled town." I took a sip of coffee. "We have the letters my father left me, but they're cryptic at best. He didn't give any information that could be considered useful. And since he had a nearly photographic memory, he didn't keep a journal. Even his notes about his work were quite cryptic—he was the only one who knew what they meant, and we don't have those in any case."

"But does everyone else know that?" Redvers did enjoy playing devil's advocate, but it was also a useful exercise.

"Probably not. I don't think it's normal for an academic— from what I recall, they seem to do extensive note-taking." I thought about what we did have from my father. "Who did we show the letters to?" I cast my mind back, trying to replay the events.

Redvers considered for a moment. "No one."

"Not even Ziya Bey?" Had we shown him anything that we had from my father? I was struggling to recall even though very little time had passed.

"Not even Bey," Redvers confirmed. "And who knows what he related to his brother. As far as things stand now, we've only *told* our companions what any of the letters contained."

"And if they didn't believe our recounting of what my father said . . ."

"They might have been curious enough to search for the letters. Or any other papers from your father they believe we have."

"This could be anyone." I sighed. I'd been hoping we could narrow down our field, but no such luck.

"It's an extreme response, searching everyone's luggage, but yes. It still could be anyone," Redvers agreed.

I was going to need more coffee.

The rest of the day passed slowly, my nerves keeping me on edge despite the comfort of the accommodations. I could tell that I was driving Redvers to distraction and interrupting his reading, so I spent quite a bit of time wandering the halls and gazing out at the passing countryside from the women's lounge, taking in exactly none of it. What was perhaps more conspicuous was that I didn't see any of our traveling companions all day. Not that I was going to seek out anyone's company, but it did strike me as strange that everyone we were traveling with was absent from the common areas.

When the porters called everyone to dinner, all of our traveling companions did show up and sat at their appropriate tables, although they seemed subdued. Even at my own table, I was allowed to sit quietly instead of being badgered by my aunt to join the conversation. The food was once again exceptional, and I managed to enjoy it before we retired to the lounge for an after-dinner drink. Aunt Millie and Lord Hughes played a hand of cards while Redvers and I watched.

By nightfall I was still too anxious to sleep, so I lay in the berth staring at the ceiling, Redvers sound asleep beside me for once—he was normally the one who slept very little. But I'd never been terribly good at waiting for something to happen, and that was compounded by my anxiety over whether my father was all right. Redvers' suggestion that having our things searched pointed toward the fact that my father might still be traveling under his own steam had done a lot to alleviate my worry about him. But he had still disappeared without his things and the bank was still going to repossess our row house. How were we going to come up with the money to repay them?

My brain could not stop brooding, so I was still wide-awake when the knock at the door came. Redvers didn't even stir and I was glad I was sleeping on the outside as I quickly pulled a wrap over my nightgown and answered the door. It was a train porter, although not ours and not one I recognized either.

"I'm sorry to bother you." The porter kept his voice low out of deference to our sleeping neighbors. "You've been requested in the car of Miss Aslanyan."

I raised my eyebrows—whatever had happened must be quite serious for a porter to come and wake up another passenger. I turned and looked behind me to see whether Redvers was still asleep—he was. He didn't sleep for very long, but when he did it was obviously quite sound. The porter glanced behind me at Redvers' sleeping form but said nothing.

I followed the porter through several other passenger cars and I realized that it was later than I'd initially thought—nearly every compartment was darkened, the occupants sound asleep. The only sounds were our quiet footsteps and the gentle sound of the train itself on the rails below us. Exactly how long had I been staring at the ceiling?

The man knocked on the door before opening it and holding it open for me to pass through, which I did before stopping in my tracks. There was no one in the car, and it took me only a beat to realize this had been a trap before I whirled around. The porter stood in the doorway, a small black gun in his hand. He pushed the door closed behind him, although it didn't latch.

"Onto the seat," he said as he reached for a pillow stashed on the rack above, his eyes never leaving mine and his hand never wavering.

I froze, body and brain. I didn't open my mouth to scream because I knew instinctively the man—who obviously wasn't a porter at all—would have shot me right there. I didn't have a chance to make any kind of decision, however, because the door swung quietly back open. Moments later the uniformed man's mouth opened in surprise with a gasp before he collapsed to the floor, a large knife buried squarely in his back.

CHAPTER TWENTY-NINE

I looked from the body on the floor to Maral standing in the doorway, hands on hips. She glanced at me. "You're welcome."

"How . . . how?" My brain hadn't quite processed anything that had happened in the last few moments and certainly wasn't producing full sentences.

She shrugged. "I don't sleep well on trains, and I heard a scuffle in the hallway earlier. I peeked out and saw this man shoving my porter into the bathroom."

"Is he dead?" I asked.

"The porter or this man?" Maral asked before bending down to grab the man's gun. "This one looks dead. I'm not sure about the porter." Her calm reserve was more than a little unnerving and I realized I wanted Redvers there before I asked her any further questions.

"One of us needs to wake Redvers," I said.

"I'll go." Maral passed me the pistol, leaning over the body to do so, and I took it from her, sitting heavily on the seat staring into space.

It was only minutes before Maral returned with Redvers in tow, and I was grateful that I'd had the time to process the scene before me. I was shaking now but felt better prepared to form complete sentences.

Redvers stepped over the form of the man lying on the

compartment floor and Maral scooted through the door and pushed it closed behind her before leaning back against it. There really wasn't room for the three of us plus the figure on the floor. Redvers was already squatting beside the man and checking for a pulse. He looked up at me and shook his head before standing back up, hands on hips.

"How did this come about?" Redvers asked mildly.

Maral was still entirely composed as she explained how she'd come upon us. "He was obviously going to shoot Jane, so . . ." She shrugged, made a stabbing motion with her hand.

Redvers was no longer so calmly composed, intensity and worry shining from his eyes as he looked at me. "Are you okay?"

I nodded, then turned to Maral. "Where did the knife come from?"

"My bed."

"Do you always sleep with a knife in your bed?"

"Don't you?" Maral met my eyes steadily. "I keep it under my pillow."

I did not, but it wasn't an issue worth discussing at the moment. Right now, I was incredibly grateful that she did sleep with a weapon—I didn't want to think about what would have happened if Maral hadn't been awake with something at her disposal to rescue me with.

I could tell that Redvers was thinking the same thing, but he did nothing more than reach out and give my hand a squeeze before turning back to the form on the floor. We were all quiet for a moment, wondering what to do with the dead man. He was facedown on the floor, head turned away from us.

"He's obviously not a porter," Redvers said.

Maral shook her head. "I'll check on the real porter in the bathroom."

I watched as Maral stepped from the room. I found it more than a little disconcerting how calmly the woman was taking this. Did she keep a knife under her pillow when my father was around? I had a brief moment of panic that my father had met the same fate as the dead man before I pushed the thought firmly away. It was both unhelpful and unlikely. Not only that, the woman had just saved my life. I should be grateful, not suspicious.

Although, just how much did my father know about this woman?

Maral returned a moment later. "He's starting to wake up—he was just knocked out."

"Good," Redvers said. "I'll go inform the conductor."

"Do you think he'll keep it quiet?"

"Oh, I'm certain of it. The real question is whether he'll feel that the police will need to be called."

I stiffened. I was not a fan of speaking with police in foreign countries. But this was an obvious case of Maral coming to my defense.

Redvers noticed my discomfort. "I don't think there will be any issue. It's clear what happened here."

I hoped he was correct. I was still not keen to find out what a Turkish jail looked like. And here I'd thought we'd avoided that possibility when we left the last crime scene behind back in Istanbul.

Redvers quickly searched the man's pockets that were immediately accessible.

"Anything?" I asked.

"Just the usual; some change and a handkerchief." Redvers pulled a slightly crushed packet of cigarettes from the man's pants pocket. "And this." He held it aloft and then leaned across the body at his feet to hand it to me. A matchbook had been tucked inside the cigarette box, and I pulled it free. There was nothing remarkable about it except that it was from Maxim's—the very place where we had met Ekrem Bey, and where another man had been murdered in the alley.

"Another coincidence?" I held the matchbook up for Redvers and he grunted and narrowed his eyes a bit. There was nothing written inside the matchbook so I tucked it back into its place and returned it to Redvers, who put it back where he'd found it in the man's pocket. I shivered a bit, glad that I wasn't the one searching the body.

His inspection completed, Redvers left to fetch the conductor. Maral came and took a seat next to me and she and I sat in uncomfortable silence. I considered telling her that she should make her way to the bathroom to clean the drying blood off her hands, but on second thought decided that the conductor should get the full picture first.

Maral and I stepped into the hallway when the men returned since there wasn't really room for all of us plus the dead body sprawled on the floor. And if I was honest, I was happy to get a bit of distance from the bloody man. I did, however, leave the door cracked open enough that we could see what the men were up to.

I'd wanted something to happen, but this wasn't what I'd hoped for.

As soon as he saw the body, the conductor let out a string of muttered expletives, which I felt were entirely appropriate for the situation, although he immediately apologized for his language. Both Redvers and Maral shrugged.

"We should turn him over." Redvers grabbed the man by the shoulders, the conductor squatting down to assist in rolling the body over. Even once the man was faceup, I didn't recognize him and said as much.

I looked at Maral and she shook her head as well. But a glance at Redvers told a different story. His face was pinched and his eyebrows had drawn together.

"Redvers?" I asked.

Redvers' voice was low. "I do know him. Or at least, I used to."

Chapter Thirty

The conductor and Maral seemed shocked, but after a moment's thought, I realized that I wasn't. Given the nature of Redvers' work, and the fact that his cover was blown the last time he'd been in Istanbul, it was more surprising that he didn't know more of the parties that had been following us around town. Redvers continued without prompting.

"He's Armenian, but his loyalties were . . . fluid, to say the least. Arman something . . . I don't recall his surname. But based on the little I know of him, I'm not surprised he was willing to be paid for this." His eyes flicked to me and I knew he was again thinking about what might have happened if Maral hadn't been there. I hoped he wouldn't blame himself for it—he wasn't responsible for my charging off into the night unaccompanied. It was entirely my fault for going without waking him up and letting him know where I was going. It was something we would discuss later—at length.

"When is the last time you saw him?" I asked.

"When I was last in the city." He didn't elaborate and I knew he was being deliberately vague in front of our two companions.

I looked to Maral. "You're sure you don't recognize him?" I thought perhaps he'd been one of the men following my father and she might have seen his face before.

"Because we are both Armenian? We don't all know each other."

That wasn't at all what I meant, and I said as much, explaining why I thought she might recognize his face.

"I'm sorry. It's just that things have been difficult for my people, and I'm sorry that I had to kill a fellow Armenian." She shook her head. "But I had no choice."

I was tempted to reach out and touch her shoulder, but something about her posture stopped me. I didn't think she would welcome the gesture at this moment.

"Many claim the genocide of the Armenians never happened," Maral said, bitterness evident in her voice. "But it did. Thousands, hundreds of thousands of Armenians were killed. Not to mention the forced displacement." Maral took a deep breath, having glanced back down at the dead man. "So many Greeks and Armenians were shop owners, restaurant owners in Istanbul. But they forced everyone to pick up their lives and leave their property and move to a country we have not seen in generations." She shook her head again. "Devastating for so many." Maral gestured at the man. "Forcing them into positions like this."

I thought it was a bit of a stretch that their tragic past had forced this man to try to kill me on someone else's orders, but I kept that to myself. I didn't want to minimize Maral's pain. I was curious about her experiences, however. It was something we hadn't discussed.

"How did you come to be back in Istanbul?" I asked.

"My father, he had an employee take over the restaurant as a placeholder, vowing to return. And he did. We falsified some papers and managed to return."

I wanted to ask about how that had worked, but her lips were pressed tightly. She would not be discussing how they'd managed to get back to Istanbul and it wasn't really relevant to our current predicament, so I held my tongue, attention refocused on the dead body at our feet.

We were all quiet for a few more moments, Maral's story hanging heavy in the air, but then practical considerations won out. "Jane, can you take Maral to the bathroom to get cleaned up?" Redvers asked. "And take her to our compartment once you're finished in the bathroom. We can talk more about what will happen next." Maral had buried the knife in this man's back at a close distance and blood had sprayed her clothing as well as her face and hands. Her dress would probably be ruined, but she could wipe down everything else.

I held out my hand for Maral. She didn't take it, keeping her arms wrapped around herself instead, but she followed me from the compartment to the bathroom, shutting herself inside. I stood in the hallway listening to the water run for long minutes. I was grateful that the conductor had dismissed the porter from this hallway since it meant we didn't have to offer any explanations for the state of Maral's clothing. I wasn't keen to clean the bathroom after Maral was finished, though, but I also didn't think we should leave any traces of what had happened. Maral finally reemerged and I peeked into the room—she had left the sink and surrounding areas as spotless as the porter would have. I breathed a small sigh of relief.

The two of us walked in silence through the other cars to the compartment I shared with Redvers. I was pleased to note that no one else appeared to be awake—the only people we passed were a couple of porters, asleep at their posts. I let the two of us into my compartment and took a seat on the edge of our open bunk.

Maral hovered uncertainly for a moment, clearly uncomfortable with being in the compartment I shared with Redvers, especially when it was made up for sleeping. "I think I'll go back to my own compartment. We can wait until morning to discuss what will happen next."

I looked at her for a long moment. She had been remarkably calm—eerily calm, really—until Redvers had announced the ethnicity of the assassin. That was the first time she'd shown any emotion about having stabbed a man to death. My gratitude for her actions warred with suspicion and I was reluctant to have her leave. But it wasn't as though she could leave the train while it was moving.

I hated that that was my first instinct—to worry that she would try to escape when all she had done was save my life.

I hoped none of this internal battle showed on my face, so I quickly nodded. "That sounds good. I need to get some sleep. We can discuss how to deal with the police in the morning."

Maral turned to leave, but I stopped her. "Maral . . . thank you," I said. I didn't think I needed to elaborate on why I was thanking her.

She looked over her shoulder at me and gave me a single nod but said nothing before taking her leave.

The door shut softly behind her and I was left alone with my thoughts. I'd maintained a reasonable level of calm myself until then, but now that I was alone and able to think about how close I'd come to a quick and fatal end, I began to shake with some vigor. I pulled a blanket off the bed, wrapped myself in it, and huddled in the back corner of our bunk.

It seemed like an eternity, but it was probably only half an hour before Redvers returned to our compartment.

I breathed a huge sigh of relief just at the sight of him. The man closed the door and came straight to me, wrapping me in his arms. We sat like that for a long moment, saying nothing, and I realized I had finally stopped trembling.

"I don't even want to think about what might have happened," Redvers finally said.

"Then let's not. Nothing happened to me and I'm fine."

He just shook his head, then leaned back against the wall, mind switching to practical matters although he didn't release me, keeping me tucked in tight against him. "It's unfortunate that anyone we might be able to get answers from keeps dying on us."

"Very inconvenient. Maral certainly appears to know what she's doing with a knife," I said. I hadn't really considered how much force it must have taken for her to stab the man hard enough to kill him nearly instantly. It was almost as though she'd been trained for such a thing. But once again I pushed the thought from my mind—it felt traitorous since I was sitting there only because of her.

But I couldn't help wonder yet again just how well my father knew his paramour.

"We'll have to speak with the police when we stop, but I think it will be pretty simple and we won't be held up too long. What happened is fairly straightforward."

"Except why an apparent stranger was trying to kill me."

"We'll find a way to explain that."

I was glad Redvers was so confident. But I was now feeling entirely wrung out and ready to go back to sleep, or at least try to. Everything else could be dealt with in the morning—or whenever I saw fit to wake up. I lay back down, my eyes already sliding closed, but I did have one last question for Redvers.

"What did you do with the body?"

"We put him in the refrigeration section of the baggage car. For now."

I shivered again.

The next morning, I awoke earlier than I would have liked given how little sleep I'd had. It wasn't just the interruption—I'd slept hard for an hour or two, then tossed and turned for the rest of the short night despite being exhausted. Now I rushed to get ready since Redvers had obviously been up for some time and was waiting for me. The man was stealthy as a cat—I'd heard nothing, but here he sat, fully dressed and reading his book, waiting for me to wake up. Once I'd donned my burgundy wool day dress with a pleated skirt and my black T-strap kitten heels, we made our way to the dining car. I was pleased to see that it had emptied of nearly all its occupants, except Aunt Millie and Lord Hughes.

"Perhaps you should take a sleeping powder at night, Jane." Millie's lips were pursed. "You're obviously not getting enough sleep. I know it's difficult to get used to at first—sleeping on a train. But you must find a way to get some rest before we get to Hungary this afternoon, or you won't be of any use to anyone."

The waiter was already approaching so I was able to focus on him instead of attempting to formulate a reply to Millie. I ordered as much coffee as he could carry before returning my attention to my tablemates.

"Haven't you already eaten, Aunt Millie?" I asked mildly.

"We have, but I wanted to speak with you this morning. I heard some mutterings in the hallway this morning that something happened last night."

I cocked my head slightly. "What sort of something?"

Millie's voice dropped to a whisper. "Someone was killed."

I'd been hoping that the news wouldn't spread at all, but I supposed it was inevitable—there was a body in cold storage, after all. The gossip probably began with either the porters or kitchen staff and spread outward. One person quietly mentioning it to the next until everyone knew.

"That was fast," I muttered to Redvers, attacking the coffee that had just been set before me.

"The coffee or the gossip?"

I gave him a small smile. "Both."

Redvers put a little milk and sugar in his tea, stirring it casually as he took over the conversation with Millie and Lord Hughes, allowing me a moment to enjoy my coffee in relative peace. "Yes, someone was killed last night. We're not entirely certain who he was or what his role was."

I nearly raised an eyebrow since very little of that statement was true, but I managed to restrain myself, concentrating on my coffee instead. There was not much benefit to telling my aunt that someone had tried to kill me the night before and I'd only managed to avoid it because my father's girlfriend had stabbed the man to death. I wasn't sure what exactly her reaction would be, but I was certain it would be more of a hindrance to my day than anything.

"You'll investigate further today?" Lord Hughes asked.

"Certainly," Redvers said. "Jane and I will search his compartment immediately following breakfast to see if there's anything to be learned."

I brightened a little. I did enjoy a good search, even if the man had tried to kill me. And I was ever hopeful that we might find something useful among his things—something to point us to who might have hired him.

Despite my mixed feelings about the woman, I felt a pang for Maral and made a mental note to check up on her later. She'd seemed entirely composed the evening before, but she *had* stabbed a man to death. Regardless of the circumstances, I wouldn't feel good having that kind of blood on my hands if I were in her shoes.

The waiter arrived with our food and Millie ordered another round of tea, which caused me to sigh internally. No chance of Redvers and I enjoying a quiet breakfast alone then.

"Did you see Mr. Bey at breakfast this morning?" Redvers asked.

Millie frowned. "I didn't notice if he was here."

Lord Hughes, however, nodded. "He was at breakfast. So was Miss Aslanyan."

"Excellent," Redvers said.

It left me wondering what exactly the man had in mind that required Ekrem Bey.

Chapter Thirty-one

Millie and Lord Hughes finally excused themselves, and once I found myself adequately caffeinated, Redvers and I headed toward my attempted assassin's compartment. Arman had been sharing the second-class space with a young priest who happily excused himself to the observation car when we knocked at his door.

I watched the man in black robes and white collar go. "Not another suspicious character, then."

"Not so far. But one never knows." Redvers' eyes twinkled before he turned himself to the task at hand. "From what the conductor told me, Arman had the upper bunk." The priest's bunk had been folded away for the day, but the porter had left the top bunk as it was and Redvers started there.

I started on the other side of the compartment, but there wasn't much to search, truthfully. The room was small and I finished my side in a matter of minutes with nothing to show for it. "Nothing on this side, I'm afraid," I said, hands on hips.

Redvers had finished searching Arman's bunk, then turned his attention to a battered leather hand case he'd found. He emptied the contents onto the small side table. "Might be something of interest here." Redvers held a small piece of paper aloft briefly before continuing his scrutiny of said paper. "It's a list. Physical descriptions of all of us, even me."

"What?" I stood on tiptoes to read over his shoulder before deciding that was silly and physically moving him to the side so that I could look at the paper with him. He placed it on the table where we could both read it.

He was correct. It was a list of the names of each of our traveling companions with a vague sketch of what each of us looked like. Ekrem Bey wasn't listed, but that wasn't surprising since he'd joined us at the very last minute. Next to Redvers' name, however, was written "you know him."

"Hmm." I pointed to the phrase.

"I agree," Redvers replied.

I looked at him. "You don't even know what I was thinking."

"Oh, but I do. You're thinking this suggests that someone else wrote this list and gave it to him. Suggested by the use of the word "you." It also means that whoever hired him knows me."

I made an impolite noise, refusing to come out and agree that that had in fact been what I'd been thinking. I didn't want the man getting cocky that he could actually read my thoughts.

Redvers had already turned his attention back to the bag. "Perhaps there's something else in here with handwriting on it, so we can compare the two." Redvers continued emptying the bag but came up short on anything useful.

There was nothing else of interest among the man's belongings—a small Bible, a newspaper, and a Hungarian train schedule were the only things that could be considered even vaguely interesting, and all the latter meant was that he'd planned to follow us beyond Budapest. Of course, that begged the question of how he knew we were going elsewhere in Hungary, but again, there was no one left to ask. We packed the things back into Arman's bag except for the list, which Redvers slipped into his pocket. Securing the top, Redvers moved toward the door, bag in hand.

"Where are you taking that?"

"I think we'll want to hang on to it. In case we're missing something."

I nodded. I was glad Redvers was on top of things.

I wanted to check in on Maral after the night before so we went straight to Maral's compartment in the second-class car, although I stopped Redvers just before he knocked on the door. "What about Arman's trunk?" I whispered. "Did he have something in the baggage car?"

"He did. And I searched it last night," Redvers mock whispered back. "Nothing to report."

I gave him a little shot to the arm. It covered a variety of offenses, but mostly for conducting a search without me. As well as the mockery.

Redvers knocked on the door and Maral's voice came from within, telling us to enter. She was seated by the window, staring at the countryside as it passed by. Her compartment was somewhat narrower than our first-class accommodations, and it was obvious that there was an upper and lower bed for sleeping in—I would have been nervous about tumbling from that top bunk, especially if the train was forced to make any abrupt stops. But the compartment was also done in fine woods, with a modern floral pattern repeating on the walls and floor.

As we entered, Maral turned her attention to us and I couldn't help but notice the black circles under her eyes. They were entirely new, and I wasn't surprised she'd spent a sleepless night. But her voice was still clear and direct, no trace of a tremble.

"We just wanted to see how you were doing," I said.

Maral waved us in, indicating that we should take a seat.

As we sat down, I noticed a cup of tea on the table that appeared to be nearly untouched. Lord Hughes had seen Maral at breakfast that morning, but I wondered if she'd managed to actually eat anything. Just how heavy was the previous night weighing on her? She obviously hadn't slept, but was that the only side effect of killing a man that she was experiencing? I'd tossed and turned all night, but my appetite hadn't been affected. But I hadn't wielded the knife.

"Did you eat something?" I asked.

Maral gave me an amused look. "Is that what you came here to ask me?"

I flushed. I'd only been concerned that she was looking after herself after such a traumatic incident.

Maral gave me a small smile to show she was teasing me. "I had something to eat earlier at breakfast. But thank you for your concern, Jane." She looked at Redvers. "And what would you like to talk to me about?"

"I'm afraid that we will be unable to avoid speaking with the police once we arrive," Redvers said.

Maral raised an eyebrow. "And we are making sure we have the same story?"

Redvers gave a small shake of his head. "We're going to tell the truth and explain exactly what happened. This man dressed as a porter lured Jane from her room and tried to kill her. You heard noise and . . . took matters into your own hands."

"When I stabbed him, you mean." Maral wasn't dancing around what happened, that was for certain. "What will we say about why the man wanted to kill Jane? I assume we are leaving out any mention of Henry."

"You're correct. We're going to leave out any mention of Professor Wunderly or the sultan's heart. They aren't really relevant—not to the police anyway." Redvers had been holding my hand between us on the little settee and he gave my hand a squeeze. "As for why the man wanted to kill Jane, we will say it was simply a robbery."

Both Maral and I gave him skeptical looks. "I don't have anything worth stealing," I said.

Redvers shrugged. "The police don't know that." He was quiet for a moment, and I felt the pressure from his hand increase. I wasn't going to like what came next. "There is another option. We could say that the man found Jane attractive and lured her to the empty car for . . . more nefarious purposes."

I felt my stomach dip. There were a host of unpleasant things that might have happened the night before if Maral hadn't intervened.

CHAPTER THIRTY-TWO

An hour later, we had hammered out what each of us would say to the police when we arrived in Budapest later that day. According to Redvers, the conductor had considered making an extra stop to offload the body, but it seemed like a better plan to get to a city where there were more resources—both police and mortuary, despite the fact that we would cross the boundary into another country from where the incident had taken place. But the only stops between where we were currently and our destination were tiny outposts barely outfitted with train stations, let alone a police force.

After we left her compartment, we stood in the hallway for a second. "She's entirely too calm. She was even teasing me this morning while a man's body is lying in a refrigerator," I said quietly. I was still unsettled from our conversation and was having trouble shaking the knowledge that I'd narrowly avoided death or something equally as unpleasant.

"People react in different ways," Redvers said.

That was true, but I still couldn't help but find Maral's calm in the face of—well, everything—incredibly disconcerting. My memories of my mother were fading, but I couldn't help but reflect that Maral seemed to be nearly the exact opposite of what I remembered my mother to be like. Mother had been warm and funny, and I couldn't imagine that she would have been so callous about taking a man's life. Of course, I couldn't picture her in a scenario where that would be necessary, either.

Altogether it made me curious about my father's choices in women. Was he attracted to Maral because she was so unlike my mother? That didn't sit well with me, and I tabled the entire topic as something to ruminate over later.

"What next?" I asked.

"I think we should chat with Ekrem Bey," Redvers said.

I nearly excused myself from the conversation since I found the man so unpleasant, but ultimately, I didn't want to miss anything. Even if it meant another uncomfortable encounter. "Lead the way."

After checking Bey's second-class compartment just down the hall from Maral's, and finding no one there but Ekrem's roommate, we continued through the dining car and into the sitting lounge. The elegant décor was perhaps amplified here, with a beautiful wooden bar along one wall and ample bottles of alcohol at the ready for the bartender standing behind it. The leather chairs scattered about the room were deep and plush, and the beautifully carved panels of wood between the car windows were more prominent with less furniture to detract attention from them. We found Bey there, sipping something brown in a cut crystal glass—if I had to guess, I'd say it was whiskey.

"Rather early for a highball, isn't it?" Redvers asked.

Ekrem Bey gave him an amused look as he swirled the liquid in his glass. "I will not ask you to join me then."

We sat at the chairs gathered around his small table anyway, sinking into the plush leather.

"You never did say why you decided to join us on this journey," Redvers said. "We assume it is because you are searching for your brother's killer."

Bey gave an elegant shrug, his dark eyes glittering. "I decided that the answers I seek are not likely to be found in Istanbul."

Despite not wanting to draw this man's attention, I couldn't help the question that escaped my mouth. "And why is that?" I was fully convinced that this interview was going to be a total waste of time. The man was entirely too self-possessed and would never answer any of our questions seriously.

"Because I think your father is responsible."

I had some choice responses to that, but Redvers put a restraining hand on my leg and I managed to bite back what I was going to say. But only just.

"What makes you say that?" Redvers asked.

Ekrem gave me one of his unpleasant smiles. "I don't mean that your father killed him with his own hand, Miss Wunderly. But he was responsible all the same."

Redvers hadn't removed his hand from my leg, which was for the best since I was finding everything Ekrem said to be incredibly incendiary, and the gentle squeeze of his hand was helping me to hold my tongue. Ekrem looked meaningfully at Redvers' hand, one eyebrow arching mockingly, although he didn't comment on it.

"Again, what makes you say that?" Redvers' voice was level.

"I did some more looking into things regarding your father and his 'investment' into that expedition." Ekrem took a sip of his drink and I found myself wishing that I had some alcohol for this conversation as well. "My brother felt guilty that your father lost his money, but I am starting to believe that your father is the one who got my brother involved with it, not the other way around. My brother lost some money as well, although not nearly as much as what your father threw away."

I closed my eyes briefly, trying to get my temper under

control, despite my desire to throw a punch at this man's face. It had only been a drink on previous occasions that I'd been tempted to throw at Ekrem Bey, but now it was definitely my fist. The insinuation that my father had been the instigator of our troubles and that he'd thrown money away when it could potentially lose us our home . . . it was too much.

"That doesn't mean Professor Wunderly was responsible," Redvers said.

"Not in itself, no. But the man who absconded with the money was an associate of your father's. My brother did not know him at all."

Could this be true? Could my father have been swindled by his own associate and gotten Ziya involved in his mess? Why would Ziya have felt guilty about my father losing the money then? And what did it really matter if the money was gone anyway? We weren't going to be able to recover it regardless of who got who involved. Somewhere in the back of my mind I'd begun wondering if my father was correct—perhaps finding the sultan's heart meant that we wouldn't lose our home. Of course, we needed to find both him and it before our clock ran out with the bank. We were losing time even as we spoke.

Ekrem gave a flick of his hand. "Either way, my brother's murder has to do with your father and his quest for the sultan's heart. And since you are traveling to Budapest to find your father, I am more likely to find his killer by following you."

I couldn't argue the point. In this, he was probably correct.

"A man was killed last night," Redvers said. "Did you know him?"

Ekrem's face actually sobered. "I heard that someone met an unfortunate end. But I do not believe that I am acquainted with him."

"Are you certain?" Redvers asked. "He seemed to spend

quite a bit of time at Maxim's." At least, that was what the matchbook we'd found in his pocket indicated. I assumed Redvers knew something of the man's habits as well.

"So does half the population of Istanbul," Ekrem said airily. "I do not know every character that comes in."

The answer was evasive and Ekrem wouldn't quite meet either of our eyes, a dead giveaway that he was lying. I could tell from the little line between Redvers' eyebrows that he thought so too, but what I couldn't figure out was why Bey would lie about knowing the dead man. Ekrem claimed he was here because he was looking for his brother's killer, but did he have some other motivation as well? Was it possible that he was after the heart too, as some sort of compensation for losing his brother? Or simply because it would make him a wealthy man? It was something I'd never considered before.

The only thing I knew for certain was that the man was giving me a headache. "What do you know about the sultan's heart?" I finally asked.

Ekrem took a long sip of his whiskey and regarded me for a moment before putting the glass back on the table. "It is not a secret that your father is searching for the heart. Although I do think it will be a miracle if he actually finds it."

"Why do you say that?" It went without saying that the man knew more than he was ever going to tell us. But he had to have heard something about whoever was trying to get father to lead them to the heart. Or whether someone meant to stop father altogether—someone willing to murder several people along the way.

But Ekrem shrugged casually. "Because people have been searching for the heart for hundreds of years. And still, it has never been found. The odds are not in his favor."

I felt myself deflate at this anticlimactic pronouncement. That wasn't the least bit helpful—I should have known he wouldn't tell me what I wanted to know.

"But I will say this. I have heard rumblings, and your father is not the only one interested in finding the heart. The box that it is buried in, that alone would fetch enough money to make someone a very rich man. I would advise both of you to be very careful so you do not end up like my brother." He threw back the rest of his drink. "And no, I cannot give you names."

Wouldn't give us names was much more likely.

Ekrem stood. "Thank you for a charming conversation. I will see you at lunch. Perhaps afterward we could play some cards, Mr. Redvers." He grinned, his teeth white against his dark beard. "It helps *kill* the time."

Chapter Thirty-three

Ekrem left, and despite the early hour I seriously considered ordering a drink before deciding against it. The man truly set my teeth on edge.

Redvers had the same idea, but he went ahead and signaled the waiter, ordering himself a whiskey neat and a gin rickey for me. I didn't stop him, despite just having decided against an early drink.

When we had our beverages, he leaned back in his seat, fingers tapping against the glass. "He knows more than he's telling us."

"Do you *really* think so?" I said sweetly, chin propped on fist. I batted my eyelashes dramatically before rolling my eyes at him. He grinned at me and I couldn't help my own grin before becoming serious again. "My guess is he actually knows who is after the heart or at least has a good guess. And by extension, he knows who is after my father and possibly even who killed his brother."

Redvers agreed. "It's a fair guess. It's also a safe bet that he's not going to tell us."

"If he knows who killed his brother, why would he still join us on this trip?"

"You're not going to like the answer."

I sighed. "Because if Ekrem does know who it is, and Ekrem is here, that means the person responsible for his brother's death is also here or has left Istanbul to follow my father." He was right; I didn't like it. Maral had eliminated our immediate danger, but that didn't mean there wasn't more around the next corner. In fact, it was likely.

"My next question is whether Ekrem knows because he's part of it, or whether he knows simply from his other dealings around the club."

"You're suggesting he had something to do with his brother's death?"

I cocked my head and gave that some thought. Ekrem did seem passionate about finding his brother's killer, but that didn't mean he wasn't still mixed up in the affair somehow, and I said as much.

"I suppose we can't rule it out. It would be pretty bold of him to join us if he was involved, though."

"But you've seen him—I don't think there's much he wouldn't do boldly."

Redvers inclined his head in agreement. "When we get to Budapest, I will stop at the telegraph office and send a message to the office. See what we can find out about Ekrem Bey as well as Arman. I'd like to know who Ekrem does business with, and exactly what kind he dabbles in."

"We should be so lucky."

"We've been pretty lucky so far."

I gave him my most skeptical look. "If by 'lucky' you mean we haven't been killed yet, then yes, I suppose we have."

Redvers sobered immediately. "I don't know what I would have done if I had lost you."

The stark emotion in his voice was my undoing and I felt my eyes get wet before I blinked the tears furiously back. I understood that Redvers loved me—he'd told me as much— but it was rare for him to show this depth of emotion, and I was deeply moved. I reached out and took his hand, the free one that wasn't gripping his whiskey glass. I took a few breaths, waiting to speak until I was sure that I could.

"I hope you aren't blaming yourself for what happened," I said.

He squeezed my fingers but stayed quiet, clearly trying to decide what to say next.

"Redvers, you cannot keep me safe at all times. And you are not responsible for when I hare off into the night without a thought for my own safety." It wasn't the first time it had happened either. This time, however, I believed I had finally learned my lesson.

He sighed. "I know that logically, but it's difficult not to feel responsible for keeping you safe."

"Even while you sleep? That's ridiculous. You don't sleep enough as it is." I gave his fingers a squeeze of my own. "But I will promise you this. I will not disappear off into the night again without telling you where I'm going."

"I'm going to hold you to that."

I was a little relieved that the humor had returned to his voice—I was ready for the intensity of this interaction to be over for now. "And how do you intend to do that?" My voice was teasing now.

"I'm going to make you sleep on the inside of every bed so you have to jump over me to get out," he said, eyes twinkling.

I laughed. "At least you have a plan."

There truly wasn't much to do for the rest of the morning until lunch and our eventual arrival at the station in Budapest besides eat, drink, and play cards, so that is precisely what we did. Millie and Lord Hughes joined us in the lounge not long after Ekrem left us, and Redvers suggested we play a few rounds to pass the time.

It may have passed the time, but I couldn't keep my mind on what was happening in front of me—there was simply too much to process, not to mention the fact that our imminent arrival in Budapest meant making a statement to the police while the body on the train was offloaded. I found myself worrying that the police would detain us and we would lose even more time in our quest to find my father.

It was obvious that I wasn't able to concentrate on my hand and Millie was becoming increasingly frustrated with me, so I finally bowed out of the game and simply watched before further abuse could rain down upon my head. Instead of defending myself, I held my tongue. We'd been keeping Millie and Lord Hughes in the dark about much of what was taking place—both back in Istanbul and now on the train. There didn't seem to be any reason to alarm them, and for once Millie didn't push to know everything.

In fact, Millie only brought things up once. "After all this trouble, we had best not find your father sitting in some bar enjoying a drink when we get there," she said.

I was fairly certain Millie was just posturing, so I didn't say anything, but as far as I was concerned, that was the best-case scenario. There was nothing I would have loved more than to find him safe and sound and enjoying himself. Wherever that might be.

Of course, it would be even better if he'd found a way to repay the bank as well.

Chapter Thirty-four

After a lunch of veal with *petits pois*, crispy rolls, and slabs of excellent cheese, we pulled into the station at Budapest. We exited the train and I heard Millie make a noise behind me. It sounded much like a harrumph, and I hid a smile. The station had soaring ceilings overhead but was otherwise quite modest. The walls were stone with pale green doors and windows running the length along either side. Redvers and Lord Hughes saw to our luggage, ensuring that it would be transferred to the train going south to Szigetvár, and the passengers disembarking were led through one of the doors.

"This is the royal waiting room," the porter said. "They will take care of you here."

Taking care of us appeared to mean a glass of champagne before we left the station, and I accepted mine while taking in the surroundings.

"This is more like it," Millie said to Lord Hughes. He smiled and sipped at his champagne.

The scattered chairs were upholstered in rich red velvet, matching the patterned red-and-gold carpet beneath our feet. The marble walls were ornately carved, and above the columns and arches were round stained-glass windows high overhead. It was a beautiful room, certainly fit for royalty, but I couldn't entirely enjoy the experience knowing that I needed to speak with the police.

Lord Hughes and Millie had taken a seat at one of the tables, and I noticed that Millie had the waiter with the bottle
of champagne standing nearby as well. Maral came over to
stand with Redvers and I, which is how the conductor found
us a few minutes later.

"If you'll come this way. The police inspector will speak
with you in the station manager's office." The conductor kept
his voice low so as not to alert any other passengers.

I glanced at Millie. "Do you think we should tell her something?"

Redvers looked amused as he watched my aunt get a refill.
"I think she might not even notice we're gone. Especially if
they have another bottle or two somewhere."

The three of us followed the man out of the room into the
main part of the station. It was a beautiful space, although
not as striking as the one we'd seen in Istanbul. Still, the high
arching ceilings and numerous windows made it light and
airy. We moved in a little group through the hustle and bustle
of the ticketing area and into an area much less grand that
was for staff only. A police inspector was waiting for us, having taken up residence behind the station manager's desk.
The station manager himself was nowhere to be seen.

The police inspector wore a dark navy uniform with silver
buttons and blue-and-silver epaulettes. He had a dark bushy
moustache that tipped up at the ends.

"I am Inspector Kovács. I am here to take your report on
what happened aboard the train."

"The body . . ." Redvers started to ask.

"The body has already been removed. It will be taken care
of," Kovács said. "Now. One by one I would like you to tell
me what happened, and we will write it down. Then you will
be free to go."

I was suspicious that it not only seemed so easy, but that
the man was showing us such deference as well. It was not at

all what my experiences had been like in dealing with the police in the past, but after a few minutes I felt my shoulders drop as the tension leaked out of them. He was doing exactly as he said—typing up our statements as we went, his fingers flying across the keys. Kovács barely asked any follow-up questions, simply had us each sign our statements and thanked us for our time.

The three of us left the office and looked at one another.

"That was . . . faster than I anticipated it would be," Maral said, and I nodded my agreement.

"We're passengers from the *Orient Express*," Redvers said with a shrug, but didn't elaborate. We both looked at him for a beat, expecting more, but when it wasn't forthcoming, we moved on.

"I'm going to go for a walk," Maral announced. "I would like to stretch my legs before we get on the next train." With that, she set off, not waiting for a response.

Redvers and I watched her go, then he gave me a quick kiss to the temple.

"I'm going to head to the telegram office. See if anyone has left word for us."

"Without me?"

"Without you. But perhaps you should stop at the luggage room here and make inquiries. Just to be safe." He gave me a winning smile. "Divide and conquer, my dear."

I shooed him off with a bemused look. We still had a little bit of time before our next train departed, but it *would* be more efficient for us to split up. I watched him go for a few moments, enjoying the view before turning to take in the area, looking for the luggage room. I assumed Redvers was hoping that perhaps my father had left some sort of package for us, although I didn't think we would get lucky enough that he might leave us anything as important as, say, the map. I caught sight of Millie and Lord Hughes at the small café opposite me, and even from where I stood, I could see that

Millie was already ordering the waitstaff about. Those two would be occupied for a bit, at least.

I spun slowly, taking in the station and looking for a sign that would direct me to the luggage room, spotting it out of the way of the ticket office. A man with a dark fedora was ahead of me at the counter, and I waited while he retrieved a small carpetbag. He didn't look at me as he swept past, and I moved up to the counter where a middle-aged man with a tidy moustache waited for my request.

"Is there anything here for Jane Wunderly?" I asked.

"Do you have a ticket?" He peered at me over his half-moon spectacles.

I shook my head.

"Hmmph," he said, but he bent down to take a look just the same. I could hear the sounds of rifling through papers before he stood back up, holding an envelope in one hand.

"I shouldn't give this to you without a ticket." He looked me over and held the envelope for a few extra moments before reluctantly holding it out.

"Thank you." I dug in my bag to hand the man a few bills, belatedly realizing that they were Turkish lira instead of Hungarian currency. He gave me a sour look but accepted them anyway.

I was tempted to immediately rip the envelope open and read the contents, but I restrained myself. I had no idea who was watching, so I tucked the envelope securely into my bag and held it close as I wound my way back to where Millie and Lord Hughes were having tea. There was no sign of Redvers yet, so I joined my aunt and her fiancé at their table, mentioning nothing about our conversation with the police or the note that had been left for me even though it was burning like a living flame, flickering at the edge of my consciousness.

"Where did you two disappear off to? You missed out on the champagne."

"I had a bit of it," I said. "It was quite good. But I thought I would avoid overindulging—it sometimes gives me a headache." I didn't answer the rest of her question, hoping she wouldn't notice. We were keeping quite a bit back from Lord Hughes and Aunt Millie, including the fact that I'd nearly been shot the night before. We had never discussed this decision outright; it was simply unspoken between Redvers and me that they didn't need all the details of what was going on. There was certainly an element of wanting to protect my aunt—both mentally and physically—even though I knew she was tough as old shoe leather.

But if I were honest, there was a larger element of not trusting Millie—she would undoubtedly stick her nose into things and make them even more complicated than they needed to be, and I was eager to avoid that. Not to mention my deep desire to remain unbeholden to her, which would not be the case if she were to bail us out of our financial pickle with the row house. It might come down to asking her to do just that, but we still had a little over a week to try to solve the problem ourselves. I held out a small spark of hope that Father could actually find the heart and save our home.

We were just finishing up our beverages when Redvers returned from the telegraph office to escort us to the train.

"And now where have *you* been?" Millie asked.

"Checking to see if there were any messages for me," Redvers replied easily.

"And were there?" she asked with no hint of feeling that her question might be inappropriate or invasive.

I was always impressed with Redvers' ability to take my aunt in stride no matter what she threw at him.

"Nothing of any interest." Redvers winked at me as we left the café and headed toward the next leg of our journey. Millie harrumphed and I had the sense that she didn't believe him, but she also didn't press him on it. I knew he had at least something to share, but I also knew he would wait until we were alone in order to do so.

The train was much less luxurious than the *Oriental Express* despite our first-class accommodations. But I was grateful that we once again had our own sitting compartment even though we wouldn't be spending the night on board—we still had a several-hour ride ahead of us, and at least the seats were padded here. Once we were safely alone and the train had begun to move, I pulled the envelope from my bag. I was almost surprised that it wasn't actually warm to the touch—it was an ordinary envelope with an ordinary piece of hotel stationery inside. The Pera Palace logo was at the top, which meant that my father had written it before he'd even left Istanbul. Or he'd taken this stationery from the hotel but not his luggage, which seemed unlikely.

"What does it say?" Redvers asked.

I glanced at him, then proceeded to read the letter out loud. This was no great trial since it was more like a note than a letter.

> *"Jane dear. If you've found this message as well, I hope you will stay where you are in Budapest. I beg of you not to follow me any farther than this. I have things in hand and it will only do us both a disservice if you come after me. Stay in Budapest and I will find you shortly. Your loving father, Henry"*

"He really must be worried for my safety—he really doesn't want me to come after him."

"Hmm," Redvers replied. He said no more on the subject, but I could tell he didn't think my suggestion was what had motivated my father's directive to stay in Budapest.

I sighed. "It's too late; we're already on the way. And it's not as if I would have stayed in Budapest even if I'd read this before we left."

Redvers had a small smile on his face. "I certainly know that to be true."

I could feel my brows pulled together in a furrow as I thought about the crumb trail of messages my father had been leaving me. But instead of leading me somewhere, they were telling me to stay put. Didn't he know that telling me repeatedly to stay where I was would only push me to do the exact opposite? It was almost like he didn't know me at all.

That was an uncomfortable thought. I was glad when after a moment I remembered that Redvers probably had news as well. "Were there any messages for you?"

"There were." He paused, pulling a pair of papers from his inner jacket pocket and passing them over. Before I could look at them, he continued. "Ekrem Bey is indeed associated with an underworld criminal organization. A couple of them, really. He's known as a dealmaker."

"What does that mean?"

"He negotiates deals between different factions."

I thought about the man's charm and smooth manners. Well, I assumed they were smooth when dealing with other people—I found them intensely discomfiting, but I suspected that was purposeful. This role made perfect sense for the man, however. "And is this the organization that's been following us?"

"As far as our people can tell, it is not. They are strictly involved with other types of vice." At my raised eyebrow he continued. "Women and drugs, but not ancient artifacts. The sultan's heart is completely outside their area of interest."

That was something of a disappointment. It would've been quite convenient to have identified the group we were up against. But just because the organization Ekrem associated with wasn't after the heart didn't mean that Ekrem wasn't interested in it for his own gain. In fact, I would have been shocked if he wasn't.

It occurred to me that I hadn't seen the man in a while. "Did Ekrem get on this train?"

Redvers shook his head. "I spoke to him before I joined you, but I haven't seen him since. I assume he made it on to the train. Maral as well."

I had such mixed feelings about our companions—wanting to keep an eye on them, but also not trusting them as far as I could throw them—that I wasn't sure whether to hope they'd both made it or not.

CHAPTER THIRTY-FIVE

We arrived at the station in Szigetvár, a small outpost that nonetheless had a very charming train station to welcome us. It was a long cream-colored building with stone columns holding up a sheltering roof over the platform. We managed to find a local with a horse and cart who was willing to transport our luggage for a few Hungarian korona. The town was so small that there were only a couple options for places to stay, so we directed the man to take our things to the place with the nicest accommodations. This was no small feat since the man spoke no English, although it was finally determined that he spoke a little German, so Lord Hughes was able to step in and communicate for us.

"I didn't know you spoke German, Edward," Millie said as we followed behind the cart the few hundred yards to the hotel.

"Picked up a little during the war, my dear," Edward said, patting her hand where it was nestled in the crook of his elbow.

"That might come in handy," Redvers said quietly.

I looked at him, but he gave his head a little shake.

From what I could see, the town of Szigetvár was entirely charming. There was a small square surrounded by long buildings with red roofs and numerous windows framed by shutters. A small white church sat at an off-kilter angle to the buildings, its steeple capped with dark, bulbous towers with the typical cross reaching into the sky. The trees were already bare, but I imagined that they were quite lovely when it wasn't so late in the season. The farmer deposited our bags at the corner of the square in front of a square two-story building painted cream with brown accents. At the front desk we inquired about rooms, Lord Hughes' German once again coming in handy—it seemed English speakers were light on the ground here in Szigetvár. Eventually we were able to determine that there were only two rooms available, so Maral and Bey elected to find lodging at the place a few doors down. I thanked both of them, but Maral brushed off my thanks.

"We both only need a small room with a single bed. It is no trouble," Maral said, glancing sideways at Bey. He didn't acknowledge either of us, simply picking up his small piece of hand luggage and walking out the door.

We'd been correct then, that Ekrem hadn't packed much for this journey.

Back at the front desk, Lord Hughes was attempting to ask the man if he was familiar with Henry Wunderly. I couldn't understand what he was saying in his broken German, but I did recognize my father's name.

The man shook his head and replied in equally broken German. As he spoke it looked as though he might swallow his bushy moustache. I watched in fascinated horror as it somehow stayed on his upper lip, and almost missed when the man pointed down the street, nearly leaning over the front desk to get his point across. Lord Hughes thanked the man, then turned back to us.

"I think he's saying that we should try a place down the street," Hughes said while Millie beamed at him.

Redvers took our room key from Hughes.

"Good work, Lord Hughes." The men shook hands and we agreed to meet back in the lobby in an hour or so once we'd settled into our rooms. Redvers and I had no need of a porter and carried our bags to the room ourselves. As soon as we passed the threshold, we each set our things down, looked at each other, and nodded before setting off down the street in the direction the clerk had pointed without needing to say another word.

The rooming house the clerk had seemed to be indicating was much simpler accommodations—it looked like a large home that was simply renting out their spare rooms. We knocked and an older woman came to the door.

"No rooms," she said, starting to close the door. I was pleased she obviously knew at least a little bit of English.

Redvers stuck his shoe in the crack before she could close it all the way. The woman glared down at his foot, then up at the man himself. She was unimpressed.

"No room," she repeated more forcefully.

"We do not want a room. We are looking for Professor Wunderly." Redvers was enunciating clearly, since it was clear that English was not widely spoken in this small town, and this woman's vocabulary was most likely extremely limited.

"Professor, yes. No here now." She reached up to tuck some stray hair back beneath the patterned kerchief she wore on her head.

I felt a wash of relief that we'd at least found where my father was staying. It seemed that he'd gotten here under his own steam, and hopefully he hadn't been followed.

Of course, I hoped that we hadn't been followed either.

Redvers thanked the woman and retrieved his foot from the doorway. The woman gave him one last dark look before closing the door.

"At least we know where he's staying," Redvers said.

"It's a relief, although there is still the issue of how to repay the bank."

Redvers took my arm and led me away from the stoop of the house. "Yes, that is certainly still an issue. Not to mention whether one of our own companions is after the heart for himself—we brought him directly to your father."

I sighed. "I do hate it when you're right about things."

This earned me a chuckle. "I know you do."

"Is there a way to keep Bey in the dark?"

"If I think of one, you will be the first to know," he replied.

We strolled back to our hotel where we investigated our room in more detail—plain, but serviceable—and cleaned up a bit. Days of train travel—luxurious though the *Orient Express* had been—had left me yearning for a soak in the bath, but I made do for the moment by scrubbing my face clean and changing into a new wool day dress in burgundy. It was even colder here than in Istanbul and I would not have been surprised if the sky suddenly released a flurry of snow on us. It occurred to me that it was a terrible time of year to dig in the ground, if that was what my father was up to.

We returned to the lobby and found Millie and Lord Hughes waiting for us.

"Are we heading to the boardinghouse the clerk directed us to?" Millie asked.

I looked to Redvers for help, but for once he too seemed to be unsure how to handle my aunt. I decided to handle this one. "We took a little walk down there. She didn't speak English, so we'll just keep an eye out for him."

I felt Redvers' hand pat my back in approval. It was still best that we didn't tell them what we had discovered about where my father was staying, although I wasn't sure just how long we could keep Millie and Hughes in the dark. Not to mention our other companions as well. This was a small town, and continued skullduggery was going to be difficult. But on the walk back I'd decided that we should stick to our plan of keeping things to ourselves. I wanted to talk with my father first and try to figure out if he had a plan to deal with the bank before setting Millie on him.

I insisted that we stop and see if Maral wanted to join us for dinner.

"Why should we? She's an adult," Millie said.

"Because . . ." I faltered, unable to explain to Millie that Maral had saved my life and I felt a debt of gratitude toward the woman, despite still having mixed feelings about her as a person and as my father's paramour.

"Because I believe Professor Wunderly would want us to include her," Redvers said.

I gave him a smile for coming to my rescue as Millie harrumphed but agreed. The number of things we were hiding was exhausting to keep track of—I hoped this would be over soon for a multitude of reasons, not least was that I was looking forward to being able to speak freely again without having to consider every word that came out of my mouth.

We stopped at the small hotel down the street, but Maral wasn't in her room when we inquired. I didn't bother asking if Bey was around—I was hoping to avoid him as much as possible.

The four of us found a restaurant on the charming square and enjoyed a simple meal of goulash, a warm, hearty stew filled with beef, paprika, onions, and potatoes. Even Millie was hungry enough not to fuss about the lack of options available to us, and we all enjoyed a bottle of red wine with our meal, although I was careful to have only one glass. Afterward, Redvers and I excused ourselves, telling Millie and Lord Hughes that we wanted to take a stroll, purposely giving the impression that it might be a *romantic* stroll. Millie gave a knowing nod, and the two of them went back to the hotel alone.

My eyes were narrowed watching my aunt and her fiancé walk away. "That seemed too easy."

Redvers quirked an eyebrow at me. "They might want their own romantic evening."

I was happy for them, but that was a notion that I didn't need to entertain. "Now what?" I asked.

"Now we wait," Redvers said, directing us back toward my father's lodgings.

We set up in a small park opposite the building where we'd inquired earlier about my father. There was a wooden bench with a decent view of the front door where we huddled together for warmth. Because the trees were bare, we didn't have a lot of protection from being seen, but it was already dark and we could pretend to be a pair of lovers there for some time alone.

Which truthfully, we were. Although we kept our attention focused on the boardinghouse.

"Assuming Father has the map," I started to say.

"Which he told us he does."

"Yes, so if he has the map, he'll have to suspend his search soon now that the sun has gone down."

"There are such things as lamps, you know."

I poked him in the ribs with my sharp elbow and heard him chuckle next to me. But I'd been correct in my guess that Father wouldn't be back until after dark. We heard the cart well before we saw it, a wooden contraption similar to the one our luggage had ridden on to the hotel, this one pulled by a pair of oxen with large horns. The slow plodding of the oxen announced their arrival, and when the cart creaked to a stop in front of the boardinghouse, I could see that it was in fact my father that had arrived. Even in the dim light I recognized his lanky form.

As he hopped off the back of the cart he was riding on, I jumped up from where I'd been sitting and had already taken a step forward when I felt Redvers' hand on my arm, restraining me. He didn't have to speak—it only took a moment for me to realize that my father wasn't alone. Two very burly men had also stepped off and were standing on either side of my father. They followed him to the door, and one took up a post to one side of it, while the other followed my father inside.

All the relief I'd felt a moment before popped in my chest like an overfilled balloon. While I was glad to see that my father was alive, the two men he was with were an indication that all was not well. Not well at all.

Chapter Thirty-six

Redvers and I waited in the shadows until my father and his companion reappeared. I could see that my father was now carrying his satchel, a brown leather bag that already had been battered looking ten years ago, although he refused to let me purchase a new one for him. His reasoning was that it was still holding things, so there was no need to replace it.

In other words, it was unmistakably his.

The three men got back into the cart they'd arrived in, and the driver flicked the reins, the oxen plodding off, carrying my father away with it. I looked around frantically, knowing full well there was no chance of finding our own transportation at this time of night in a town as small as this one. I had to stuff down my shriek of frustration.

The cart moved off down the road and Redvers and I stepped out of the shadows.

"I was afraid of that," Redvers said.

I didn't even need to ask what he meant. It explained Redvers' earlier reluctance to get excited about finding my father's lodgings. He must have suspected all along that my father had found trouble here in Szigetvár. I'd been worried that we were bringing along trouble by having Ekrem Bey follow us here, but I hadn't considered that Father might have stumbled into trouble of his own here.

"Now what?" I asked, hands on hips. "How do we figure out where they went when no one in this town speaks a word of English? We can't very well set up out here until he returns. *If* he returns."

"It's not as though he has much to return for either. We have his trunk, so he can't be carrying much."

And we'd just seen him leave with the satchel that I'd noticed missing from his room at the Pera Palace. It was a fair bet that he wouldn't be returning to this lodging house, especially since he was being escorted by two very large men. I had no doubt they were controlling his movements since one of the men had escorted him inside. It was something of a surprise they'd allowed him to return for the satchel, frankly, unless there was something in it that they wanted. Or more likely, whoever these two worked for.

We walked back to our hotel, both lost in our own thoughts and quiet. "We could really use Ziya Bey's language skills right now," Redvers muttered as we mounted the steps toward the front door.

"Do you think his brother has the same aptitude for languages?" I asked.

Redvers held the door open for me and I moved through, then came to a dead stop. There in the tiny sitting area off to the left was none other than Ekrem Bey.

I turned back to look at Redvers behind me. "How did you do that?"

"Magic." Redvers offered me a slight smile before his expression became serious.

We approached the man, and for once, he stood. All this small courtesy did was make me even more suspicious of the man.

Ekrem pursed his lips. "Why don't we go somewhere we can talk?"

"Capital idea." Redvers glanced at me. "Why don't you lead the way, Jane?"

I wasn't sure where this conversation was supposed to take place, but I gave a little shrug and headed up to our room. It was as good a place as any, although I wasn't keen to have the man in my quarters. But there didn't appear to be a better option for a completely private conversation.

I unlocked our door and led our little party inside, Ekrem directly behind me and Redvers bringing up the rear.

Inside our room, I glanced around. There was one chair and the bed—no other seating options. "Should I try to have some chairs brought up?" I asked while I hung my heavy wool coat in the small wardrobe. Redvers slung his onto the bed while Ekrem took a seat in the chair.

"Not necessary," Redvers said, leaning against the wall near the door, arms folded over his chest. He looked casual, but I knew he was poised and ready for whatever might happen. I could feel it in the way he held himself.

I perched on the edge of bed and wondered what was going to happen next. I suspected that whatever it was, I wasn't going to like it.

"I'm guessing you are here to tell us about something you've learned in the few hours since we've seen you last," Redvers said.

Ekrem's teeth shone as he bore them at Redvers. "Not a bad guess, although it is less about what I have learned and more about what I can do for you."

I heard myself give a little snort. "And what might that be?" It was pretty late in the game to be offering us information. He didn't know who had been following my father, which was likely who was responsible for the men who were escorting Father. Without that, what could he offer us at this late stage? We'd laid eyes on my father, and just needed to determine where in the area he'd gone.

"I speak a little Hungarian," Ekrem said.

I felt my face wrinkle in distaste—that was the one thing

he could offer us that we needed. As we had just been discussing.

"You don't believe that I can speak the language?" Ekrem asked, mock offended at my questioning his skills. He proceeded to rattle off a few sentences in what could have been Polish, for all I knew.

"And why should that matter to us?" I asked, still not willing to concede the truth or give up my combative take against this man.

"Because you need a translator." Ekrem was now simply amused.

"How do you know we need a translator?"

Ekrem gave a casual laugh. "How else will you ask the locals anything? There is maybe one person here who speaks even rudimentary English. I was there, remember, when I watched you all fumble around? You are lucky Hughes speaks some German, but that won't be of much more use to you."

"Why didn't you step in before?"

Bey smiled again. "It was amusing to watch." He gave a shrug. "But if you want to ask questions around town, you are going to need someone who speaks the local language."

I couldn't argue with him. I thought the chances were good that we were going to need a translator—we certainly were going to need to talk to the locals to see if we could determine where in the area my father was working. As we had walked back to the hotel, I had considered whether we might be able to find the ox-cart driver tomorrow and ask where he'd taken the men. But Ekrem was right; we wouldn't be able to do that without speaking some of the language.

"And just how is it that you speak Hungarian?" I asked.

"I had an aunt who married into the family who was from Hungary. I liked to spend time in her kitchen, and she taught me her language, not to mention some cooking skills." Ekrem smirked. "I also have a, shall we say, knack for languages. My brother was not the only one."

I'd been sorry when Ziya had been killed, and it was terrible to admit this, but I'd never been sorrier than in that very moment that Ziya had been the one murdered in that elevator, knowing that we might have been dealing with him instead of Ekrem. I pushed away my awful thoughts and focused on the man before me.

"What do you want in return?" Redvers asked. It was exactly what I'd been wondering myself.

"A cut, of course." Ekrem held up a hand at the look of outrage on my face. "Just a very small percentage."

"That's assuming that Father has anything to give a cut of. You know very well that he lost the money he invested." I'd wondered before whether Ekrem knew that we might lose our home because of the money my father had taken out.

"This will be much harder to lose, I think. And I have no doubts that he will have something to split."

But Ekrem would say nothing further on the subject, no matter how we pressed the issue. We might never know if he'd heard something about Father in the few hours since we'd been here or if he was simply making a guess based upon what he'd already learned. I continued to refuse to agree to his terms, but even that didn't seem to bother him. He seemed to think it didn't matter what I thought—in the end it only mattered whether Redvers would agree later.

I couldn't think of the last man I'd met that had raised my blood pressure so thoroughly. Especially not one whose help we were actually in need of.

CHAPTER THIRTY-SEVEN

We agreed to meet the next morning. Even though we clearly couldn't trust the man, and I was not willing to give him a percentage of anything, the truth was we needed Ekrem's translation skills—that was all there was to it. We were stuck with him.

The next question was how we could redirect my aunt Millie while we questioned the townspeople? There was nothing in the way of local tourism for her to do, and I wasn't particularly keen on the idea of her accompanying us on our rounds about town asking questions. What could she be tasked with?

It turned out that once again I was expending energy worrying about something that took care of itself.

"Edward and I are going to tour a local winery today," Millie announced as soon as we'd taken our seats at the breakfast table. Our options in town were limited to a few places—we'd decided to try a small café three blocks away this time. The seating and décor were fairly rustic and simple, but I hoped the food would be as good as it had been the night before.

"That sounds lovely," I said, pleased that they'd eliminated the need for us to make up some sort of excuse to get them out of the way.

"It appears the only thing worth seeing in this area of the

country. Besides the castle, that is." Millie spread her napkin on her lap. "I assume you will be talking to the locals today, and you hardly need us for that task."

My jaw had apparently come loose, because Redvers reached over and tapped it gently and my mouth closed again.

"Unattractive, Jane." Millie commented before turning her attention to buttering a piece of bread from the basket that had been delivered. "As I was saying, we'll have a fine time at the winery. Perhaps we will see you back here for dinner this evening."

I wondered just how much wine Millie was planning on drinking, but once again decided to accept the gift I was given.

"I hope they have a nice port," Lord Hughes mused.

"Who can say if they've even heard of port, this far out in the middle of nowhere," Millie retorted. "We'll be lucky to get anything better than bathtub moonshine."

"I enjoy your optimism, dear." Lord Hughes was obviously teasing my aunt. But instead of the biting comment I anticipated, she smiled at him.

I couldn't stop my head from giving a little shake. Wonders never ceased. I couldn't completely wrap my head around the pairing of these two, but it obviously worked for them.

"It's too bad that we couldn't simply go to the castle and look for Henry," Millie said as her eggs came. She poked at them for a moment with her fork, then reached for the salt and pepper. I watched suspiciously, worried she might send them back if they weren't up to her standards, but she took a bite and gave a brisk nod before continuing with what she was saying. "Perhaps Edward and I will tour the fortress if we are here many more days."

I murmured something polite and turned to my own food.

After breakfast, Millie and Lord Hughes found a structurally sound horse-drawn carriage that met my aunt's approval and the two headed off in the direction of the winery that lay some miles out of town. I hoped the carriage driver was willing to wait for their return, otherwise I wasn't certain how they would get back. But that was not my concern.

I turned to Redvers, about to comment that I hoped Ekrem Bey actually kept his word, whatever that might be worth, when I heard footsteps on the wood planks behind us.

"Good morning," Ekrem said. "You thought I would not come?" The sardonic tone was back, along with the raised eyebrow.

I narrowed my eyes slightly, but Redvers stepped in before I could reply. "Pleased to see you. I presume you slept well?"

Ever the diplomat, Redvers.

The men made some more polite small talk, although Redvers did ask if Bey had seen Maral that morning.

"I saw her at breakfast," Ekrem said.

"Did you speak to her?"

"For what purpose?" Ekrem asked.

I shook my head impatiently, eager to get moving. Redvers glanced at me, then smiled at the man, which was more than I was willing to do. "Jane is anxious to get to work. I suggest we start with Professor Wunderly's landlady. I believe the only words in English she understands are 'rooms' and 'no.'"

When we knocked on the door, the same woman answered in the same kerchief and apron. Only her dress had changed. She was even more forceful today, perhaps disbelieving that we still didn't understand. "No room."

Ekrem stepped in and spoke to her in what sounded like reasonably fluent Hungarian. The woman was taken aback, dropping open her mouth a bit to show that most of her teeth were missing, but she did open the door nearly all the way to look at him and then us. She rattled something off in reply and Ekrem answered once more before turning to us.

"She says that Professor Wunderly was staying here, but he is not any longer and she already cleaned his room."

If she had already cleaned, there was little sense in taking a look at it. I doubted this woman left a single dust bunny to be found.

"Did he leave anything behind?" I asked.

Ekrem repeated the question, and the woman shook her head no quite firmly. Bey spoke again, I assumed to thank the woman for her help, and she gave a small nod before shutting the door once more.

"He did not."

We stepped away from the front door and paused in the street. "Who next?" I asked.

Apparently, the answer was everyone because it seemed as though that was who we spoke to—nearly every single person in that town, including those that had nothing to do with anything we needed to know. We never did get any direct information, but we picked up a few tidbits here and there that felt like they might be useful.

Such as there had recently been an influx of strange men— or at least, men who were strangers to the area. Then, just as suddenly as they'd taken over the rooming houses of Szigetvár, they'd disappeared. One or two of the townspeople speculated that they were a group of smugglers, although it was hard to tell whether this was simply the excitement that type of enterprise might provide an otherwise sleepy town, or something that might be true.

Either way, it seemed that Ekrem had decided to drop the sarcasm and toying attitude and appeared to be offering straightforward translations all day. Of course, it was impossible to say whether or not that was true, but it felt more sincere than any other interaction we'd had with the man so far. It was entirely possible that he was holding back information for himself, but given the little we'd collected—and the general demeanor of the people we'd spoken with—I didn't think he was getting anything of great value.

What made Ekrem Bey tick was an absolute mystery to me. But not one that I was interested in getting to the bottom of.

By the afternoon we were tired and dusty from the dirt roads we'd been treading, but at least all the moving around had kept us warm. I could feel that my cheeks were rosy from the wind and the exercise, and it actually felt good to take off my wool coat when we regrouped at the same restaurant from the evening before. I decided on the stuffed cabbage leaves and a small bowl of goulash since all the walking and interviewing had left me starving.

"Your father isn't in town anymore," Redvers said once we'd ordered.

"And we're obviously at a disadvantage since we don't have the map and none of us ever laid eyes on it."

"Except possibly Maral," Ekrem said darkly.

"You think she saw it?" I was surprised at his accusation, but it did make me wonder how she was passing the time— we hadn't seen her since we'd arrived the night before, although Bey had seen her at breakfast. I had no intention of asking for her assistance or even letting her join us in our search, but I also didn't like being in the dark about what she was up to. Could she have known all along and simply joined my father? It wouldn't be the first time that it seemed as though she knew something and kept it to herself, letting us flounder.

"Perhaps after lunch we should inquire about her." I went back to our original discussion. "Wherever my father is being held, it's within driving distance of a horse and cart."

Redvers agreed. "Probably within several miles of here."

"But that's still too large of an area to search."

The scraping of a chair being dragged to our table interrupted my meditation on the matter. I looked up to find my aunt Millie settling herself into a chair.

"Not to worry," Millie said. "I think I know where he is."

Chapter Thirty-eight

"You do?" Those two words could not have contained more surprise.

Millie smiled, hands folded comfortably over her stomach, looking like the cat who got the canary. Lord Hughes had squeezed another chair into our group and was taking his own seat. "These chairs are quite uncomfortable," Millie told him.

"Hang the chairs, Aunt Millie! Where is he?" I asked.

She pursed her lips but continued without chastising me. "I think he is at the winery. And if I'm not mistaken, he's being held there."

I remembered that we hadn't shared any of our concerns about the trouble Father might have found here—including the two large men we had seen him with.

Redvers spoke up. "Why do you think that?"

"Because we were not allowed into the main house where the owners reside."

"That's not so strange that they wouldn't allow people into where they live," I said.

Millie gave me a quelling look. "But they also would not let us into the wine cellar. Now, what kind of winery does not let people tour the wine cellar? The *wine cellar*. Preposterous."

I had to admit that she had a point there. Was it possible

that my father was being held in a cold, dank wine cellar? In late November? This only added concerns for his health to my list of worries—not only was he being held captive but he was also running the risk of catching pneumonia on top of everything else.

This trip seemed to deliver nothing but bad news on top of bad news.

But I was curious why Millie had decided that Father was being held there. "Why do you think he's being held? Even if he is at the winery, maybe he's fine."

"Obviously you haven't been telling us everything," Millie said, not even bothering to give me a lecture about this. "And Henry is not exactly the most observant person—he never has been—so I can't imagine that he would have gotten this far without being followed." I was going to open my mouth to say something, but Millie barreled over me. "And there were two very large men, had a very caveman look about them, and they seemed to be simply lurking on the property. I couldn't get an answer from our tour guide about what they were there for." Millie sat back, looking pleased with herself. "I can only assume that Henry has found some trouble here. And that he's being held there, or he would have heard me and greeted me."

If my father had been on the property, there was little chance he would have missed my aunt's voice. She certainly wasn't wrong about that. Millie had taken a lot of leaps in her conclusions but had arrived at basically the same place I had, and I had all the information.

I didn't confirm or deny anything she'd said. But I did admit that we needed to come up with a plan to infiltrate the winery and search it thoroughly. All sorts of suggestions were floated, including a Trojan horse type scenario that was immediately shot down by Redvers. It was ultimately decided that simply sneaking onto the grounds after nightfall and taking a look around was our best bet.

The real battle was over who was going to participate in our little venture.

"I am perfectly capable of being quiet," Millie insisted, quite indignant that we were trying to exclude her.

"Of course, you are, dear." Lord Hughes sounded more sincere than I think any of the rest of us could have managed. "But I just don't want to risk seeing you hurt." Millie gave him a suspicious look but seemed slightly mollified by his concern for her safety.

There was not even a small chance that I was going to be so easily talked into staying behind. Redvers knew this, and I caught his raised eyebrow and amused look, giving him a little shake of my head in return. I was going—there was no use in his even suggesting otherwise.

After some time, we finally managed to hammer out a plan. Ekrem would find us a horse and cart that we could hire for the evening, since the winery was over an hour's walk outside of town, and if we did find my father, we might need to make a quick getaway. We didn't want a driver with the cart though, so it was going to prove challenging to find a local willing to let a group of strangers take their conveyance off into the night without supervision. Either very difficult or very expensive.

It was decided that waiting until nightfall was our best option. There had been quite a bit of argument about whether we should go during the day, perhaps take another tour of the winery as a cover, but it was finally agreed that it would be even more conspicuous if one or two of our party left the tour to go investigating. We were much more likely to get caught, especially since whoever was holding my father would be even more alert during the day with strangers on the property. It was astounding that they were still conducting the tours if they were holding a captive, which caused some doubt in my mind as to whether we were correct about this whole scenario. But there were too many warning signs for us to ignore it completely—we had to check out the winery.

Ekrem Bey and Millie would stay behind. I had insisted that Ekrem not join us since I didn't trust the man and never would. There was no way that I was taking the chance that he might be working for the other side—we needed people on this trip who we could trust at our backs. Ekrem Bey was not one of them, despite the apparent help he'd given us that day. He'd argued briefly, then given up with a casual shrug. I made a mental note to pull my aunt aside and ask her to keep an eye on the man so that he didn't ambush us from behind.

Our group broke off for the afternoon, and I insisted that Redvers and I check on Maral. She didn't answer the knock at her door, and the clerk at the front desk spoke just enough English for us to understand that the last time he had seen Maral, she appeared to have gone for a walk. I wanted to ask more questions, but that would have required entirely more English than the man understood. It was the first time that I wished Ekrem was with us, but he'd gone off to complete his own task.

There was nothing left to do but to wait.

It was nearly dinnertime when Ekrem reported back that he'd found a farmer on the outskirts of town willing to let us take his donkey and cart off into the night. I didn't ask but I imagined a significant amount of money had to exchange hands to secure the deal.

"Can you ask at your hotel about Maral?" I asked.

Ekrem looked between Redvers and me. "You did not find her?"

"The clerk said she had gone for a walk, but I would like to talk with her," I said.

Ekrem looked exhausted but agreed to make inquiries at the front desk about the woman's whereabouts and get back to us. I had the feeling that something was wrong, although it may have been an overreaction on my part. Ekrem saw her at breakfast and then the clerk saw her in the afternoon. I relayed my thoughts to Redvers.

He frowned. "It is strange that she isn't trying to get involved with our search."

"Unless she really did see the map and simply joined Father without telling us."

Redvers didn't comment on this, but the crease between his brows deepened.

Millie and Lord Hughes joined us for a quiet dinner after nightfall, conversation at a minimum, which did nothing to soothe my nerves about the task ahead of us. I did ask Millie to keep an eye on Ekrem while we were gone, and she agreed to do her best. I could only hope her best was good enough.

When we'd finished eating, we met Ekrem in front of our hotel. He'd fetched the donkey and cart from the owner while we ate.

"Here you go. Good luck," he said, handing the reins to Redvers. "It's not the most agreeable animal."

I watched this exchange and then asked what he'd learned about Maral.

"Nothing. The clerk did not see her return from her walk, and I checked her room and she wasn't in."

I wondered aloud if we should have gone into her room to see if anything was amiss, but it was too late now—we needed to go ahead with our plan.

"I can do that while you're gone," Ekrem said.

I narrowed my eyes at him suspiciously. He'd been entirely too helpful since we'd arrived here in Szigetvár, the sardonic attitude mostly having fallen away. I didn't trust it.

"I'll go with him," Millie said decidedly.

I nodded. That was the best we could do right now. I just hoped Millie watched her back.

Lord Hughes and Redvers sat on the bench in front and I

perched on the uncomfortable wooden seat in the back. We set off, the cart bumping over the unpaved dirt roads out into the countryside, where we were quickly swallowed by darkness once the smattering of lights from the town disappeared behind us. The silence was eerie, the only sound the rhythmic clop of the donkey's feet and the rattle of the cart, none of us saying a word, concentrating on the task ahead of us and trying to ignore the cold. After what felt like an eternity, I heard Lord Hughes mutter, "Nearly there."

We didn't dare bring the cart too near the house where the owners lived, so instead we pulled off the road next to a field of ground-hugging grapevines, twisted and menacing in the moonlight. Redvers tied one end of the donkey's reigns to a fence post and threw some straw we had brought along at its feet, giving the animal enough slack that it could graze on the straw if it so desired. Instead, it twitched its large ears back and forth several times before shutting its eyes and appearing to go to sleep. It certainly didn't seem as difficult as Ekrem had warned us it would be—I hoped the animal wouldn't change its attitude while we were gone and find a way to take off. I also fervently hoped nothing would come along and spook it, for that matter. We were going to need this donkey later, one way or another.

A dirt track off to the left led away between fields of bare vines and up a hill, and we followed it on foot. These fields were probably lovely in the summer months, vines covered in lush leaves and hanging heavy with grapes, but I was not enjoying them now, bare and shrunken in the cold. I shivered, listening intently for any noise beyond our own footsteps.

We said nothing as we walked. It wasn't necessary since we had already discussed our plan of attack hours before. We would search the wine cellar first; then, if there was nothing to be found there, we would attempt to search the house. It had seemed wise to leave the residence for last—if we could avoid where the owners lived altogether, all the better.

The main house, built of stone with the signature red roof, was near a dirt road at the front—we had approached from a different road running along the backside of the fields. Some distance behind the house was what I could only assume was the winery, another stone building sitting close to the fields, ready to process the grapes from the acres of vines we walked amongst. The three of us cautiously approached a small brick outbuilding that stood a few yards from the winery, nothing more than a shed, really, that barely offered all three of us cover. There we waited, watching for movement on the property.

It was not long before we were rewarded for our efforts. A man stepped from the heavy wood door leading into the wine cellar. There was no urgency to his movements, and the brief, bright spark and ensuing small glow indicated that he had probably just come outside for a smoke.

But he had come out of the building where we knew the wine cellar was located. And there was no good reason to be in a wine cellar at this time of night unless you were searching for something.

We were still at a bit of a distance, but even from our vantage point and in the darkness, the man looked large and well-muscled. I would have wagered money that we were looking at one of the men who had escorted my father from his lodgings the day before. But where was the other man, and how were we going to get past the burly pair?

Redvers leaned close to Lord Hughes and whispered in the man's ear while I wrinkled my nose with impatience. Once he had finished, Redvers moved to my side and began whispering in my ear.

"Hughes and I will make our way around the back and subdue the guards. You stay here and I'll signal you when it's safe."

I thought about arguing but glanced down and saw moonlight glinted off a pistol in his hand. I decided in this instance that Redvers probably had a good point—he was armed, and there wasn't much I could offer by way of subduing the two giants without a weapon of my own. Although I made a mental note to complain later that I hadn't been armed as well—especially since I could see that Lord Hughes was also carrying a gun. Redvers would certainly hear about this later.

I gave him a nod, and Hughes and Redvers slipped from behind the shed toward the house, keeping to the row of trees that lined the edge of the property. They soon disappeared from my view, but I mentally tracked where I thought they were and within a few minutes I caught a glimpse of movement in front of the wine cellar where the man was now finishing up his cigarette. He turned to go back through the door but there was a flash of movement and he fell to the ground instead. Redvers had brought the butt of his gun down hard on the back of the man's head and both he and Lord Hughes now each had an arm and were dragging him behind the building.

One down, one to go. Or so I hoped.

Chapter Thirty-nine

Redvers didn't send me any kind of signal, but I made my way all the same through the line of trees along the property back to where the men were hiding the body of the guard. They had just dropped the man's arms to the ground when I arrived where they stood. From here we weren't visible to the main house or any of the other outlying structures.

Redvers gave me a dark look for ignoring his instructions, but I shrugged. "You need a guard for the guard," I whispered.

He ignored this and bent down, rolling the guard onto his side to tie the man's arms behind his back. I wondered where he'd found the rope, but it was entirely possible that he'd brought it with him and hidden it inside his apparently bottomless pockets. I hadn't known that the men were armed either—so who knew what other supplies they'd brought along?

"Can you manage to stay here at least?" Redvers pointed to the ground where we stood.

"Certainly." My whisper was indignant, and even in the dim moonlight I could tell that Redvers was clenching his teeth. Lord Hughes simply looked amused.

Redvers and Hughes set themselves up at the corner of the building and I sat down with my back to the rough stone wall, the guard tied up and unconscious at my feet. He was out cold, not even stirring when I nudged him with the toe of my T-strap shoe, so I turned my head to watch the men.

They didn't have long to wait before the other guard appeared, looking for the first. The first man had clearly been expected back after he'd finished his cigarette, which was exactly what Redvers and Hughes had been counting on. The second guard stepped into the moonlight and I could see he was carrying a shovel. I hoped he wouldn't be able to get a swing in before Redvers and Lord Hughes were able to subdue him. It was a large shovel and looked as though it could do quite a bit of damage.

Redvers obviously had the same thought because instead of waiting until the guard approached the back of the building where we were hiding and taking an open swing at the man, Redvers simply stepped from the shadows brandishing his gun.

"Don't move." Redvers' voice was quiet but authoritative, and the large man immediately stopped in his tracks and held up the hand that wasn't clutching the shovel's handle. "Drop the shovel," Redvers instructed, and the man did so slowly. The guard was seemingly trying to decide what his odds against Redvers were when Lord Hughes stepped from the shadows as well, pistol at the ready. The man's body relaxed into a posture of resignation and I felt my shoulders drop as well. The guard might have taken a chance against one man with a gun, but he wasn't prepared to take on *two* armed men.

Not a complete fool, then.

I stood up and again toed the guard that was laying on the ground at my feet. He didn't move, although I did cautiously put a hand to his chest to make sure he was still breathing. It only took a moment for me to decide to leave him there unattended and follow Redvers and Lord Hughes. Hopefully the guard wouldn't wake up before we determined what was happening in the wine cellar.

I stuck my head around the corner and watched as Redvers indicated with his pistol that the man should lead us back into the building. I hurried to catch up with the men, falling in behind Lord Hughes. Our guard started to drop his hands at one point, but Redvers reminded the man to keep them up and he complied. From what I could see, Redvers' gun never wavered from the man's back, nor did he get too close, which would have opened him up to being suddenly disarmed.

Immediately beyond the doorway into the wine cellar you could see that we were going to be descending, and quickly. The entrance was only a small room immediately leading to a brick-lined passage leading down. I took a deep breath and reconsidered whether I wanted to subject myself to what was clearly going to be close quarters. I didn't do well in tight spaces.

But in the quiet I could hear the sounds of work being done—metal against hard earth, and faint voices. They were still too distant to make out who they might belong to, but my heart picked up. Could one of them belong to my father? I took a deep breath, thought about lengthening out my breathing, and stepped into the passageway after the others.

We descended the narrow passage in a little phalanx. It was obvious that we were proceeding belowground as the air here felt stale and smelled of earth, although I was surprised that it wasn't much colder than it already was outside. The floor was hard packed dirt, smoothed over from many years of foot traffic, and the ancient, discolored bricks arching above us and down the walls were lit with occasional torches. After an initial sharp descent, we came into an area where the floor leveled out and the walls widened out—my breathing evened out as well and I was able to stop counting each inhale and exhale. Looking around, I could see large barrels of wine lining the walls; some looked quite old and I briefly wondered how long they would sit there aging.

The faint voices I'd heard earlier were getting louder and I was now able to recognize one of the speakers—the loudest in fact—as my father. It took everything in me not to race ahead of the men, but I managed to stay back, reminding myself that they were the ones who were armed and we still had a captive.

The men slowed, and I braced myself for whatever we might find around the bend.

CHAPTER FORTY

The trio of men ahead of me came to a rather abrupt stop at the bend in the passage just beyond the last large wooden cask. I took a bracing breath before stepping out from behind them. I'd feared we would find my father weakened and under guard, but instead he was hale and hearty, leaning against a shovel as he watched a small group of people dig along the foundation of the far wall. The room was well lit with lanterns and more torches along the brick walls that had been darkened by soot and age.

"I think we might need to move farther along to the west." Henry Wunderly pulled a folded paper from his pocket and tilted it toward the light for a better look.

I stood in shocked silence. I was obviously delighted to see my father alive and well, especially after the anxiety and worry that had dogged me this entire journey. But not only was my father fine, he appeared to be enjoying himself. I had to admit that this got under my skin and rankled—was I the only one concerned that we were about to lose our home?

"Father?" I finally said. He didn't hear me so I repeated myself, louder this time to be heard over the sounds of the shovels. He turned and gave a start at the sight of us. I wasn't sure how he'd missed our approach, although like Millie had pointed out earlier, Father wasn't the most observant of men.

The other individuals behind him were hard at work, so it was understandable that we hadn't been noticed.

"Jane?" He came forward, stopping when he realized that Redvers was still holding his gun on the burly guard. "Jane, why is this man pointing a gun at Andor?"

"Andor?" I asked incredulously. "You mean this man is with you?"

"Well, certainly. We hired him and his cousin to assist us with security. Can't be too careful, you know." My father frowned. "Although it seems they aren't quite worth what they're being paid, are they?"

At my continued silence, which was punctuated by my mouth hanging slightly agape, my father continued, brow creased. "Hired them back in Stamboul, you know, although they are Hungarian. None of the locals here really speak any English."

"So we discovered," I said wryly, finally recovering my wits enough to step forward and give my father a hug. I held on tightly for a moment, reassuring myself that he was all right. After giving myself that moment, I stepped back again and found the presence of mind to start asking questions. "Then you're fine?"

"Absolutely, my dear." My father still had an arm around my shoulder, but he let it drop and looked at me shrewdly. "Although I do wish you hadn't come. Didn't you get my messages?"

By this point, the digging behind him had stopped, everyone watching the scene we presented. A glance to my right showed that Redvers had dropped his weapon to his side and Lord Hughes had done the same. Their expressions matched how I felt—confused and perhaps a little bit irritated.

My father's question lit the spark of my anger. "You wish I hadn't come?" My voice was disbelieving. "I've spent *weeks* worrying about the mess you've made! You left Istanbul without your things, Ziya has been killed, and we're about to lose our home." The words had left me before I remembered that we didn't want Hughes and Millie to know that part of things. But I maintained my indignance—fine, now Hughes knew that our row house was at stake.

He smiled at me. "Well, you can see that wasn't necessary, Jane. I'm quite fine." Then he frowned. "What do you mean Ziya was killed? He said he would help you, but no one was supposed to get hurt."

I sputtered, but he ignored this and turned back to the group that was now leaning on their own shovels, watching us with avid interest. I took a moment to actually look at the men and realized that I recognized two of them—Professor Matthew Kelley from the anthropology department and Professor Michael Blanchard whose specialty was the classics, specifically ancient music. Both men worked at the same university as my father.

"You remember Professors Blanchard and Kelley." Both men gave me friendly waves but continued to watch the proceedings. My father tipped his head at the last man. "And that's Michael Dillman. History professor, you know." Dillman gave a smile and a nod and the three men returned to digging, although somewhat slowly. I could tell that they were still keeping one ear on what was happening over here.

I glanced at Redvers and found that his face was unreadable. I sighed, then cast about looking for Andor, realizing he was now gone. Redvers answered my unasked question. "He went upstairs to untie his comrade. And to retrieve his shovel, presumably."

I hoped he came back with only his shovel and no hard feelings. Lord Hughes had wandered closer to the digging site, asking questions about whether they had found anything so far.

"We have. It's obvious that this vineyard was built on top of Turbek," Professor Kelley started to explain before my father broke in excitedly.

"Turbek was built by the Ottomans on top of Suleiman's burial site. It was an entire little city with a mosque and all, right there, but one hundred years later it was destroyed by the Crusaders. We knew that it had to be some distance from the fortress in Szigetvár, and on a hilltop, but we couldn't determine the exact location until we had the map." He pulled the folded paper from his pocket once again and passed it to Lord Hughes. "This is a copy, of course."

Hughes studied the map while Professor Kelley took over explaining what they'd found so far. "We've found some sherds and building blocks from the original walls, but not what we're after, obviously," said Professor Kelley. "We're optimistic that we're closing in, though."

Lord Hughes said something encouraging and they continued their discussion, Blanchard and Dillman chiming in here and there. Redvers stood bemusedly at my side, hands clasped behind his back, taking in the scene. I felt like flapping my arms in frustration. What was happening here? None of these men were archaeologists, and how had the four of them come to be together in the countryside of Hungary searching for the mystical sultan's heart?

My thoughts were interrupted by my father, who had returned to my side. "Aren't you going to introduce me to your friend?" he asked.

I stared at him for a moment, quite close to snarling, when Redvers laid a hand on my arm. It grounded me and I took a deep breath and made the introductions. "Father, this is Redvers. Redvers, this is my father, Professor Henry Wunderly."

The men shook hands and I rubbed my forehead. This was all incredibly surreal. I started mentally running through all the things we hadn't been able to figure out up until now— and there were many.

"Why did you leave your luggage at the hotel?"

"As a ploy, my dear. So it would look as though I'd disappeared." He rocked back on his heels. "I thought it was quite clever of me."

"To who? Why would you need to make it look like that? Do you know who was following you?" I looked at Redvers, then back to my father. "Redvers picked up on the men following us right away."

My father cleared his throat. "Yes, well, about that." I stared at him until he continued, looking slightly abashed. "I might have had something to do with that."

CHAPTER FORTY-ONE

"Do you mean to tell me that *you* had us followed? What on earth for?" My voice had reached an unpleasant pitch and I took a deep breath.

"Because I couldn't take the chance that you'd lead the bad guys right to us." My father gave a little shrug and looked at Redvers apologetically, then frowned. "Now what's this about Ziya being hurt?"

"He was murdered at the Pera Palace after helping us translate the tile. One of the men following us was killed as well," Redvers said.

"What?" Father finally looked shocked. "I didn't think Jane was serious."

I didn't have a civil response to that.

"I'm very sorry to hear that," Henry said soberly. "I liked Ziya; he was a good translator. And something of a friend." He was quiet for a moment. "Do you know who did it?"

Redvers related what we knew about both of the incidents in Istanbul, leaving out the part about Maral saving my life by stabbing a man on the *Orient Express*. I assumed he was leaving that for me to relate to my father, although I thought Redvers was doing a fine job explaining things in a concise manner and should just go ahead with it. My tongue was fairly tied with frustration at the moment.

After hearing the description of the man killed in the alley, my father rubbed his chin. "He wasn't one of ours. I'll bet he was working for the other side."

"One of ours? The other side? Father, what are you talking about?" I was reaching the limits of my exasperation.

My father motioned us both closer, glancing behind him at his friends who were hard at work digging at the foundation behind him. It was obvious he wasn't keen for them to hear what he was about to relate to us.

"I did take out a loan against the house and invested it in what I thought was sure to be a lucrative investment."

"And you were swindled instead," I couldn't help saying.

Father ignored me, focusing on Redvers and keeping his voice low. "The fellow turned out to be a thief and made off with my money. Ziya's, too."

I nearly sighed out loud. So Ekrem had been right that my father had been the one to get Ziya involved in this scheme. I said a silent apology to the dead man, then muttered aloud, "I never should have left you alone."

Henry ignored that, too. "Now, I know the bank wants their money, but I knew that if I could actually find the heart that I would be able to recoup my money."

"How do you figure that?" Redvers asked.

"Oh, any museum will pay a fortune for it," Father said, but his voice was just a little too loud.

"I thought we were going to give it to a museum," Blanchard broke in. "Donate it, like we discussed."

My father's face flamed a bit red, just as mine did when I was embarrassed. "Well, I ran into some trouble, so we'll have to discuss that later."

Professor Blanchard's blue eyes gave my father an icy stare before giving up a moment later and returning to work with a shake of his head. It would appear that his friends knew him well.

"You invested all the money you took out against our house to find the heart, and when it was stolen you decided to do it yourself," I said.

"Yes." My father smiled at me, looking pleased. "And since we have the map now, we're sure to succeed. Especially since we're here ahead of the others."

"That's insane," I told him. "For one thing, none of you are trained archaeologists."

My father looked offended. "Dillman there has studied some archaeology, for your information." I glanced over, but Dillman hadn't even looked up from his work. "And we're doing good work. We've already recovered one other artifact that I'm sure has some value on its own."

I rubbed my forehead again. "How did you talk these three into this crazy scheme?"

Redvers didn't give my father a chance to answer, which was fine since I wasn't certain I wanted the answer. "Andor has been gone an awfully long time," Redvers said.

"Perhaps he couldn't wake his cousin up." Even as I made the suggestion, I was also trying to calculate just how long the man had been upstairs. Redvers and I held eye contact, each of us obviously concerned that something else had happened, but my father waved a hand.

"Oh, I'm certain everything is fine," he said. "Who knows, the pair of them might have left after being treated so roughly by you lot." Father looked amused at the prospect of his muscular guards being handled so efficiently by the three of us, but he didn't inquire as to why Redvers was so well-equipped to do so. I wasn't sure how I would have explained Redvers and his profession anyway.

Lord Hughes rejoined our group. "That man has been gone an awfully long time." Hughes looked at my father and held out his hand. "Edward Hughes. I'm engaged to your sister."

My father shook Lord Hughes' hand politely and the men

exchanged pleasantries. But as soon as he was able to, Father hissed in my ear, "You brought Millie along?"

"Did you think I'd be able to stop her from coming?" I whispered back.

My father sighed. "I suppose not," he muttered as we both put on smiles for the others. Father picked up his shovel and stepped over to the trench the other men were standing in, obviously intending to finally lend some support. The clank of Kelley's shovel brought everyone to a momentary standstill as Kelley and Dillman began to dig around something solid and square in shape. Everyone's breath held as they tried to determine what they'd found.

I realized that despite the emotional ups and downs of the last few minutes, even I was excited to see what they'd uncovered.

The only one who wasn't paying attention was Redvers. His attention was focused behind us on the staircase at the far end of the cellar. I didn't see anything and turned back to the men, stepping closer so I could get a better view of what was happening. In my peripheral vision I saw Redvers step beside a cask and pull his gun from his pocket, letting it hang at his side.

"Just another brick," Blanchard said in disgust, sticking the head of his shovel firmly in the ground. "I'm done for tonight." He ran a hand over his reddish blond hair, then removed his spectacles to clean the dirt off of them with the edge of his shirt. I wasn't sure the shirt was much cleaner than the spectacles, but he seemed pleased with the results.

Dillman started to argue with him. "Come on, let's keep going. We've barely done anything today. And if you hadn't drunk so much this afternoon, perhaps you wouldn't be so tired."

Blanchard shot back that his afternoons were none of Dillman's concern, and their argument continued from there.

Kelley ignored everyone and continued to dig in his corner, having moved the large brick out of the trench with my father's help. The momentary excitement that the men might have actually found the sultan's heart had turned to disappointment quickly, and I turned to see that Redvers had moved back around the bend and ducked down behind a wine barrel.

Which is when I realized that someone was coming down the ramp. I followed Redvers' lead, stepping to the opposite side of the room, and taking cover behind the large cask of wine opposite Redvers'. In the dim torchlight I could see that it was most likely a woman, but for some reason her hands were being held behind her. When the woman stepped fully from the bottom of the sloped passage and came to stand on the packed earth floor, I could see that it was Maral. I nearly stepped out of my hiding spot, but Redvers put out a hand to stop me. I glanced to my left, but no one else in our party had noticed that we were being joined by another person.

Make that *persons*. Other feet were descending the ramp behind Maral, and when she turned back toward the person descending behind her, I could see what I hadn't before.

Maral's hands were bound behind her.

CHAPTER FORTY-TWO

What had seemed like one set of feet turned into many, as an entire group of men came down the ramp behind Maral, initially using her as a shield but eventually pushing her out of the way. They were armed, and if I had to guess, made up the "other group" my father had mentioned. But how had they gotten a hold of Maral—and when? While she was out on her walk? It had to have been, although I wondered how they would have managed to subdue the woman— there was no way Maral would have gone without a fight.

The group was advancing toward us and Redvers cleared his throat loudly from his place behind the cask. My father's friends finally stopped what they were doing and my father cocked his head at them in confusion. Even without being able to see everything from where I crouched, I realized we were desperately outmanned. The newcomers were armed and my father and his friends were academics. It was unlikely they would be useful in a fight, and especially not one against armed thugs.

Redvers had disappeared into the shadows immediately after giving the warning signal, and I was hopeful that he hadn't been seen at all. We needed at least one secret weapon. Because whoever this group was, I didn't think they were here for a polite chat about the winemaking process.

Maral was being pushed forward, and my father said her

name in surprise, starting to rush forward, but I stepped out from my place of cover and caught his arm before he could get very far. He tried to shake me loose.

"Jane, I know this woman," he started to explain, but I cut him off.

"Yes, I know exactly who she is," I said, refusing to release my iron grip. He stayed tense but eventually stopped trying to pull away from me.

I was irritated that I'd had to leave my place of cover. I could now count just how many men we were up against, which was four, but I also realized there was another woman in their midst besides Maral. This woman was dressed all in black and stood nearly a foot shorter than the men around her.

Katerina Semenov.

"I should have known it was you," I said once Katerina had stepped out from behind her hired thugs.

She gave me a cheerful wave with her free hand. The other held a small black pistol. "Silly of you, really. Although I am quite a good actress. You shouldn't entirely blame yourself."

My father opened his mouth at our exchange but nothing came out.

Katerina noticed. "This must be your father then. Professor Wunderly, I've seen you numerous times at Maxim's, but we've never been properly introduced."

I had no doubt that her civil tone and demeanor were carefully calculated to keep us all off-balance, and I could tell that my father was confused by the whole scenario.

"Why is Maral tied up?" he asked.

"Because she's my captive," Katerina said conversationally. "We had to use a handkerchief covered in something to knock her out. Not an easy task, really. Now, have you managed to locate the heart yet?"

"I don't know what you're talking about," he said stiffly.

"Please do not be foolish," Katerina said, her voice chiding. "It is a simple question. One that I recommend you answer." She waved her gun in Maral's direction. "There is a reason I have your lover captive."

I made a face at her choice of words, and Katerina chuckled.

"Because you'll do what?" My father's voice was challenging, and I gave my head a little shake. I didn't think it was a good idea to antagonize Katerina—especially given the situation we were in. I desperately wanted to look to Redvers for reassurance, but I kept my eyes fixed straight ahead so that I didn't give away his position. I could feel that the rest of our group had gathered behind us and I could only hope that they hadn't left their shovels in the trench. They were the only weapons we had besides the guns that Redvers and Lord Hughes had been carrying.

"I'll kill her," Katerina said. This time her voice had dropped the sweetness, and I didn't think anyone standing there doubted for a moment that she meant what she said.

Her eyes raked across our group. "Drop your weapon." Katerina pointed her weapon at Lord Hughes and I sighed. Now we were down to one gun, and I had no idea where Redvers had hidden himself.

Redvers and I were going to have a discussion in the future about leaving me without a firearm in this type of situation. If there was a future. I wasn't feeling terribly confident in that respect at the moment.

"I'll ask only one more time," Katerina said, stepping toward Maral and pointing her pistol at Maral's head directly behind her ear. I could hear Maral whimper, the first time the woman had shown a bit of fear despite everything we'd encountered. "Have you found the heart?" Katerina clearly enunciated every word.

My father was shaking violently at the sight of Maral with a gun to her head, and I wasn't sure he was even able to answer, so I took matters into my own hands. "No, they haven't. We can't even be certain it's here, Katerina. They've done quite a bit of digging already and haven't found anything."

Part of that was true, part of that was a lie. I nearly crossed my fingers in the hopes that none of these men would contradict me. I held my breath for a beat and was relieved when everyone stayed silent.

"Well, there's still more to go," Dillman said, and I shut my eyes. So close.

"Excellent," Katerina said, eyes gleaming, although she stepped back and dropped the gun from Maral's head, giving her a little push to the ground. "Then you'll simply carry on." The men around her fanned out with their weapons aimed directly at us. We had more in numbers, but it was obvious that we were outgunned, and it was no surprise when my father and his coterie of academics picked up their shovels and got back to work. It was difficult to argue at the motivation found on the other end of a gun—or several, as in this case.

"Where's the map, Henry?" Katerina called. I shivered at her use of my father's first name and recalled that I'd had a similar reaction in the bathhouse when she'd spoken about my father, but I'd dismissed my instincts.

I needed to learn how to listen to my gut.

My father grunted as he picked up a shovel of dirt. "I burned it."

"That is nonsense," she said. "I am going to ask you to hand it over, or it will be taken from you."

My father didn't respond, so I called to him from my seat on the block Kelley had found earlier. "You'd best do as she says, Father."

My father paused, his shovel full of dirt, before dropping it all to the ground. The others around him continued digging while he reached into his trousers pocket and removed the folded paper. He tossed it in Katerina's general direction, although it didn't get far.

"Jane, go fetch that for me."

I stood slowly, not wanting to make any sudden movements and get myself shot, although my mind was racing with how I might use this to my advantage. I bent down and retrieved the paper, then headed toward Katerina.

"Don't even think about it, my dear."

"I never would," I said, passing the paper to her before taking a few steps back.

"Now we both know that's a lie." Katerina barely took her eyes off of me to look at the paper after she gave a flick with her wrist to unfold it. "This is a copy, Henry. Where is the original?"

My father took a long time to answer, and I almost spoke up again, but he finally answered. "In the farmhouse."

Katerina didn't take her eyes from us but tipped her head toward the man standing next to her. He wore a thick peacoat and had a bushy black beard. "Go find it, Kiril." The man left without a word, heading back up the ramp.

It had improved our odds, but only by a little.

Chapter Forty-three

"Now, Jane, don't think I'm unaware that Redvers should be here somewhere."

I nearly flinched since I had been holding out hope that Katerina hadn't realized he was missing from our party, but I managed to maintain a neutral expression. "Redvers is in the farmhouse. You aren't the only one who wanted to see the original map."

"Hmm." Katerina tapped her little gun against her chin before aiming it in my direction and pulling off a shot that blasted dirt into a spray awfully close to my feet. I made a noise and started shaking but shook my head.

"He is, I swear it."

No one behind me said a word, and I didn't take a chance to look either, although I could just barely see Maral's face. I couldn't quite interpret her expression, but she held my gaze from where she sat on the ground behind Katerina and her men. One of the men was standing back and to the side, casually holding a gun on her. I looked back at Katerina when suddenly we heard a small thump and Maral give a little shriek of surprise.

Katerina flinched, but didn't otherwise move or even turn her head, instead calling to her side. "Maral? Is everything all right?"

"Yes." Maral seemed to choke a bit on her response. "It was just a rat. It ran over my foot and I am frightened of them."

Katerina seemed to consider this for a moment, then gave a single nod, seeming to accept this story. Clearly Katerina didn't know Maral—there was little chance a rat could make the woman shriek in fear. The same woman who'd stabbed a man in the back without a second thought and with very little regret? No, a rat wouldn't scare Maral.

But when the silence continued long enough, I let out the breath I'd been holding. If I had to make a guess, the "rat" that startled Maral was human sized and Redvers shaped. I silently prayed that he'd been able to take out that third guard and even up the odds a bit.

If Redvers had been able to take out that guard, I thought about what the next part of his plan could possibly be, conjuring up several possibilities then discarding them. The trouble was that Katerina Semenov was standing dead center in the aisle that ran the length of the cellar, rows of casks on either side. It would be difficult to sneak up on the woman and disarm her. Unless I could distract her.

So I just started asking all the questions that had been tumbling around in my mind. "Was it you that killed the man in the alley? The one who had been following us?" I asked.

Katerina looked at me for a long moment but then a smile crept onto her face, wide enough that her dimple peeked out at me. "Yes, of course. As soon as you left the table, I went out a different exit. Threw on a quick disguise—I find it's helpful to have dark clothing at the ready."

She would have had to move fast, but I supposed it was possible, especially given how well she had to know the building. "You followed us and shot one of your own men," I said.

"I could tell you had decided to corner him, and I couldn't

take the risk that he would talk." Katerina's smile faded to a look of grim satisfaction. "I know Redvers well enough. I know he would not have hesitated to do what was necessary."

I couldn't help but wonder if what the woman was saying was true. Would Redvers do what was necessary to get information? Including . . . torture?

My stomach felt sick at the thought. I didn't want to believe it was true of my fiancé, but it wasn't something to focus on now. I could worry about it if we made it out of this cellar alive.

Katerina continued, and I hoped that she hadn't noticed my reaction. "Ivan was one of the weakest members of my team. It was no great loss." She frowned. "Although I'm regretting not shooting all of you that night."

A glance behind my shoulder told me that my father had stopped working again and was standing stock-still. His pinched face told me he was worried for me.

"Henry," Katerina said warningly. "Did I say you could stop?"

He blinked several times but slowly went back to shoveling dirt. The men were silent as they worked, their shovels moving a little more slowly at this new threat but still moving.

I wondered how long these poor men could keep up this level of physical labor. None of them were youths.

"Why *didn't* you shoot us all that night?" I asked. It was one of the things I hadn't been able to figure out—why we hadn't been eliminated that evening.

"I was hoping that I might . . . rekindle things with your handsome fiancé. It would have been a nice perk to this entire enterprise, finding myself back in his arms. I decided to let him live in case that might be possible."

He'd told me that there'd been nothing between him and this woman, and I chose in that moment to believe him. And while something had obviously happened between them, I also believed that this ploy was nothing more than Katerina trying to get a rise out of me—she enjoyed it.

I didn't bother asking why she didn't shoot me. There was no truth to be had by asking the question. But perhaps she'd clear up some other things.

"Once you find the heart—if we find the heart—what will you do with it? Use its powers?" I asked.

Katerina scoffed. "I have heard of these mystical powers. Foolish nonsense." She shifted on her feet. "No, I want that gold box. I can sell it for quite a bit of money. I might not be able to return to Russia, but I can get back some of my lifestyle."

I must have looked confused because Katerina became irritated, her arms dropping to her side in frustration. "I was a noble in Russia. A very wealthy noble. I had everything I wanted, anytime I wanted it. And then I was forced to come here and start from scratch. Sing in a *nightclub*." She spat out the last word, and I stiffened at her growing fury. I had unwittingly kicked the hornet's nest.

"So I do what I have to do." Katerina nodded. "I start working at Maxim's, I learn the players. Soon, I'm the one making deals and giving orders. It did not take long—people are very stupid about things like drugs and women."

This woman had set herself up running a criminal enterprise. If I wasn't afraid that she was going to kill us I might have been impressed.

"Wasn't that bringing in enough money for you?"

She laughed, a little less angry now, which let me relax ever so slightly. Especially since the hand that had been clenched around the gun had also loosened. "Ahhh, what's ever enough, Jane? What will be enough that I can get my life back?"

I made a noise, not even sure what I was agreeing to. But

I'd decided it was better to stay agreeable and avoid topics that would further inflame our volatile captor.

"What about the man on the train who Maral killed?" I asked.

Katerina opened her mouth to answer but she never got the chance because my aunt Millie stepped from behind the nearest cask and swung at the woman's head with a shovel, making a direct hit.

Chapter Forty-four

At the sound of Katerina hitting the ground, the guards turned toward her. At that moment, Redvers burst from behind the last cask and dove for the knees of the guard standing nearest him, taking him to the ground. Millie ran forward and grabbed my arm, trying to drag me to safety behind a row of wooden barrels, although I pulled free and grabbed the shovel she'd dropped to the ground. A shot rang out, followed quickly by another, and I dropped into a crouch as Millie, cursing quite colorfully at me, took cover herself.

Another shot from somewhere to my right blew a hole into one of the wine barrels, shooting splinters into the air, and the scent of wine filled the air as the liquid poured from the container into the dirt below. To my right, Redvers was sitting on the back of the man he'd tackled, holding his gun on the second guard who held his hands up, although he still had a grip on his gun. My father and Professor Blanchard were still grappling with the third guard, both men fighting to gain control of the gun. I stayed in a crouch but scuttled to a position behind the second man, standing and raising the shovel menacingly.

"Drop it," I said. Redvers indicated with his weapon for the man to do so, and he did. I picked the gun up with my free hand, momentarily unsure of what to do with the shovel.

"Toss it here," Millie called. I turned and gently tossed the shovel in her direction. "I meant the gun, Jane," I heard her mutter, but Millie grabbed the shovel and stood guard over Katerina.

I quickly turned my attention to the last guard, who had finally been subdued by Professor Blanchard and my father. Blanchard was now holding the gun on the man, although not too steadily since both he and my father were breathing quite heavily.

Taking a deep breath and feeling like things were under control for the moment, I did a quick inventory and realized that Michael Dillman was lying in the dirt and not moving at all. I rushed over, tripping over a clod of earth in my haste to get into the trench. There had been three shots, and at least one of them had obviously found Dillman—he wasn't breathing and the bloodstain on the front of his shirt stretched across the whole of his chest.

"How's Dillman?" my father called to me.

I put my fingers to his neck and leaned my ear down over his nose hoping to catch any signs of life. But there were none. From the wounds I could see it looked like he'd been struck right in the heart, plus at least one other hit. I looked up at my father and shook my head sadly. My father choked back a sob and made a fist, looking like he was going to take a swing at the guard.

"Father, no!" I nearly shouted. "No," I said again more quietly. We had things under control and needed to keep them that way. In fact, we needed something to tie the men and Katerina up with. I was going to suggest to Millie that she go and see if she could find some rope, but one look at my aunt told me that she was not giving up her post guarding the little Russian woman. I gave a little sigh and headed for the stairs myself. I hadn't made it far when Maral appeared at the landing above me, carrying some lengths of rope.

I brought the rope to Redvers, where he tied up the man he

was still sitting on. I took over guarding that particular man while Redvers went about tying up the rest of Katerina's group. I left him to that task since his binding skills were superior to mine.

Katerina Semenov still hadn't regained consciousness, and I caught Maral's eye over the body.

"I'm sorry I couldn't return the favor," I said. I really should have said *didn't return the favor,* since I could have if I'd taken the time to investigate where Maral had disappeared to.

Maral looked at me for a moment. "It is okay," she said. "You do not owe me anything. Although I do think we got off on the wrong foot. I would like to change that." She cocked her head at Katerina. "Maybe later, though."

I smiled, a grim one, but a smile nonetheless. "I'd like that." I still had mixed feelings about the woman, but my father obviously cared about her. And that meant I should at least try.

In fact, I was a little surprised that my father wasn't attending to her, since she'd had a gun held to her head not thirty minutes earlier, but Father, Kelley, and Blanchard were kneeling in the dirt next to Dillman's body.

"He didn't have any family left," Kelley was saying.

"I still think we should send him back to the States," my father replied.

I felt terribly that we had lost someone, but I also felt relieved that it wasn't Redvers or my father, and then felt guilty for that relief when someone lay dead.

Nothing was ever simple.

By the time we had secured the four men—not only bound but also lined up outside the building with Professor Blanchard standing guard over them—Katerina had come around. We left her bound and gagged while we decided whom to contact to haul this little gang of criminals away.

"Whom should we contact? Will the local police even care?" I asked Redvers.

Millie had come to stand next to us. "They certainly should," she said. "I sent that Bey character to fetch them after I had him leave me here, so I imagine someone should be arriving shortly."

I looked at my aunt in astonishment, but Redvers seemed amused and not all that surprised.

"How did you get here?" I asked.

My aunt's mouth pursed in disgust. "Horses."

Millie never had been one for horseback riding. "How did you know to send for the police? There may have been nothing going on here."

Millie shook her head at me, then patted her hair to ensure nothing was out of place. It wasn't—you'd never be able to tell that she'd taken out a woman with a shovel and watched a gunfight. "Those two men, they were quite large and spoke very little English, but they were leaving just as I got here. One was helping the other who seemed to have a wound to the back of his head." Millie looked back and forth between Redvers and I but neither of us felt like offering an explanation. It was late and we were both tired, so Millie huffed and continued. "Anyway, they left in a hurry and I realized something was wrong." She fixed me with a dark look. "It was a good thing I decided to come anyway."

I opened my mouth to protest that I wasn't the one who had insisted she stay behind, but decided against arguing. I just hoped Lord Hughes saw some of the same admonishment—although I doubted he would. He seemed better equipped to handle Millie and charm her out of her moods. And I had to admit that she had really come through in a pinch—Millie was no shrinking flower and could hold her own. She'd swung that shovel like she meant it.

"Thank you, Aunt Millie. I'm glad you came to the rescue," I said. Millie preened for a moment, and instead of rolling my eyes I excused myself and walked over to where Katerina sat slumped against the wall. I had no idea how long it would take Ekrem Bey to scare up some local authorities, but I thought it would be advisable to ask some questions before they arrived.

I bent down and pulled the gag from Katerina's mouth, quickly stepping to the side as it looked like the woman was preparing to spit at me—I think the only reason she didn't was because her mouth was dry from the gag. I stood and regarded her for a moment, trying to decide what I wanted to ask first.

Before I could ask anything, however, Redvers came and stood next to me, then reached down and pulled her gag back up, causing her to shake her head violently back and forth, her dark hair falling loose around her face and her eyes spitting mad.

"It's not worth asking her anything. Nothing she says will be the truth, anyway."

I looked at him for a long moment, thinking about what she'd said about this man and his willingness to "do what it takes" to get information. Then I reached up and gave him a kiss, while Katerina made a noise of disgust from the ground.

"You're right," I said. "Nothing this woman says is the truth."

Chapter Forty-five

Ekrem Bey did eventually arrive with two local authorities, but not before I wondered whether he would come back at all. Neither of the officers was in uniform, but Ekrem assured me that they understood that our group of captives were under arrest.

"Looks like I missed all the fun," Ekrem said.

I didn't bother to respond.

Bey had arrived with the officers in a tiny conveyance so they commandeered the donkey and cart we had come in to take their five prisoners back to town. There was a one-room jail that the group would be crowded into until further arrangements could be made. I wondered if they would be taken back to Istanbul or face charges here, and which would be preferable. Then I decided that it was a worry for another day.

We all stood and watched the prisoners being loaded into the cart, and I saw Bey pull my father to the side. They commenced what looked to be a heated discussion, and at one point my father put his hand on Bey's arm, but Ekrem immediately shook it off. I was tempted to join them and mediate, but decided it was ultimately between the two of them. Bey's brother had been murdered, and whether my father had any moral responsibility for it or not was questionable. But they would have to work things out themselves.

Once the prisoners were removed and the cart had creaked off down the bumpy road, we all made our way back to our respective sleeping arrangements via horses and took advantage of what little night was left.

At least I know I did.

The next morning—late morning, nearly afternoon—I awoke and lay in bed for a long time, trying to wrap my head around what had happened the night before. Redvers was, of course, nowhere to be seen. but for once I was very nearly grateful. I needed a minute to myself.

I wondered if Maral would tell my father about how she had stabbed a man on the train in order to save my life. I had decided that it was her place to tell him, since it was something that she would have to carry with her, regardless of her cavalier attitude about it. She had taken a man's life and that was no small thing.

And I'd meant what I'd said the night before about trying to start over with Maral, even though I was still nervous about the woman. Truthfully it was hard to untangle my feelings about Maral from my feelings about my father having moved on from his memories of my mother. That was clearly my issue—my mother had died years ago, and just because my father had found someone new didn't mean he would forget my mother. He deserved happiness, and I needed to stand out of the way of that.

Should he be concerned about Maral as a person, though? She'd defended me, but her reaction had been somewhat troubling. But just because her reactions didn't match what my own would be, did that make it wrong? Or just different? I thought about it for a while, but I didn't come up with an answer, and decided that I might never come up with one, and that was okay.

I turned my mind to what Katerina had told me about

Redvers, but only for a moment. It wasn't even worth bringing it up to him, and I quickly laid the issue aside entirely. Redvers was right—there wasn't any truth to it. The woman was a consummate liar. I just hoped those skills didn't get her out of the punishment she was facing.

Not least there was still the issue of the bank wanting to repossess our house. It was still looming over my head and we only had days left to sort it out. Father and his friends had already done so much digging down in the wine cellar— what were the odds that they would actually find something? And if they did find something, would his friends insist that he donate the heart instead of accepting money that would repay the bank? I grimaced, remembering that I'd said something about it in front of Lord Hughes the night before—I hoped he would keep it to himself and not tell Millie about it. I didn't want to hear the "I told you so's" that would follow us to our graves.

I didn't come to any grand conclusions and I decided all these were topics best pondered after coffee. So I went in search of some, as well as my fiancé.

Millie and Lord Hughes, Ekrem Bey, as well as Redvers and I all gathered at our hotel after the morning meal—it was late enough that I wasn't sure it could be characterized as breakfast any longer. Ekrem had spoken with the owner of the donkey and cart from the night before and arranged to keep them both for another day. I imagined the owner was thrilled with the money that was being thrown in his direction, even if the donkey seemed less than enthusiastic about pulling all of us. We rode back to the winery mostly in silence, with Redvers driving and my aunt Millie perched on the bench next to him. The rest of us bounced on the wooden benches in the back, all of us suppressing grimaces when we hit the inevitable potholes in the dirt road.

*   *   *

We arrived back at the winery, a little worse for wear from the jolting ride, and went straight to the wine cellar. We found my father and his companions back at work already, digging in the same place they'd been the night before.

"Where's Maral?" I asked, looking around. She'd stayed behind with my father the night before.

My father's face flushed a bit. "She'll be along later."

I decided not to ask any more questions.

Because the temperature of the cellar was so cool, Michael Dillman's body had been wrapped in a sheet and taken to the far corner until he could be transported back to the States for burial.

"He would want us to keep digging though," my father insisted.

Kelley agreed with this sentiment. "He would indeed want us to finish what we started." They both looked at Blanchard, who gave a shrug.

"I think we need to look at the map again. It doesn't seem like we're going to find it where we've been digging," Blanchard said.

My father looked like he wanted to argue but decided against it. He'd brought his satchel with him today, and opened it, digging around for a moment before pulling an ancient-looking piece of parchment from it.

We all crowded around it, none of us able to get a decent look since there were too many of us. Glancing around, my father gave a grunt of frustration, then grabbed a trowel and bent down. "Stand back," he instructed, and everyone moved back several steps. He then replicated the map in the dirt, muttering to himself as he drew the lines. But he did so from memory, without looking at the original.

"We're here." He scratched a little star in the dirt.

Millie had picked up the map and looked between it and what my father had drawn. "Henry"—her voice was scolding—"have you been working from memory?"

"No, I made a copy," Father said. "But I may have drawn that from memory," he admitted a moment later.

"You've got it backward." Millie handed him the parchment and pointed to where my father had just indicated we were and then to the map. "We need to be on the other side."

My father looked ready to argue but he studied the map for a moment then shuffled his feet sheepishly. "I guess I'm getting a bit old. My memory is not quite what it used to be."

I was surprised that his friends didn't stage a coup right then—all that work for nothing, but once again they just rolled their eyes, picked up their shovels, and moved to the other side of the cellar. I admired their patience with my father. I hoped it would extend to what would happen to the heart if they managed to find it.

It didn't take long once digging started in the correct area. While his friends weren't outright angry about their wasted time and effort, they did give him a hard time while digging in the new section. My father took it in stride, obviously understanding that he deserved the ribbing. Luckily, there were many more hands available now for doing the actual work, and everyone—including Millie—pitched in to help in shifts.

I didn't quite believe there was anything to be found but I was willing to give them this last day to attempt to finish what they'd started. If they couldn't find the heart, I would be forced to either come to terms with the loss of our row house or ask Millie and Hughes for help. I couldn't decide which was worse. Losing our home would be an enormous blow to my sense of security, but having to ask Millie for the money and deal with the repercussions of that would be a blow to not only my pride but my father's. And we would never hear the end of it.

These thoughts plagued my mind while we worked on digging. My father took the opportunity to lecture us further on Suleiman the Magnificent and the month-long siege that had taken place in Szigetvár before his death. I'd heard it many times before so I tuned out and watched the digging instead. When Professor Kelley hit something solid for the second time that morning, he didn't bother interrupting my father, but elbowed Professor Blanchard who turned and assisted with digging around the object. I watched as the two men unearthed a small rectangular object, much smaller than the bricks they had been finding.

Blanchard and Kelley were quite calm, although I could feel their excitement from across the room. I tried to interrupt my father, but he was not paying the slightest bit of attention to me.

"Henry!" my aunt finally shouted. "Quiet yourself for a moment."

My father looked quite offended, until he looked behind him and nearly fell directly into the newly dug trench in his haste to reach his fellow academics and their discovery. The three of them scrambled to get the item brushed off. I held my breath. Could this actually be it?

And it was. Little by little a gold box encrusted with a row of jewels revealed itself. It was dull with age and dirt, but I imagine it would be stunning once it was cleaned up. Not to mention priceless.

"Do you really think it's in here?" my father asked breathlessly.

I wasn't surprised that my father was more interested in the mummified heart itself rather than the jewel-encrusted box that it came in. But I also decided that I didn't need to see what was inside, so I took myself back upstairs to take in the sunshine and fresh air.

Over an hour later I was still huddled in my coat against the cold on a wooden bench I'd found, enjoying the sunshine on my face and the feeling that things had mostly been resolved.

I was sorry that Professor Dillman had lost his life to this cause, and I hoped that my father and his remaining friends would realize that this had been a foolish venture and not attempt such a thing in the future. Even though they *had* managed the improbable and found the heart—and perhaps more importantly, the box. I was hoping that my father would be able to convince the men that they should accept money in exchange for their find, and that it was enough to resolve our troubles and also compensate everyone fairly.

Except Ekrem Bey. I still didn't believe that he should receive a cut at all.

I struggled with the idea of accepting money for a historical find, but in the end decided that needs must when the devil drives, as the saying went. As long as the box and the heart weren't sold to a collector, and a museum was willing to front the money for it, I decided I would put my moral objections to the side. I would discuss this with my father when I found a moment alone with him—which looked like it might be difficult, since he and Maral were attached at the hip.

I didn't know what lay ahead for my father and Maral. I had no idea if their relationship would survive the distance, especially now that it looked like my father had few other reasons to return to Istanbul. It seemed complicated, but during my time in the sun I'd also decided it wasn't my concern. My father would make his own decisions, just as I would.

Ekrem Bey had returned to Istanbul that morning, a decision that frankly had shocked me. I had thought for sure he would stick around to see whether my father managed to locate the heart—he'd demanded a cut of the profits after all. But he'd seemed quiet and even introspective that morning when he'd taken his leave of us. Ekrem had thanked us for our efforts in finding his brother's killer, even though it had been sort of peripheral to our overall scheme. He mentioned ensuring that Katerina didn't escape the justice coming to her, and I had the sense that he would follow through with that promise, even if he was entirely untrustworthy otherwise. Ekrem didn't ask again about the heart, and I wondered if he'd decided that he had gotten what he'd ultimately come for—justice for his brother. I didn't know what he'd spoken to my father about and what sort of agreement—if any—they had come to, but I let him leave without asking.

I was still pondering questions about our companions when everyone joined me upstairs. Professor Blanchard was holding the box quite tenderly as everyone else hauled up the various shovels and supplies that had been carried into the cellar. I wondered if they'd filled the trenches or if the owners would allow further excavations. This winery was built on what was once a small city—there were likely other finds to be made, although none as valuable or famous as the heart. But there would undoubtedly be other things of interest to discover.

"Do you want to see the heart?" my father asked me. I was certain he thought he was doing me a favor, but I couldn't stop my grimace.

"No, I'm fine without seeing a desiccated heart."

"It's more mummified, really," Father said, as though that would change my mind on the matter.

I shook my head and he gave a shrug, then came to sit next to me on the bench. The professors continued to the house with the box, chatting excitedly about cleaning the box up to reveal its full beauty. Millie trailed in their wake offering advice on the best way to do that; I couldn't help an amused smile. Lord Hughes and Redvers followed quietly behind her, and for the first time I was surprised to find myself alone with my father.

"Have you talked to the men about what will happen with the heart?" I asked.

"I have, and they've agreed that we will only let it go to a museum."

I breathed a sigh of relief, and he smiled at me. "I know your feelings on the matter—I've taught you well. I wouldn't be keen to accept money in exchange for the find if I hadn't gotten us into such a mess," Father said. He studied his hands, poking at a blister that had formed on his palm from digging. After a moment's silence he looked up at me. "I am sorry to have caused you so much worry."

I nodded, accepting his apology. "I just wish you had trusted me with the truth from the beginning."

Father's mouth quirked into a lopsided smile. "I wish you could trust me with the finances." We both chuckled, but I wondered what would happen once Redvers and I were married. Who *would* look after my father's affairs?

"Do you think we'll get money in time to repay the bank?" I asked. We only had a few days left, and I was anxious to return to Budapest where we could make arrangements for a wire transfer of money. Assuming it could be arranged with a museum so quickly.

"Not to worry. Hughes pulled me aside, and he will take care of the wire transfer once we're back to civilization, in plenty of time." I grimaced again, and my father patted my arm. "He said I can pay him back once the museum money comes through, and I will," he said.

And if Father didn't, I would make sure it was repaid.

"But Millie—" I started to say.

"Hughes said Millie doesn't need to know everything about what he does with his money." My father's face split in a full-fledged grin now. "It seems he knows my sister well."

I matched my father's grin with one of my own. "He does."

"I'm glad she'd found someone who understands her," Father said. "Speaking of which, I hear you're to be married again."

"When did Redvers manage to talk to you about that? While everyone was shooting at us?"

My father chuckled. "Actually, your aunt brought it up first."

"That figures."

My father was quiet for a moment, then patted my hand. "I'm happy for you. I think Redvers is a good choice. He asked for my permission this morning, and I gave it to him. I could hardly say no—the man did save our lives."

I thought Millie would argue with that interpretation of events, but held my tongue.

He cleared his throat. "I'm sorry I didn't see that the last one wasn't . . . a good choice. Or a good man, for that matter."

We'd never fully discussed my first marriage, although I'd intimated to my father that things had not been good. I suspected that he'd read between the lines of the little I'd said about it, although I doubted I would ever let on fully how bad things had really been. This was the closest we'd ever come to talking about it openly, and my first instinct was to make a joke—perhaps about how he liked Redvers because he'd tackled a man with a gun and that was a handy person to have around. But instead, I took a breath and answered sincerely.

"Thank you." I struggled for what else to say but settled on leaving it at that.

My father had the same instincts though, and his tone lightened considerably. "If your aunt has anything to say about it, you'll be hitched tomorrow. Or, heaven forbid, you'll be having a double wedding with her and Lord Hughes."

I gave my father a look of pure horror and he burst out laughing.

"Best hop to it, then, my girl."

Perhaps the man had a point.

Author's Note

Language is tricky, and it was difficult to decide exactly what to call Istanbul since the name was officially changed from Constantinople to Istanbul in 1930, but the city was commonly called Istanbul (and sometimes Stamboul) for many years before that. Hemingway wrote about the city as "Stamboul" in the early 1920's, and from what I could tell, many locals called it Istanbul, which was closer to the Turkish name. And so I decided to largely go with Istanbul.

It was difficult to determine exactly how long it would have taken them to get from Boston to Istanbul in the 1920's and what the best route would have been, so I ballparked this to be about ten days via ship and train and then more ship.

Regarding the *Orient Express*—they most likely would have had to switch trains to get to Budapest, but for simplicity's sake I made it a direct route. It was also quite fast, and I added extra time for plot's sake rather than how quickly it would have actually travelled. Agatha Christie's first trip on the train was in 1928, two years after this novel takes place, but I wanted to tip my hat to her, so I fudged those dates as well.

While I was in Istanbul conducting research, the Basilica Cistern was closed for renovations so my apologies for anything I didn't get anything exactly right there.

The names of the Turkish rug dealers are real—they work at a shop near the Basilica Cistern and not only sold me a lovely rug, they gave me a space to write for a few hours and provided me with plenty of Turkish coffee. Many thanks for their hospitality, and admiration for their sales skills.

ACKNOWLEDGEMENTS

Huge thanks to John Scognamiglio, my editor extraordinaire, as well as to Larissa Ackerman and Jesse Cruz, my outstanding publicists. Thank you to Robin Cook, Lauren Jernigan, and Sarah Gibb. Further thanks to the rest of the Kensington team who work so hard to get books into your hands.

Thank you and big love to Ann Collette, my amazing agent who always makes me feel grateful to not only simply know her, but to get to work with her. You bring me joy.

So much love and thanks to Zoe Quinton King, my dearest of friends and editor and boo. I'm so lucky to have you on my team both in my life and my career. I'm grateful for you every damn day.

Big love and thanks to Jessie Lourey, Lori Rader-Day, Susie Calkins, and Shannon Baker. Midwest ride or die squad.

Immeasurable thanks for the friendship, love and support to Tasha Alexander, Gretchen Beetner, Lou Berney, Mike Blanchard, Keith Brubacher, Kate Conrad, Hilary Davidson, Dan Distler, Steph Gayle, Daniel Goldin, Juliet Grames, Andrew Grant, Glen Erik Hamilton, Carrie Hennessy, Tim Hennessy, Chris Holm, Katrina Holm, Megan Kantara, Steph Kilen, Elizabeth Little, Jenny Lohr, Erin MacMillan, Joel MacMillan, Dan Malmon, Kate Malmon, Mike McCrary, Catriona McPherson, Katie Meyer, Trevor Meyer, Lauren O'Brien, Roxanne Patruznick, Margret Petrie, Nick Petrie, Bryan Pryor, Andy Rash, Jane Rheineck, Kyle Jo Schmidt, Johnny Shaw, Jay Shepherd, Becky Tesch, Tess Tyrrell, Bryan Van Meter, and Tim Ward.

Thank you to the amazing booksellers and librarians who've supported this book and especially to the folks who hosted me for a real-life tour this time. Special shout outs to Jane and Joanne and Charlotte at Mystery to Me; Daniel, Chris, and Rachel at Boswell Books; Barbara at the Poisoned Pen.

Thank you and big love to my amazing family, Rachel and AJ Neubauer, Dorothy Neubauer, Sandra Olsen, Susan Catral, Sara Kierzek, Jeff and Annie Kierzek, Justin and Christine Kierzek, Josh Kierzek, Ignacio Catral, Sam and Ariana Catral, Mandi Neumann, Andie, Alex and Angel Neumann. Special thanks and love to my dear friend Gunther Neumann, who is truly a rock.

So much love, gratitude and thanks to Mike B. for being the amazing person that he is. To the bones, babe.

And all the love and thanks to Beth McIntyre, the Laverne to my Shirley, the Thelma to my Louise—although let's not drive off a cliff. Much as we love to drive—Beep, beep!